An Ex-citing Proposition

A Date My Ex Novel

Kelly Ohlert

Linda Floyd

Cover Illustration by Ali Shearer

Published in the United States by Beryllium Sphere Press LLC.

ISBN (paperback): 979-8-9918973-1-0

ISBN (ebook): 979-8-9918973-0-3

Printed in the United States.

www.kellyohlert.com

For Judy and Pete,
Who paved the way for us and taught us that can't never did anything.

Also by Kelly Ohlert

To Get to the Other Side

Let's Get Quizzical

Chapter 1
Moxie

Zombies. At least, they might as well be. The dude at the far end of the bar is close to passing out and drowning in his drink. The other men are ashen and unappealing, though the general darkness of the room doesn't help. The lurkers on the dance floor are like a herd of corpses milling aimlessly, waiting for fresh flesh to appear. My booze goggles appear to be malfunctioning.

"Hey Murray, what's with the crowd tonight?" I ask the middle-aged bartender. The hole-in-the-wall is a frequent haunt of mine. It's usually a good place for picking up men, but tonight's options are lacking. The atmosphere feels stale in a way that makes my muscles twitch. The sameness weighs down on me, and I suck in a deep breath to fight the sudden claustrophobia squeezing me.

"Same old stuff," Murray replies, rolling his eyes like, *Don't give me shit today, Moxie.*

Maybe I need to change things up. I mostly follow a one-and-done policy. Getting close with someone leads to a natural entwining of lives and a reliance that makes my skin crawl. Dependency is not my jam; thanks, dear old Mom and Dad.

"Hook me up with some tequila," I say. If the vodka didn't

do the trick, tequila definitely will. Heck, enough rounds with my buddy Jose Cuervo, and I'll probably forget the men entirely and start dancing on the pool tables.

A woman bursts through the door and throws herself at the bar a few stools down. Physically, she's my complete opposite. Her wavy, sandy-blonde hair is a sharp contrast to my own jet-black pixie cut with blue highlights. She wears a white skirt and pink sweater on her thin frame, while I'm rocking jeans and a black tank top over my curves. Tears stream down her blotchy face.

This is not a silent suffering kind of cry. This girl is in shirt-drenching, snot-producing, ugly cry mode—and I know her.

"Lady, are you okay?" Murray asks.

"May I please have some alcohol?" she asks between sniffles.

Murray stares at her dumbfounded and looks at me like I'll have a solution for him.

Hannah doesn't wait for a response, just throws her head into her arms and shakes with the violent heaves of her sobs. Damn it.

I need to find a bar further away from work. I bump into an acquaintance too often. Each time, I vow to frequent a new bar, but Murray's is in easy stumbling distance from my apartment. I have a feeling I'm going to regret my laziness tonight.

Hannah is the self-appointed welcoming committee at the casino and is always kind to me. She's quick to offer help to everyone. We aren't close, but she regularly waves to me from her post at the customer service desk. Her smile is always bright, and she has Donkey-from-*Shrek* kind of energy.

Meanwhile, I deal out cards and shoot the shit with my players. It sounded like such a fun job. I've worked my way to the best tables, but the players blend together. Instead of the hitting-the-jackpot high I sought, I'm stuck on a losing streak with not much chance of the cards turning.

Hannah hiccups loudly and Murray stands with his hands frozen helplessly on an empty glass. Doesn't he know bartenders are supposed to be every drunk's sounding board? The last thing I want is to spend my night off consoling a coworker. The girl clearly needs someone to talk to, but we don't talk. I deal cards, she signs up new members. Acknowledging each other in passing doesn't qualify me to break out a notepad and leather sofa and talk about her feelings. Tonight was apparently a bad night. She'll have "some alcohol" and wake up tomorrow ready for her Miss America act, all without any needed intervention from me.

When Murray doesn't make a move to play therapist or bartender, Hannah's bleary eyes search the room like a player down to their last chips frantically scanning the table for the winning card that will be their salvation. We lock eyes and my stomach twists. Her lips tremble, and her eyes widen and glisten in an absurd puppy dog stare.

This is a lost cause. I blame you Cuervo. I toss it back before trudging over to Hannah.

"Get her a chocolate cake shot," I say, and Murray nods, relieved to have direction. "And I'll have another Cuervo."

"Moxie?" she asks.

I do some unenthusiastic jazz hands. "That's me."

"What are you doing here?"

"Drinking." It's truthful and sounds better than prowling for a hookup.

"Shots come in cake form?" Hannah asks. She pulls a fresh tissue from her purse and cleans up the swamp on her face.

"Yep. There isn't any chocolate in it, but somehow it still tastes exactly like chocolate cake."

Alcohol is a topic I can handle. Her eyes light up behind the glaze of tears. "I love chocolate. And cake."

"I had a feeling," I say.

We wait in silence for Murray to pour our drinks, and she trembles with the effort of composing herself. We've reached the splotchy aftermath stage: tissues, uneven breaths, and the occasional whimper.

Murray delivers our shots, and I nod to her. We clink glasses. "Bottoms up," I say, and we toss them back.

She bites the lemon and studies the empty glass, her doe eyes wide with astonishment. "It does taste like chocolate cake."

Just like that, I'm out of conversation topics. I tap a finger on the bar along with the beat emanating from the tinny speakers.

"Do you... want me to pick out another drink?"

"No. It's okay. I'm alright."

She's not. She's going to fall apart and tell me the whole story any minute now. She attempts a discreet eye blot with a tissue. I sip my water and wait her out. Three. Two. One—

"I'm never going to find love!" she wails.

Ah, love. A topic I'm oh-so-qualified to advise her on. I spare my old stool a longing glance. Best not to dwell on the past. First things first, I need to confirm the severity of the situation.

"Are you physically okay? Did someone hurt you?" I ask.

"Only my *heart*!" She sobs.

I nearly choke but hasten to stifle my laughter. If we were at the casino, I'd be putting my money on Hannah being a drama kid in high school.

"Alright, who was it, and what did they do?"

"It was supposed to be a rebound date. The guy was a freaking sword swallower for Renaissance Faires. He has a flair for the unusual, and I couldn't see myself doing anything with him."

Ever a sucker for the wild ones, I perk up but remind myself that we're focusing on her issues right now. Tonight's mission: get Hannah's smile back.

"And... you're upset you're not getting a second date?"

"No. It's history repeating itself. My boyfriend of a whole year broke up with me because he said I was too predictable. I don't want to be boring, but how am I supposed to keep up with that?"

I can't help but laugh. Neither one of us can find the right person, but our reasons are reversed. "You're not alone. I can't find a good one either, although I'm just looking for an inter-esting guy to date occasionally. All the ones I go out with bore me to tears. The last guy I dated had a routine he refused to deviate from, including a weekly game night." A shiver runs down my spine, remembering how he'd wanted to slot me in like a cog in his perfectly-planned life.

"What's wrong with game night?" Hannah's head jerks up, jaw dropping and brows furrowing as if my criticism is a personal affront to her.

"Nothing!" There really isn't. They could be fun. My ex's game night was the same game with the same people every week, and it was a box I couldn't stand being placed in. Some-thing in his ideal system would inevitably break. "It was all too scheduled for me."

Hannah's nose crinkles at this and I laugh. "What's that look for?"

"Schedules are awesome." She's no longer crying. I smile to myself as phase one of the Hannah Project—put a stop to the sobbing— is complete. "Don't you feel lost without one?"

I work on a schedule, and that's enough for me. I prefer to go out and not know where or with whom the night will take me. Anything else makes me feel like the world is quicksand swal-lowing me whole.

"Nope. I find it freeing." I signal to Murray for two waters.

"I love schedules. And spreadsheets. I live for spreadsheets, but I can't seem to find anyone else who agrees."

Murray delivers our waters, and I blink at Hannah. "You love spreadsheets?"

"Oh yes, they're wonderful." There's not even a hint of exag-geration. She's talking about spreadsheets like she watched them save a litter of kittens from a burning building. "I would love routine dates and someone I could rely on."

"Mind numbing." I shudder. No one can be relied on, but she's so innocent and sweet, I don't want to be the bearer of that bad news.

She absently stirs the ice around the glass of water. "You sound just like my exes. Maybe you should date them." She laughs.

"Ha, yeah."

Since Hannah's ceased her hysterics, we're no longer the center of attention. The disheveled suits around the bar return to ESPN or their existential crisis fueled staring contests with the bottoms of their bottles. I tune out the clanking sounds of Murray filling drinks and the crackle of the same old songs funneling through the speakers. Hannah's hand stills, and she spins to face me. Her grin widens in a way that makes the hair on the back of my neck rise with dread.

"Hear me out," she begins.

I cringe. That can't be good.

"We should date each other's exes!"

"Yeah, okay." I laugh and look away.

"I'm serious! It makes sense. Think about it." Her eyes are wide with hope. "I need someone who moves more at my speed, and you break up with guys because they're too boring. We do a little switcheroo, and voilà! A perfect match."

"I don't know…" I shift in my seat and crane my neck in search of Murray. I've got an urgent need to cash out. "It makes sense in theory, but we don't know each other that well. We can't possibly know if our exes are a good fit."

"Not knowing each other is why this works. It'd be too weird to date your ex if I'd known you two together, but I didn't, and you never saw me with any of mine."

Seriously, where the hell did Murray go? "Fair, but I'm not looking for a relationship."

"Please?" she asks, giving me that glossy-eyed, pleading look.

No. Not falling for that. I grimace. "They're not my thing and I don't see the point in you setting me up for a hookup."

"So go and have some fun on a date. See how it goes. Who knows? Maybe one of my exes will surprise you. You said it yourself, they're right up your alley. You don't have to marry them, but you might want three or four dates before you cut them loose."

I tap on my glass and shake my head. "You're going to call up some guy who, in your own words, broke your heart, and say, 'Hey, there's this girl you should meet'?"

"No, of course not. Most of these guys didn't break my heart. We just weren't right for each other. Oh, I know! We could stage a meet cute." She leans in close, giving me the puppy dog eyes again.

The options in the bar have not improved. My inclinations meter ticks closer to *Maybe*. "It feels hella weird to go out with some guy you dated for a year."

"Who says it has to be him?" She frowns at the bar top and her eyes widen as she grins at me. "I've got it! There's a guy I've known since I was a kid. We dated briefly but weren't a good fit. I bet you would like him." She blows her nose, still experiencing the lingering effects of her sob session.

"I still haven't agreed to this."

"I'm telling you, Wyatt's the one. Please, Moxie? I can't go back into the dating world alone." She pouts.

"Can't I just cheerlead you from the sidelines? I'm not looking for The One."

"Help me believe in love, Moxie!" she yelps, drawing attention to us once again. I can't deal with these dramatics.

I might have to agree just to be done with her badgering. The thing about one-night stands is there's no pressure. No expectations. I can chat someone up, and if it goes well, I can take them home. If I'm not feeling it, I can easily walk away and find someone else just a few stools over. Hannah wants a lot more. I've got to put a stop to this now.

"I don't know. Dates are so awkward. All that small talk, or the whole 'let's ask the big questions now so we don't waste each other's time' third degree."

She bites her lip in a way that seems to move beyond simple contemplation and into fear that I won't agree.

"What if it's not a date? What if we could arrange a quick meeting so you can get a first impression. We don't have to say a word to him, so there's no pressure and we aren't getting his hopes up, either." Her voice creeps higher with each word in a way that suggests panic, so that by the end of her speech she's squealing.

My bank of excuses is running low, and Murray's taking his sweet ass time. I'm so going to threaten him with a negative Yelp review when I get my hands on him.

"It's perfect." She claps her hands. Her mood is flip flopping so fast I can barely keep track. "We could give each other intel to make sure the first date goes well."

"What happened to just a quick meet to see if I even want a date? I thought we were going the low stakes route?" I don't bother mentioning there is very little intel I could provide her on my one-night stands. What am I going to say? *Kick this one out when you're done with him, he eats too much cheese and farts in his sleep?* Or, *Let that one go down on you, he works wonders with his tongue?*

She waves her hand. "Hypothetically, of course. If you decide you want to date."

"I don't usually put this much effort into dating," I say weakly, already knowing she'll have an answer.

"That's just because you're not using spreadsheets to their full potential. Don't worry, I can plan the whole thing."

Murray finally shows up, and I lean in to ask for my check.

"Can I please have another?" Hannah wiggles her empty glass at Murray.

So much for peacing out of here before Hannah talks me into her wild scheme.

"If you're so keen on this idea, why don't you go first?" I suggest. "That'll give me time to decide if I want to be set up." I mentally scroll through my little black book, grasping at fleeting memories for someone who might be a good fit for schedule-loving Hannah.

"I still have mascara tracks on my face," she says. "I need a hot minute to catch my breath. I'll take a couple weeks to recover, and then we're in this together. But the more I think about it, the better I think Wyatt is for you."

Seeming to sense that I'm wavering, Hannah whips out her phone, taps, and scrolls.

"Okay, you want to see a picture? Here." She thrusts the phone at me, and I take it. On the screen is a very attractive man with a strong chin and the kind of wide, honest smile that can only come from genuinely having the time of your life. Long blonde hair frames his face, hanging just far enough off it that there must have been a strong wind that day. He has kind eyes that crinkle at the corners and sun-kissed skin dotted with small freckles. He's hot.

She silently waits me out, sipping the fruity concoction Murray whipped up for her. Hannah's eyes are full of confidence. Mental recap time.

Her suggestion of a low pressure meet-and-greet isn't terrible, and maybe by then I'll have come up with better excuses. Judging fully on his looks, I could certainly do worse than Wyatt.

At this point, saying no to Hannah's tear-stained face feels a bit like kicking a puppy. I may not be taking home a *Miss Compassionate* award any time soon, but I'm not that big of a monster.

I take a fortifying breath. "Fine, but just a quick meet. I meant it when I said dating isn't my thing."

Hannah pumps a fist in the air, and let's out a quiet "Yes!" I can't help but chuckle.

"Do you still talk to this Wyatt? Is he even single?"

"Only if we bump into each other, but Stitch 'N Bitch is a reliable nuisance of a news source."

"I'm sorry, run that one past me again?"

"The neighborhood moms are in a cross-stitch and gossip group. That's the central hub for the goings-on in the neighborhood, but it extends beyond that inner circle. I can't sneeze in the grocery store without getting a call from my mother to ask if I've got a cold. They've got eyes everywhere." She looks around as if moms are hiding in the corner.

The music in the bar shifts mid-song, and the abruptness makes us both look around. One of the dance floor zombies turns away from the TouchTunes jukebox as his selection plays. He locks eyes on us to the crooning of "All By Myself." Subtle. Hannah shudders, and I agree.

We spin back to the bar. "Right. Stitch 'N Bitch. What does that have to do with this guy?"

"Wyatt's mom is a member. You know how you get superglue on your skin even when you swear you were careful and there's no way you could have gotten any on you, and then you try everything to get it off, but you eventually have to accept that you're going to live with it?"

"Not really."

"Well, pretend. Even though he and I ended on good terms, our mothers hold a grudge and have clung to the dredges of our very brief affair like superglue on skin, so I hear about him all the time. He recently broke up with someone."

"I feel like you could have just said. 'Like superglue.'" The song ends and promptly restarts, dooming us to desperation in musical form on repeat.

"Forget the analogy," Hannah says. "You're stuck on the analogy."

"There are so many better examples. Like spinach on front teeth, sand in your swimsuit, glitter on... anything." What little hints of sadness that had been lingering vanish with her annoyance. Mission accomplished.

"Yes, they cling to their grudge like all of those clingy things." Hannah folds her arms and tips her nose up, looking rather pleased with herself.

An Ex-citing Proposition

"Alright," I shrug. "Wyatt it is. Now can we get out of here before we have to listen to this song a third and fourth time?"

She presses a hand to her chest in absolute bewilderment. "We can't leave now. There's so much planning to do!"

I wince, sparing a glance toward the sad sap near the dance floor and setting the over/under for his approach at five minutes. I'm taking the under.

"I seem to remember you saying you'd handle the planning. Can't you just text me when and where to show up?"

She laughs as if I've intentionally cracked a joke, but I wasn't trying to be funny. "This is going to be so much fun! Who knows, maybe he'll even be the love of your life."

I've created a monster. I glare at her, and she holds her hands up with a laugh. "Okay, okay. I'm sorry. You're right. We're going slow. First things first, we need to be able to communicate." She grabs her phone and looks expectantly at me. I hesitate for a second before giving her my number.

She's so damn sweet it's hard to be annoyed with her despite how absurd all of this is. If I'm not getting out of here anytime soon, and if I'm agreeing to this thing, I might as well go all in. I order another round of drinks as Hannah frantically searches her purse.

"I wish I had my notebook, but this will have to do. Or I could pull up a spreadsheet on my phone. No, sometimes paper is best." She is full-on babbling to herself, and I decide it's best not to interrupt her.

She taps around on her phone some more, then flashes Wyatt's profile at me. "Status recently changed to single. Gossip confirmed."

"Way to go Sew n' moan."

Hannah laughs, and a hiccup bubbles out. Maybe we should slow down on the drinks. "Stich n' bitch."

"Right, that. Hey Deejay! Give us something upbeat," I shout to the guy who has been playing us the depressing broken record.

His eyes widen, and he nods and swipes his card in the machine.

"You acknowledged him," Hannah whispers. "Now he's going to expect a dance."

"I don't owe him or any man anything. He can expect all he wants."

She raises her eyebrows but lifts her glass. "Moxie, you might just be my idol. Cheers to that."

If I'm her idol, I fear for her. Hannah busies herself with planning, doing who knows what on her phone and scribbling notes on a coaster. True to her word, she doesn't seem to need my input, so I eye the crowd.

Before long we've roped another group of women into dancing with us, and I do my best to find the perfect ratio of alcohol and water for happy and fun, but not sloppy. Hannah alternates between notetaking and dancing. I'm questioning the quality of her notes as tipsy Hannah takes the wheel. She appears to be a shouty and lovey-dovey drunk.

"I think we're going to be best friends," she shouts at me for probably the sixth time.

"And I think you should drink some water." I shove a glass in her direction.

"You don't believe me, but just call me Kool-Aid Man because I'm going to break right through that wall you've got around you."

I have no idea what she's talking about, but I tug at her elbow and steer her toward a corner of the room away from the chaos I've stirred up. "Right. Drink that water."

"Ooh yeah!" she bellows.

We tumble into a booth and she rummages through six coasters covered in her looping script. Finding the one she wants, she shoves it in front of me, where she's written:

County Fair Expo
This Saturday

An Ex-citing Proposition

Meet Cute

Saturday already? My chest constricts with anxiety. While playing the entertainer, I almost forgot what we were doing. The reality of starting this project so soon slaps me in the face and sobers me up fast.

She hits me with that hopeful stare, her smile loose from the alcohol, and once again I nod with a resigned sigh. "Saturday, huh? At the fair?"

"Yep. Wyatt and his buddy Noah have an adventure tourism business. They'll have a booth there. It's the perfect opportunity for you to meet him without it seeming like a setup."

I have to admit, it's a good idea. "Alright. I'm in."

"I was hoping you'd say that. Let's meet at one o'clock at the entrance to the expo."

"I can do that," I say.

"Oh! And Wyatt is on the rugged side, so don't wear anything that screams high maintenance."

"Noted."

Hannah puts the rest of her note-coasters into her bag. "I already emailed you a map of the fairgrounds. I'll send you another email soon with more information."

I can't imagine what else I could possibly need, but I'm ready to wrap this up. "Sounds good."

We cash out, and I make sure Hannah gets into her rideshare before taking the short walk to my own apartment.

The unfamiliar pressure of a dating scenario that isn't just picking up a random guy at the bar has my thoughts swirling once again. I remind myself that I don't have to go on a date. I simply agreed to meet him. I only hope I don't regret it.

Chapter 2
Wyatt

My phone's ringtone echoes off the canyon walls, breaking the serene late afternoon stillness, and "Dad" glows on my watch screen.

"Don't answer it," Noah, my best friend and business partner, calls out from the ground twenty feet below me.

"Wasn't planning to!" I shout back and shift my foot up to the next hold.

My fingers burn with the ache of clinging to the rock. I was tired before I even started climbing thanks to the earlier hike to set up the top rope. Sweat covers my skin despite the chill in the air.

I scan the jagged cliff face taking more time with my moves than I normally would. I'm trying to figure out the puzzle to guide less experienced climbers so they can have the thrill of a challenge but not end up careening off the rock face. We don't have a climbing excursion in our repertoire yet, and this would be a perfect one to add.

Another sound breaks the peaceful mountain silence; this time it's a high-pitched chirping.

"Eagle?" Noah asks.

"Yep. Over there." I nod my head in the direction of the stunning bald eagle drifting across the sky. For a moment, the bold greens of the trees and the mountain valley take my breath away. I'll never get tired of this.

"You sure you don't want to climb? You should see it up here."

"Not today," Noah says.

"Is something on your mind?" I grunt as I lunge for a new handhold that's too far a leap for the newbies I'm planning to take here, but a guy's got to have a little fun. "Look at this place, man. Nowhere better to solve the world's problems."

"All is good. You should pay attention to where you're putting your feet," he says.

"Is there trouble in paradise? Six months of marriage, and already there are ripples in the smooth waters of love with you and Mindy?" I doubt that's the case. The two of them have been head over heels since the moment they met. Only five months into their whirlwind romance, he put a ring on it. He saw his chance and he took it. I don't blame him, either, because nobody knows that opportunities are fleeting better than I do. My best friend has found the love of his life, but I've yet to find mine. I'd be jealous if I wasn't so damn happy for him.

"No way. You know Mindy is the best. There's a good foothold by your left knee."

I glance down, and he's right. I step up into the hold and boost myself higher. "If I'm honest, I thought with you two getting married and the new house, she wouldn't want my big feet tracking in mud all the time, but she's been super cool about it."

"It's been going great other than the home improvement projects that keep popping up," he says. The eagle screeches again, and we both go silent for a minute. I cling to the rock as the eagle flies by, leaving us behind as effortlessly as it some-times feels like my friends do, when each day someone else announces new marriages, homes, kids.

"I was thinking it might be time for me to get married too."

Noah lets out a hearty laugh. "Really?"

"For sure. I mean, you and Mindy being married, and I was talking to Carlos the other day and he's ring shopping. It seems like it's time."

"Brilliant plan. There's just one small problem. I'm your best friend and know just about every detail of your life. Sometimes too much. I could do without knowing the schedule of your bowel movements."

"That's what you get for sharing an office with me."

He ignores me. "To my extensive knowledge, you don't have a girlfriend at present."

I look down at Noah from my perch halfway up the cliff face. "What's your point?"

"Are you kidding me? How can you think you can get married when you aren't even casually dating anyone?"

I sigh. "I didn't say I'd worked out all the details yet, just that I thought it was about time. You tend to get hung up on the minutia of a master plan."

Noah scoffs. "Minutia? I think the bride-to-be is a pretty big detail in a wedding." The rest of his lecture gets cut off by ringtone of Kip from *Napoleon Dynamite* shouting, "Your mom goes to college."

"It's my mom."

"Yeah, I figured. You can call her later." Talking with Noah while climbing is one thing, but while Noah gets along well with my parents, dealing with them while hanging on a cliff goes against his idea of safety.

But if they both are calling in a span of a few minutes, my cell phone is about to become a revolving door of parental missed calls if I try to avoid it. "She's just going to keep calling."

"You should have turned off your phone," Noah says, bracing himself for me to let go of the mountain and put my weight on the rope.

"If I'd done that, she would have sent helicopters out here

looking for us." It might sound like I'm joking but it's a real possibility.

"You might want to tell her your life is literally hanging by a thread right now and she should wait to talk to you later."

"I hope it's hanging by a lot of threads."

I don't bother looking down. I know the eye roll is there, and so is the grumbling that I can't hear. Such a worrier, but I love him.

I lean back and let the harness catch me, then tap to answer through my watch.

"Hey, Mom. It's not the best time. Can I call you back?" The question may as well be rhetorical. I brace myself for the latest gossip about her friends, what my dad has done to drive her up a wall, or inquiries into my dating situation, the latter of which I'd prefer to avoid.

"This will only take a minute." I shake my head and laugh to myself. It will not take a minute. "Your dad thinks we should put a hot tub in the backyard. What do you think?" Mom calls out over the clank and clatter of bowls and pans as she presumably prepares breakfast. To purchase or not to purchase a hot tub. This is definitely a problem that needs to be solved while I'm swinging in the breeze.

"Uh, sure, why not? It sounds fun." They live in the same house I grew up in and have lifelong friends all over the neighborhood. Unfortunately, that means the whole neighborhood feels they have a right to know everyone's personal business.

"Well Honey, here's the thing. I think it would be great for us and I'm all for having fun stuff around the house."

I let the sun hit my face, spreading my arms wide and relishing the beauty around me while I dangle like a spider on a string.

"Great, then go for it."

"I'm not sure."

Now is not the time for me to wait for my mom to get to her

point. "Listen, I should pay attention to what I'm doing right now. Can you give me the short version?"

"Oh, come on. Her short version is a marathon, not a sprint. I'm not going to hold you up forever!" Noah shouts.

"I just know *that woman* is going to bring it up to the home-owner's association and they'll say we can't do it. Or she'll bring it up at Stitch 'N Bitch and find a way to turn everyone against me." My mom's so-called crafting group really just gets together for the wine and the whine, but they do have an incredible amount of pull in the neighborhood goings-on.

"Don't you think this has gone on long enough?"

"I'm not going to dignify that with a response. But that's not the only problem."

"What else?" I roll my eyes and shrug down at Noah, who exaggeratedly taps his foot with impatience.

"Your dad's breakfast buddies will come over every weekend to soak, and then before you know it, I'll get roped into making breakfast for them and that will get old fast. And they would all be out there soaking in their swim trunks. I don't want to start off every day with six old men simmering in my backyard asking for bacon and eggs. Can you imagine?"

"Mom, that's a visual I didn't need." I rub my eyes as if that will wipe away the image now burned in my brain.

"How do you think I feel? I can't wake up to that every morning. They'll be nearly naked! In. My. Backyard!"

"Mom–"

"What happens to my quiet weekends enjoying the mountain view? Good grief, they would never leave! Can you talk to your dad and tell him this is a bad idea? Please?"

I sigh, knowing she'll call me every morning if these guys are over there, and probably send pictures too. "Okay, I'll talk to Dad and see if he can encourage Mr. Lewis to put it in his yard."

"As long as it doesn't get back to Ava that we suggested it. She'd never forgive me!" Mom takes a deep sigh. "I feel better. Now that we've settled that, any news on the dating front? It's been a while since... what was her name?" So much for avoiding this topic.

"Jessica. No Mom, there's no one new."

"What happened with her? She seemed nice."

Noah groans, "Don't get into this with her, man. Tell her you're going into a tunnel or something."

"Yeah, she's nice. Just wasn't the right fit." I can't say *I brought her over to meet you and Dad and she panicked.*

"That's too bad. Although, if I'm honest, remember when you brought her over for chili that time? She wasn't very friendly at all."

I take in a deep calming breath of mountain air to remind me that I can handle my mom's version of love, which involves way too much participation in my life.

Still, it wasn't a great loss. I liked Jessica but was she my one true love? No. I can't say I felt a strong connection with her or any of my past girlfriends, really. I'm not too picky but every time I try to move it to the next level, I end up getting dumped. It sucks.

"Any day now," Noah shouts from the ground. I shrug, plant my feet against the wall, and bend my knees to bring myself back in to climb.

"Why don't you give Kayla a call? Her mom told me she's not dating anyone right now."

Despite my recent proclamations about marriage, letting my parents set me up probably isn't the way to go. "I really need to get off the phone or Noah's going to drop me." Frustration bubbles in my chest and I kick the rock face. Noah grunts with the force of the sudden catch.

"Okay, no Kayla. How about if I ask around? I'm sure I can set you up on a date with someone. You can come over on Saturday."

I take a second to secure some footing from my new hand-hold and catch my breath before responding. "Absolutely not. Been there, done that. I can find my own dates, thanks." This hell will not end. Mom means well, but if she gets started talking to her friends about who I should date, I'll have to leave Colorado to find a deserted island with no cell service. That woman has a lot of friends.

"But–"

"I'm good Mom, but I've got to go."

The eagle makes another chirping pass.

"What was that?" Mom asks.

"An eagle."

"Where are you?" Concern tinges her voice.

"On the side of the mountain."

"What on Earth are you doing talking to me while climbing?" she shrieks.

"I told you it wasn't a good time!"

The line goes dead. That's one way to get her off the phone, I guess. I return to my climb, and before long, I reach the top. An endless sea of rockface stretches before me, and deep trenches cut by the river create a picture-perfect view of Colorado. A laugh escapes me. I have to blink a few times to keep my eyes from watering. I truly have the best job in the world. I get to experience beauty like this almost every day, and better yet, I get to watch the absolute wonder on other people's faces when I guide them through those experiences.

Even though my camera roll is full of hundreds of similar pictures, I pull out my phone to snap a few more shots of the valley from my perch at the top. I take in one more deep breath of that sweet mountain air while I spin in a slow circle to get a full 360-degree view before reluctantly preparing to descend.

"On belay," I call down to Noah.

"Belay on," Noah calls back. I take hold of the rope and rest my feet on the edge of the cliff, then slowly lean back until I'm standing against the side of the rock. My phone rings again.

"Let it go until you get down," Noah calls out.

"I got it, don't worry. It's just my dad, so this will be quick."

After ensuring I've got a good grip, I tap my watch back onto speaker.

"Hey Son, you aren't on the mountain right now, are you?" I should have guessed it would be Dad.

"Yeah, actually. I'm climbing down now. What's up?"

"Oh shit, call me back when you get down."

"It's okay, I can talk."

Without looking I can tell Noah is glaring at me. He calls up, "I should drop you."

"Mom got to me first about the hot tub and Noah is threatening to let me plummet to the ground, so I'll call you later."

"Later, but back me up on this one!" The line goes silent.

"Thanks for not actually letting me fall," I say.

"I definitely considered it," he grumbles. "It sounds like your mom's got you covered with this marriage idea of yours."

"See, that's another reason why it's time. You wouldn't believe the list of people she wants to set me up with. I can't take it. I know you think I'm joking but I'm serious."

"I know you're serious but I'm not sure you've really thought it through. Are you planning to just fall in love with the next girl you meet? It isn't something you just decide to do. Besides, in a week, you'll be on to some other big idea, and finding the love of your life will be out the window."

I land my feet on the ground and face Noah. "Nope, I want this. You never know when the perfect one will walk into your life. You never saw Mindy coming."

Noah concedes the point. "I guess that's true. But there's an issue with timing. Let's get back to focusing on work, and when there are women around," he gestures to the quiet trail, "you can consider finding the one."

I chuckle and flip him off as I gather up my equipment. "This would be an awesome tour for us to do. Check these out." I hold out my phone for him to see the shots I took up at the top.

He shakes his head. "Yeah, but you're talking a lot of new equipment. We have to do a feasibility study before you get carried away. The bouldering trail looks great, but I think it's better if we focus on the things we have going right now."

Noah is always a little hesitant to add new trips, but I love to keep things fresh.

"Let's come up with a good description and you can set a price for that at least."

"Fine, but I want to see how we do at the Expo before you go adding climbs. Business has been a little slow lately, so I want to wait until our numbers go up."

We grab our gear to start our trek back out. When the phone rings, I mime pitching it over the side of the mountain.

Chapter 3
Moxie

The combined voices of the crowd blend with the thumping and clanging of rides and the ringing of prize buzzers as I weave my way through the town's summer fair. Childhood memories climb to the surface as I slip between tents towards the building where they're housing the business expo. I'll stroll up to his booth and express a little interest. If I get bad vibes, I walk away. It's no different than saying hey to a guy at the bar, and yet my anxious belly seems to be convinced that it is.

Six-foot tables line both sides of three aisles. A few people mill about near the entrance to the exhibit hall, but none of them are Hannah. I hang my thumbs on my belt loops awkwardly while I wait. Since I'm one of the millions of cyborgs who can't seem to pass a silent moment without a screen, I whip out my phone to check my notifications. Still no Hannah. I glance at the phone's clock before shoving it in my back pocket with a sigh. It's five minutes after one o'clock. She's late, which seems very unlike her. Or maybe I've misjudged her. It never really surprises me when people let me down. It's the whole reason I try not to depend on anyone. If you don't expect anything from them, they can't disappoint you.

Another scan of the room, and three booths up the aisle,

right in my eye-line, a frog is staring me down. Not an actual slimy creature but a bright green costumed one, with eyes more disturbing than friendly. Odds of any child catching sight of that thing and wanting to come within ten feet of it are slim. I shudder and resume my search. After scanning all the rows, my eyes swing the other direction, and I jump back a step in shock. The frog is still zeroed in on me from the vicinity of the insurance booth for which it appears to be the mascot. I swear it looks closer than it was before.

I narrow my eyes at the frog. I can't say what's going on inside the massive head, but the costume eyes remain fixed, never moving. What the hell is up with this theme park reject? Finally, it glances from side to side, then discreetly—or as discreetly as a six-foot, lime green, fur covered amphibian can —beckons me.

I laugh as it hits. "You've got to be kidding me," I mutter. "This is your plan? I don't know if I can take you seriously in that."

"One, I tried to send you the plan, but your email wouldn't accept the attachment. It said the file was too large." Hannah's voice is muffled by the thick mask. I'd tell her to take it off so I could talk to her but I'm honestly not sure which would be more scarring to children: the actual mask or seeing the fake frog decapitate itself.

"How large a file could you have possibly created for a meet cute?" I ask, incredulous.

The massive head tilts and I can picture Hannah's nose crinkling in confusion. "Well, I had photos, a bio on Wyatt, and a PowerPoint with an embedded role-playing video to demonstrate recommended conversation starters. There was a minute-by-minute Excel schedule—which we're behind on, by the way —and a map of directions from the bar since I didn't know where you live, as well as of the parking lot and fairgrounds."

My jaw hangs slack as I gape at her. "You made a role-playing video? You're going to have to find a way to get me that file. I don't care if it's no longer relevant."

"I like to be prepared," she grumbles.

"What was point two?"

"I couldn't have him recognize me. You wanted to meet him with no pressure."

"Yeah, yeah. What's the plan?"

"He's at the next booth, so I can try to listen in and signal if you go off track." Hannah points her green finger at a brightly colored booth full of snowboards, kayaks, and a mannequin decked out in snow gear. The sign reads, "Shred and Tread." Maybe Hannah found someone for me who won't be boring.

"Think of me as your Cyrano; instead of a silver-tongued wordsmith, I'm an amphibian with hand signals. I researched earpieces, but your hair is too short to hide them."

"Earpieces might have been extreme. You ready?"

"Ready Freddy." She hands out a few flyers to passersby.

How the heck did she manage to become the insurance company's mascot on short notice? A mystery for another time.

I walk around her, and there he is.

The lone guy in the booth wraps up a conversation with some other expo attendees, then bends over the table, his casual blond curls falling in his eyes. He looked good in his picture, but it didn't do him justice. Hannah didn't mention the pure ease with which he carries himself, nor how badly I would want to run my fingers through his gorgeous wavy hair. And that body, naturally toned and tanned, tickles my insides. I can picture his strong arms pulling himself up the cliff walls. I make a mental note to thank Hannah later.

I slow my steps, forcing my eyes away from Wyatt and studying the gear behind him, while my heart rate returns to normal. I show enough interest for any expo booth shark to latch on to a potential customer, and Wyatt bites.

"Do you kayak?" he asks.

"I've been once before. Does that count?"

He flashes me a wide grin, and oh god. I'm such a sucker for dimples, and he's got them. "What I'm hearing is, you're practically a pro?"

I laugh. "Something like that."

"Here, take a look at this. We have two-person kayaks for our river tours, and if you want an exciting group experience, you should check out our white-water rafting."

"These pictures look awesome!" Hannah was setting me up for a date, but it looks like I'm going to have fun even if the romance doesn't work out. My eyes linger on his mouth, and I imagine… Oh shit, he's watching me. I'm probably drooling. Get it together.

"Which one sounds more your speed?" He opens a book with pictures and descriptions of various options. He got a laugh out of me right away, he doesn't give off creep vibes, and he's even more attractive than I'd expected from his picture. I should probably pay attention so I can make a decision, because while I may still have reservations about dating long term, I'm fully on board for a night with this guy. His warm smile keeps pulling my eyes back up to that handsome face.

"Rafting sounds fun."

"It's rad. We've got beginner rides that stay on Class II or III rapids, or we have expert runs that hit Class V and VI." Wyatt's face lights up as he goes through the details. Flipping through pictures of past trips, I can see his taut biceps working the oar through the water. They are the same muscles currently testing the seams on his Henley. In the photos, the sun glistens off the water spray sprinkled through his hair. Yep, I'm sold.

"I've got sign-up sheets with me if you're interested, or I can give you one of our brochures that talks about our other options. We're adding a new climbing tour soon, too." His eyes dart away as if catching himself on something.

"Can I see the times available?"

"Sure." He guides me around the table, and as I lean over the clipboard with the sign-up sheets, I stand close enough to brush against him in a way that I hope sparks his attention without being obvious.

His forearm visibly tenses as he explains the sheets to me. I inhale and get a whiff of pine tree and moss, and I tamp down the moan of pleasure that wants to escape. I half-listen as he explains the sheets, distracted by his mouth and the way his frequent grin stretches kissable lips, bringing out dimples that make me weak. If he always smiles this much and this isn't just win-a-client mode, I'm a goner.

My pen hovers over the sign-up sheet, wavering between intensity levels. On the one hand, I don't want to look like a wimp. On the other hand, I've never been rafting before.

"I think I'll sign up for the intermediate level," I say, louder than necessary. I sneak a quick glance at Hannah, who has frozen in place. It's hard to get any advice from a giant, unmoving frog. She probably had a whole alphabet's worth of signals in her failed email. I'm going to have to go with it. I lower my pen to the page, when suddenly, there's a loud crash.

Without warning, Hannah has gotten into her role of frog mascot, and while crouched down, hopping back and forth, she's knocked over a table full of materials.

"The mascot's gone berserk!" the guy running the booth shouts, scrambling to pick up the puddle of brochures. Wyatt moves to help them, but Hannah stops jumping and tries to lend a webbed hand to the cleanup effort. The costume hands can't grip anything, so she's basically pawing at the ground, but Wyatt would just get in the way now and turns back.

"That was weird," he says. I can only assume that was Hannah's absurd attempt to tell me I shouldn't take the intermediate level course. She said her exes thought she was too predictable and not adventurous enough. Is she telling me I'd better go for the expert if I want to impress him? Does she know I've never been rafting before? It's the only explanation that I can think of, so that's what I'm rolling with.

"On second thought, I think I'll try the expert class," I flip to that sheet, and write my name on the form.

"Moxie?" he asks, reading over my shoulder. "That's a unique name." He's so sexy, I'm tempted to scoot back the mere inch or so between us and lean against him. That'd be a little much for an introduction, though. Especially since he doesn't know we're dating yet.

"It is." I cap my pen and spin to face him. I rest against the table, and we are right in each other's personal bubbles.

He raises an eyebrow at me, and I huff. "It's a nickname, but we do not speak of my given name."

"Why not?"

I smirk. "Funny, that sounds like speaking about it."

"Does it?" He holds up his hands in a show of innocence. "Surely there's a loophole in there somewhere."

I tap my chin, then lean in to whisper, "If there is, I'm not going to help you find it."

"I'm good at finding things." His own whisper is minty fresh, but not overpoweringly so. My eyes flick to his lips, which he absolutely notices, and the grin is back.

"Is that so?" I ask.

He straightens and runs a hand through his curls. "Yeah, but you could help me out."

"Alright. It's not that deep. It doesn't fit. I despise it, and I'm pretty sure anytime someone calls me by it an angel dies or something."

He laughs a deep belly laugh that's like a warm hug. "So dramatic. What is it?"

"A closely guarded secret." I fold my arms, and if they nudge my breasts up the teensiest bit, it's purely coincidence.

"I'm good at keeping secrets too."

"Sounds like you're good at a lot of things. I'm still not telling you my legal name."

He pouts. "I'll get it out of you eventually."

An Ex-citing Proposition

There's a brief pause in the conversation, and I realize I'm not supposed to already know his name. "We'll see. And you are?"

His eyes widen and he inches back to increase the space between us.

"Right, sorry. I'm Wyatt." He offers me his hand, switching right out of flirtation and into professional mode. I'll have to fix that.

I grasp it firmly, holding on longer than a handshake would require, and I meet his eyes. I pitch my voice lower in a way I hope sounds seductive. "Nice to meet you… Wyatt."

I'm pretty good at reading expressions, but if we were at a poker table right now, everyone would know he has a royal flush. His face reddens, and those killer dimples reappear. "The pleasure is all mine."

"I'll see you Thursday." I walk away with my head held up confidently, and a smidge of extra sway in my stride.

"I'm going to find out that name!" he shouts up the aisle.

I shake my head. "Good luck."

"How'd I do?" I ask Hannah in our planned restroom meetup.

She removes her costume head and gulps fresh air. "Oh, he's hooked. You should have seen the way he stared after you. He leaned so far, he nearly fell over the table."

"That picture was criminally misleading." I fan my face as if that could cool the heat in my belly.

"I thought you liked his picture."

"I did, but it was underwhelming compared to seeing him in person."

"Yeah, he's a cutie. A charmer too." Hannah shimmies, struggling to free herself from the costume.

"Definitely. Thanks." I'm genuinely impressed at the lengths she's gone to for this hair-brained scheme.

She pauses in her shuffling and her muffled voice comes from somewhere in the vicinity of the costume's neck. "Which course did you end up signing up for? Did you get my signal?"

"Your extremely subtle signal not to take the intermediate? Yeah, you were hard to miss. I went with expert," I say.

Her face, sprouting from the unmasked furry green body of her frog suit, falls. Her smile is replaced with wide eyed horror.

"Oh no."

Chapter 4
Wyatt

"Thanks, man." I take the signed safety waiver from Paul and tuck it under my checklist for the adrenaline rush white water raft trip. With him and his girlfriend Kim checked in, we're only waiting on one more for our small group: the highlight of the Expo for me, Moxie.

"Are you two locals?" I ask.

Paul shakes his head. "We're from Wisconsin."

"It's our first time to Colorado."

I tilt my head. "Have you ever rafted on the Menominee?"

"Many times," Kim says. "Gotta do something to shake off the boredom from the work week."

"Desk jobs," Paul sighs.

"We try to get outside as much as we can," Kim explains. "Lots of rafting and biking. And cross-country skiing when it snows."

"My kind of people."

I excuse myself to retrieve the life jackets and helmets, but the parking lot still shows no sign of Moxie. Not that I've been replaying memories of her adorable smirk and the way she strutted out of the expo, but I can't wait to see her again.

She'd jumped for the first activity I suggested. Must have

been my charm. Not wanting to get caught gawking like a simp when she arrives, I return to Kim and Paul.

"Kim, let's try this helmet for you." I hand her a bright yellow helmet as a car pulls into the lot and Moxie slides out.

She glides up to the group in barely-there white shorts and a purple tank top. Strings from a turquoise swimsuit dangle at her neckline. My intent was not to drool but I'm having trouble tearing my eyes away.

"Hey there... Matilda?" I take a stab at guessing her name.

"Nice try, but nope."

"I'll keep thinking. Ready to take on the rapids?"

She throws her shoulders back and looks at me like a lioness on the hunt, her big brown eyes captivating. "You bet. I can't believe I haven't done this sooner."

"Wait, are you saying you haven't been rafting before?" Warning bells blare in my head. Normally I'd verify experience at sign up, but I was distracted. If her name wasn't on my list, I'd have thought I dreamed her. "This is an advanced part of the river with fast moving rapids and swells. The expert run is no joke."

Moxie looks around the group. "I've been rafting on a river before but not in Colorado, and this will be my first expert run. But it'll be fine."

I look between her and the waiver. The responsible thing here would be to discourage her from an expert run, but if I do, she'll probably never end up coming back. I don't want to miss my shot with her, but grudging responsibility wins out by a hair. "Are you sure you wouldn't rather start off on one of our easier runs? We could reschedule a trip for you. I have a nice intermediate run scheduled for tomorrow, and I'm pretty sure there are still two spots left."

"Don't worry about me. I'm a quick learner." She winks, and with mixed emotions, I hand her the forms. I did my due diligence and warned her. Ultimately, it's her choice.

"Okay, but I want you sitting close to me when we get to the raft." My doubt dribbles away as she signs the waiver and grabs a life jacket from the back of the van.

"That sounds even better." A wicked grin slides across her face.

I'm distracted by the bright sunshine glinting off the river of electric blue running through her hair.

"Come on then, let me introduce you to Kim and Paul and we'll be on our way." I hand Moxie a helmet.

"Kim and Paul, this is Moxie, and this guy over here is Noah. He's my best friend and the brains behind Shred and Tread."

"Hey everyone. I'll pick you up at the end of the run and drive you back here. I'm looking forward to hearing what a great time you all have. I'm leaving you with the best guide out there, but please pay attention as Wyatt goes over the safety review." Noah unhooks the raft from the top of the van. I unload the paddles and hand them out. "Yellow paddles with green handles are for righties, green handles with yellow paddles are for the lefties."

Noah smirks while I wait for the joke to click. Kim points back and forth in the air thinking through what I said. Moxie catches on the fastest and lets out a snort of a laugh that makes me laugh in return.

"Okay team, the four of us are going to go over our game plan to make this the safest dangerous activity you've ever done." I try to keep it light while going over the basics of rowing and the safety review. Rule number one of tour guiding: throw in as many cheesy jokes as possible. Laughs equal tips.

"The rapids move quickly on this run; that's why it isn't called a walk. So, remember, don't stop to question it, do exactly what I say, keeping your feet secured under the edge of the raft the whole time. If you go in the water, stay calm, try to grab the raft, bring your legs to the surface, and point them downriver." I love rafting, but as with all our adventures, these people are my responsibility, and that's not something I take lightly.

"We'll pull you back in the raft. Otherwise, follow the directions that I call out, and enjoy the ride. You'll get to see some beautiful scenery along with bouncing around on some great waves."

As usual, each of the participants seems to think the safety lesson is meant for everyone but them. "Even though it's small, I think you've got yourself a good group today." Noah tugs the van's sliding door shut. "Keep your mind on the rapids and not the eye candy."

I flip him off and he snickers.

"I'll see you at the bottom." He turns and heads back to the van.

I do a final check of everyone's life jackets to make sure they're on properly. A couple inches shorter than me, Moxie is built with enough muscle to lessen my concern about her experience level.

"May I check your straps?" I gesture at her jacket.

"Have at it." Even standing this close to her, she looks me straight in the eyes as her tongue glides across her lower lip, almost daring me to kiss her as I tug the straps tight. The sparks fly off her as I try to focus on my job.

We get in the boat with Moxie and Kim on the right and Paul on the left. I sit in the middle at the back of the boat so I can paddle on both sides as needed.

"Alright folks, we have a nice and easy stretch up first, so let's practice some directions to get us started. Forward!" I call out.

The group responds, and we ease out toward the center of the river.

"Great job, everyone! Let's try a sharp turn around this rock. Hard left!"

Paul and I on the left side of the boat back paddle while Kim and Moxie paddle hard on the right.

"Eep!" Moxie squeaks as the raft lurches over a slope, but then she lets out a nervous giggle.

Quickly, we fall into a groove. Moxie is doing well, but I

suspect she wasn't entirely honest about doing this before. Her muscles are tense, and she flinches with every direction I call out.

We work our way down the river, picking up speed. It turns out that it was good I put Moxie between Kim and me, because she tries to anticipate what I'm going to call out. That's all well and good for an easy ride, but not when there's hidden obstacles beneath the surface that a newbie can't anticipate. Only an experienced rafter, who knows this river like the back of their hand, can account for the fast twists and changes.

To her credit, she reacts quickly, adjusting her strokes whenever I direct her.

"Woohoo!" Moxie shouts out as we come around the bend. A full ear-to-ear grin is plastered on her face.

I burst out laughing as an impressive shower of water hits her from the next dip. Moxie quickly joins in, her laugh infectious. Paul takes on a pirate accent and soon every time I shout out a direction the whole boat answers back with an "Aye, aye Captain!" We're a raucous crew of buccaneers navigating the twists and turns. I love this ride but find myself sneaking glances at Moxie. She smiles and cheers as if this is the best time of her life. When I tell her to paddle, her brow furrows in adorable fierce determination. Then she looks at me with a proud grin, droplets of water on her cheek glistening in the sun. Her excitement eclipses the beauty of the river.

"Paddle hard right," I shout to Moxie and Kim. This part of the river gets tricky. We barely squeeze through a narrow passage between two boulders. I shout out encouragement to Moxie to try to keep her on pace.

We're a little slower than we should be on the turn when we crash against one of the rocks. As Moxie shouts out in surprise with the jolt, she twists towards me, causing her foot to slide out from under the edge of the boat where it was anchored. Before I can warn her to secure her foot, we bounce off another boulder.

I know we have a big problem before the scream leaves her

mouth. I drop my paddle and reach for Moxie as she careens from her safe seat in the raft to the rock filled river. Clutching at her life jacket, I manage to slow her descent, but not save her from splashing down into the swift current. I immediately grab my paddle and switch into crisis mode, reverse paddling with all my might while I shout out directions to Paul to paddle hard left and Kim to backpaddle.

Moxie coughs and screams as she flails around in the water. She isn't focused on the boat at all, forgetting everything from the safety lesson.

Ordinarily, I have the worst attention span, but when adrenaline hits my system, it's like the whole world moves in slow motion. All at once I factor in the waves and sharp rock edges and instantly plot out the route that I need to take to get her safely back into my boat. While the river has turned into our foe, Paul and Kim follow directions as if on the battlefield. Water rushes by as we parallel Moxie's path.

She's in a panic, arms windmilling as she rolls around downstream. I know only seconds are passing, but it feels like she's in the water for treacherous hours. She's too terrified to get herself closer to the raft. I keep my voice calm but firm as we maneuver next to her.

Sweat drips down my forehead, mixing with the surges splashing in our faces as we furiously paddle and finally get close to her. "Moxie, lay flat! Feet downriver. I'm going to grab you." Even though I'm shouting, I don't know if she can hear me over the roar of the rushing water.

A heartbeat later, I manage to grab her life jacket by the shoulder straps and haul her into the boat. She lands on top of me, coughing and spitting water as she clutches my arms in a death grip.

Our eyes lock while, gulping air, she struggles to see me through her terror. She shivers and sputters as I gently set her in front of me so I can stabilize her if I need to.

After a quick assessment of our location, I direct Paul and

Kim to paddle with me to the right where the water deepens and the current turns from racing rapids to rolling waves. Paul and Kim thankfully stay calm and keep paddling. The crisis likely took no more than a minute or two, but my heart is pounding.

"We've got you. It's okay, Moxie, you're safe." I quickly run my eyes over every inch of her to make sure nothing is broken or bleeding. Her legs have a couple of scrapes, and it looks like a bruise might form on her foot, but there's no major damage. "Does anything hurt?"

She shakes her head. "No. I'm okay."

"Good. Can you take a deep breath with me? That's great."

Moxie's breathing gradually evens out as she regains her composure. She tries to smooth her wet hair out of her face. This gutsy woman may not be as tough as she tries to appear.

"I'm okay to keep going." She retrieves her paddle and wedges her foot further under the edge of the boat.

The waves turn to gentle swells, allowing me to keep an eye on Moxie. She seems to have recovered well but keeps side-eyeing the river like it's the class bully waiting for the teacher to turn her back. I give the crew some directions to get us through the last of the rapids and on to the smooth water of a drop-pool.

"You okay Moxie? Still nothing hurting?" Now that the shock has worn off, it's possible she could notice an injury she was numb to before. Her deep brown eyes appear to have doubled in size.

"Still good." Moxie clears her throat like she's remembering how to speak. "Thanks for saving me. I thought I was taking the rest of this ride on my ass." Her laugh comes out forced but we all join in and the tension washes away. The boat gently rocks as the calm blue ripples nudge us along.

"Now I know what a fish feels like being plucked out of the water." She gives a weak smile as she furtively looks from Kim to Paul and finally me.

"Nice work scooping her up, Wyatt." Kim tucks her own feet

back under the raft edge as we prepare to head back to the main river flow.

Paul laughs. "If you wanted to get your hands on Wyatt, you should have just said so."

A flash of embarrassment crosses her face at first but then she laughs along with him. "Maybe this was a little ambitious for my first time rafting. It's possible I overestimated my abilities. I should have listened to you, Wyatt."

I manage a spark of anger. "I thought you said you'd been rafting before."

Moxie looks sheepish, "I might have fibbed a little about that."

"This is your first time rafting? No wonder you were freaked out." Kim shakes her head. "But when you tell other people about this, definitely go with the *I did it to get rescued by the hot tour guide* story."

"You know, I'm sitting right here!" Paul sends a stream of water at his wife, who sprays him right back.

"Alright." I cut off the conversation before it gets too far off the rails. "Let's get back to the ride. You know, some companies charge more for a dip in the water," I tease, attempting to recover the boisterous mood. It isn't that no one has ever gone over before, but with how frantic she was, I worried she'd get hurt before I could get her back in the raft.

"We only threw that in for free because I like you. Everyone ready to move on?" Met with nods and murmurs of agreement, I shove off the sun-bleached boulder and back toward the stronger current. Now that the urgency is over, the sun seems warmer, the sky is a beautiful bright blue, and the river is exciting rather than threatening.

About an hour later, we pull into the landing singing "Rock the Boat." Everyone laughs as we pull the raft onshore where Noah waits armed with snacks and ready to collect all the gear.

"It sounds like everyone had a great trip."

"It was the best! The scenery here is gorgeous," Kim says.

Noah nods his agreement. "Did Wyatt treat you right?"

"For sure, and Moxie's tumble was certainly memorable," Paul says.

Noah raises an eyebrow. He can go from happy to fearing the worst in ten seconds.

"I didn't fall over. I jumped in to see if you all were as good at maneuvering the boat as you claimed," Moxie says as if they've been friends for years. "With all the bragging you were doing, I wanted to see you in action. What did you say Paul, you'd been rafting since you were twelve?"

I can't help but smile at this. In the water, Moxie didn't know which way was up, but she's turned it around. This woman is amazing.

"I think we handled ourselves pretty well." Paul hugs Kim and they smile at each other like newlyweds.

"Let's not forget about our pirate captain," Moxie adds. "He made that raft move backwards over the rapids to save me. Look at those muscles." She fans herself and my brain short circuits. My cheeks burn and I squirm in my seat as Kim and Paul laugh.

Noah whispers as he grabs a life jacket, "Only you could turn a safety concern into an intimate moment."

We ride in the van back to the drop-off point with everyone telling stories about past adventures.

At the parking lot, I thank everyone, truthfully meaning it when I tell them what a great group they were and squeezing in one last joke.

"Hey, what's the difference between a pizza and a raft guide?"

"What?" they ask in unison.

"A pizza can feed a family."

It gets a chuckle and serves its purpose as a gentle reminder to tip. They agree to pose for a picture for our website, and I encourage them to go on another trip with us as we say goodbye.

Moxie turns to me as Paul and Kim walk hand-in-hand over to their car. "Thanks again for the ride, Captain." The nickname fills me with a rush of pride and desire to show her all the other ways I can take command.

"I hope you enjoyed the tour despite your dip in the water."

"Absolutely," she says.

"What made you decide to go right to the expert run?"

"I like a good thrill, and the idea of seeing you in your element was… enticing." Moxie's cheeks redden as she looks down at the ground.

I flounder around for a comeback but just stare at her. She signed up to see me? "I love it out there. I was surprised that you signed up as a single. We usually get groups of two or more."

She raises an eyebrow at me, and what started as an *Are you available?* inquiry gets awkward, so I hurry to cover it up. "What do you usually do for fun? I mean, we have lots of other adventures that you might enjoy." It sounds more like a company sales pitch than the prospect of getting to know her better.

Moxie eyes me for a moment and sweat breaks out on my forehead.

"I don't have any specific hobbies, but I'm always up for trying new things. The excitement of the unknown, you know?" She tilts her head to the side, eyeing me with a devilish grin.

I nod. She's preaching to the choir.

"And, astute observation, as I am not currently dating anyone." She meets my eyes confidently as she twirls her fingers through the short strands of shimmering blue and black hair.

"Good to know. Neither am I." I'm completely off my game and have no clue what to ask next. Thankfully, she comes to my rescue.

"I haven't done anything like this in way too long." Her eyes un-focus as she stares wistfully over my shoulder. "When I first moved here, I thought it would be a blast but lately my job has become the same old shit, you know? Even the things I used to like are blah now." She sighs and looks me over. "A ride with you was a perfect change of pace." Her fingers graze my shoulder, setting off an electric current as they slide down my arm.

I clear my throat. "Like I said, there are tons of fun things to do around here." Not my smoothest request for a first date.

"Mmm, I bet that's true." Moxie's eyes darken. She takes a small step forward, and the raft, van, and parking lot fade away. She's all I can think about. I put my hands in my pockets to keep from wrapping them around her waist to pull her to me.

Noah comes around to the back of the van. "You ready to— Oh, sorry. I'll be in the van!" He ducks back to get in the van and out of our line of sight.

"You should sign up for another tour. I'd be happy to go over the choices with you." I fumble in my pocket and pull out a business card. "I think you earned a discount with your dip in the water. Or if you ever just wanted to go out…" I throw it out there, hoping it's not too terribly unprofessional. Moxie moves even closer, leaning forward to reach for the card. Our hands linger together.

The way she twirls my business card through her long fingers has me imagining those shiny pink nails dragging down my chest.

"I might do that. I'm always up for 'fun things,'" she says with a sultry emphasis. Her eyes suddenly light up. "Actually, I have a work party tonight. Do you want to go with me? There's good food, an open bar, and some party games. We could go for an hour and then see where the night takes us."

"And is this a date, or am I your arm candy because you suspect how good I'll look in a suit?"

"I'm confident you'll wear the hell out of a suit but saving me definitely earns you a date. It'll be fun." She singsongs the last of it and waggles her eyebrows at me as if any extra charm is needed. There's no way I would say no, and I think she knows it.

"I'm in."

"Okay, I'll text you the details." She waves but turns back to lean in close and whisper, "Thanks again for the ride… Captain."

I'm slack jawed fumbling for a response as she glides across the parking lot. Her hips sway as if to her own personal soundtrack.

Noah throws a life jacket at my head and rolls his eyes. "Here we go."

"What's that supposed to mean?" I reluctantly turn my attention back to him.

"You know exactly what it means." He laughs. "I saw the sparks flying between you two."

"Yeah, I think there might be something there."

Noah shakes his head as he reaches up to check that the raft is secured to the top of the van. "If you like her, then let me suggest you take it slowly."

"I'm not rushing things. You heard her, she asked me. I just said yes."

"Based on what you were talking about last week, I was afraid you were going to say, 'Hey, instead of that, how about we head to one of those drive-thru chapels in Vegas?'" Noah chides as he heads to the front of the van.

"I just put it out there in the universe that I was ready for the right girl. I don't know why you're surprised when she drops into my lap. It's called manifesting."

"See, that's what I'm talking about. You can't go into this like you're ready to marry her. You'll sound like you're going to lock her in your basement. It's creepy. Treat it like a casual date and see what happens."

"Don't worry, I'm not thinking she's The One. I mean she could be, because she's stunning, and funny, and brave. We had fun on the raft. I have a good feeling about this."

"Nobody is The One after three hours. You've got to get to know her, and she's got to get to know you. You have to see each other on a bad day or at least for a whole day." He smirks.

"The drive from here to Vegas is eleven hours—plenty of getting-to-know-you time," I tease.

"I know you're joking, but I'm worried about you. You get your hopes so high with everything. You'll start dating her and spend all your free time with her in a whirlwind romance. Two weeks later, you'll be telling me you met the love of your life. Eight minutes later, you'll ask her to move in with you." He puts his hand on my shoulder as I open the passenger door. "And shortly after that, I'll be swinging by your house to help clean up takeout containers and pick your ass off the floor to get you back into the light of day again. If it's special, you don't want to rush it." Noah rounds to the driver's side of the van.

He fires up the van as I get in. "Besides, I need you thinking about work and getting more people signed up for trips. We should go over our books. I know you don't like doing that stuff, but we only had three people on this ride, which is concerning. We're having some issues, and I need your input."

"What kind of issues?" I'm only half listening to him as I can't get Moxie out of my head.

"I know you want to add these new tours and do an overnight trip, but we can't afford to do that right now. Today isn't the only trip that's been half-full. That's why I want you to look at the numbers. We can brainstorm some ideas to work this out."

"Hey, you know me. I'm the ideas guy," I say as we park behind Shred and Tread.

A customer pulls up and distracts Noah as we're unloading, so I haul the equipment into the storage area, but my mind is on how I'm going to remember to take it slow and keep my hands off Moxie at this work party of hers.

Chapter 5
Moxie

"Ow!" I yell, as I chuck the offending eyelash curler across the room. Why do I even own a contraption like that? I don't remember using it before and can't fathom when it would have ended up in my collection.

"Yeah, I know," I mutter to my reflection. "I don't know what I'm doing."

Why am I trying to impress him anyway? My body roils with brand-new emotions making me ignore my instincts to get the hell out of this situation. I meet my own gaze, intense and wary, and immediately picture my mother staring into her own mirror, not realizing I stood in the hallway. I watched her fight to compose herself after another argument with my father over empty wallets and stacks of bills. Her trust in others wiped away as completely as her tears over the friend that betrayed them.

Bringing a guy home from the bar is easy, but this date with Wyatt is tangled up with expectations from him and Hannah. I know better than to let myself grow close to him. I know how recklessness with my heart can leave me empty, just as easily as a careless gambler can blow their life's savings in a few bets. Yet here I am, subjecting myself to the pokes and prods of alien beauty products because a stubborn girl insisted, I take a chance and because a handsome man made me laugh and feel alive. Suddenly, I have a tiny flame of hope flickering in the damp caverns of my damaged soul.

Abandoning efforts to beautify beyond my standards, I quickly draw on some eyeliner and throw on a blue dress that hugs my curves and flares at mid-thigh. My stomach churns with nerves and the fear that I'll live to regret giving a man a chance beyond a one-night stand. I wonder what my parents would think after all their warnings to be careful with my trust, although I don't think a string of hookups was what they had in mind. Maybe I should call and cancel.

I hadn't planned on going to family night at the casino. I've skipped it every other year despite heavy peer pressure to attend. I've never felt the need to bond with my colleagues outside of work hours, but my boss needled me to attend once again. I gave a reluctant maybe, but the idea of wandering a ballroom full of my coworkers and their friends and families all alone sounds like the worst way to spend a day.

I'd gone rafting on a promise to Hannah, but I found myself hooked. I had to see him again, and I confess I wanted to show him off. I knew if I was going to the event, I wanted him by my side, so I invited him on a whim.

With the clock ticking down to event time, the anxiety over-interacting with my coworkers in a social setting makes me sick. Hannah is going to bounce around declaring herself Cupid 2.0 when she sees us together.

My intercom buzzes, and the cancellation ship sails into the distance, leaving me petrified in its wake.

"It'll be okay. We'll have fun. Deep breaths," I coach myself, then let him in.

"Damn." His eyes wander over me. "You look gorgeous."

I grin at the compliment and stand a little straighter. Take that, torturous beauty gizmos.

"Thank you." Heat rises to my face. Shit, I'm blushing. I swallow back the nervous lump in my throat and take in Wyatt. His wavy blond locks are pulled back into a bun, but one strand has already broken loose from the hair tie, as free-spirited as the man himself.

He stands proud and eager in his suit, watching me with a goofy grin. He gives his tie a nervous tug, and I wonder if he agonized over his outfit as much as I did my makeup.

"You clean up pretty well yourself," I say.

His hand relaxes, smoothing down the tie and falling to rest at his side. I wish my nerves could be so easily calmed. "Only for you."

The comment makes my heart flutter; at the same time, alarms go off in my brain. *Go on a couple of dates. Have fun, but don't fall for him.*

Nervously, I clear my throat, grab my purse from the hook, and slip out the door. "Do you think you can behave yourself tonight?"

His eyes roam my body and settle on my lips for a long moment before he answers. "I'll be completely honest. I don't know if I can."

I'm comfortable in my skin, and my ego is doing just fine without his compliments, but flattery is always nice. I smile to myself and lock the door, certain he's checking out my ass while I do.

"I came over here confident that I'd be a nice piece of arm candy for you, but you're breathtaking." Wyatt keeps staring as if I might disappear if he looks away for too long.

My cheeks heat. "Alright, don't overdo it."

"Just being honest."

"Uh-huh. I like the idea of you being my arm candy." My earlier anxiety melts away.

"I'm not just a pretty face. Wait until I turn on the charm. I'll win over your bosses, coworkers, and friends. In fact, I might be the most popular one there by the time this is done."

An Ex-citing Proposition

"Someone has a high opinion of himself." I cock an eyebrow at him, before resuming fidgeting as we walk to his car. I could use a little of his mischievous attitude tonight, stealing the show and taking the attention off me. One night to get through, and then they won't pester me into attending another event for a whole year. Wyatt's expression is so eager and open, I find myself wanting to be honest with him. "We'll mainly be with the other dealers and our pit bosses. Fair warning, I hate these kinds of things. I'm not great at interacting with coworkers outside of work. I get anxious."

I watch him for judgement but instead am met with an understanding nod. "Lucky for you I also make a great scapegoat when you want to get out of there. Just say Ebeneezer and I'll fake a phone call that the horses escaped."

I snort a laugh. There's a lot to unpack there. "First, I think we need a less conspicuous codeword. Like malarky."

He frowns. "That's way less fun, but alright."

"What are you talking about? Malarky is a great word. Second, most people would just go with *I'm not feeling well.*"

"Key words: most people. It would be too transparent. The horse thing is way more believable."

I shake my head, and even though the smile won't fade from my face, I make a mental note to try and tolerate the night without requiring Wyatt's extraction services.

His expression shifts, and in a gentle tone, he adds, "In all seriousness, if you're ever uncomfortable tonight, lean on me. That's what I'm here for."

"Thanks." I ease into the car, losing some of the anxiousness that clings to me as tightly as the fabric of my dress. He wants me to depend on him, and that relaxed me? What kind of voodoo has he performed? I eye him skeptically, but he's got that innocent grin. I barely know the man, but somehow, I don't doubt him, only my own ability to rely on him.

We make small talk in the car and soon arrive at the event. The stream of vaguely recognizable faces surrounds me, making me feel trapped even in the open air as we walk across the parking lot. The ballroom is decked out with green and blue balloons, with food and drink carts arranged in a giant circle. One of the beer carts looks like a wagon with self-serve taps all around it to get the brew of your choice from a selection of local microbreweries.

"There's a flight of three mini drinks where you're supposed to vote on your favorite to be the drink of the month for the property. Rumor around the casino today was that they're delicious. Want to try them?" I don't bother mentioning that I could use the liquid courage for my social anxiety. One-night stands with strangers I can do. A sea of acquaintances is my nightmare.

A sign for the flight mentions a Mai Tai, Aperol Spritz, and a Mango Margarita. "Absolutely," Wyatt says.

As we get in line, I look around for Hannah. In my eagerness to see Wyatt again, it didn't even cross my mind to mention to Hannah that he would be here. Now that I think about us all here together, it might have been better to let her know. She had such an elaborate plan for a meet cute, and Wyatt being here probably isn't part of it.

In the corners, there are group games set up, and tables fill the middle of the room where small groups can gather or eat. About fifty people mill around getting drinks and sampling the food stations.

"They go all-out for this event," Wyatt says.

I'd heard it had a large budget, but I must agree with him. There's everything from a brightly-colored veggie shooters station and a taco and wing stand, to a station with kebabs. A group of people crowded around the wing stand laugh like friends, and I twist to face the other way. Next to the tacos, there's even a wall of donuts. It looks like something that Willy Wonka could have dreamed up, with different colored frostings and sprinkles. A sweet, sugary scent fills the air.

Hannah is nowhere to be seen.

"It's a win-win for them. They try out different ideas for the casino on us, and we get to have fun." I return the waves of some coworkers and order two flights. I hand Wyatt his tray and take my own, and we set them down on a nearby counter-height table.

Now is the time for some liquid courage. I throw back a solid gulp from each and glance up to meet a concerned frown on Wyatt's face. Right. He's supposed to be my crutch for the evening, not the liquor. Except, I like him, and the fact that I like him is making me almost as nervous as being around all these coworkers.

I resolve not to take another sip until he's caught up a bit. He kindly doesn't comment, as I scratch down a vote for the Mango Margarita. He takes his time sipping each one and considering the delicate mix of flavors with a tilted head. His sudden serious connoisseur attitude contrasts with his typical playful grin and wonky gait. He's so tall that his lope looks a bit like a puppy still growing into its legs.

"That's a good one." He returns the Mango Margarita to his board.

"It got my vote."

"I don't know, I'm leaning toward this pink one, but I need a few more sips of them both to be sure." He clearly put a lot of effort into his appearance tonight and now is carefully weighing his options for a silly beverage vote. I normally suffer from resting bitch face, but when I'm around this guy, I keep catching myself smiling. Putting his all into this night for me feels like the greenest of green flags.

Over his shoulder, I see Hannah peeking around the edge of a large pillar across the ballroom. She holds a finger up to her mouth in a silence gesture, then flicks her hand in a jerky wave. I glance over my shoulders to make sure she's talking to me, and she bugs her eyes out impatiently in response.

"I..." I hesitate. I thought now would be the time to tell Wyatt that Hannah and I know each other, but Hannah is clearly still in stealth mode.

"I'm sorry, do you mind if I leave you to consider that for just a minute? I'll be right back."

The crinkles at the sides of his eyes fall flat with disappointment, but he smiles and nods. "Sure thing. I can test these drinks all night."

"Thanks." Before I know what I'm doing, I lean in and kiss him on the cheek. I blink in surprise at my own actions and catch his significantly brightened expression before turning to go see what's up with Hannah.

The second she sees me coming, she takes off at a power walk, and I follow her bobbing curls through the crowd like I'm some sort of spy in an action film.

Her speed kicks up, and so does mine. As we finally near the edge of the absurdly large ballroom, she ducks into a service alcove.

"Are you okay?" I ask.

She peers carefully around the wall and checks both directions. "Yes, of course."

"Of course. Because this is perfectly normal and not at all strange behavior." I roll my eyes. Then again, the last time I saw her she was wearing a frog costume for stealth purposes, so I guess I should be grateful she's wearing more normal attire.

"What is Wyatt doing here?" she hisses.

"Oh, that. We hit it off on the rafting trip, and my family is all out of state, so I invited him."

"You didn't think to tell me this?" I dropped the ball in updating her after the rafting. Clearly, I'm out of practice with the whole friend thing.

"No, sorry. But why don't you come say hi now? We were just about to grab some food."

She bites her lip. "I'll say hi to him, just not right now." Suddenly she ducks under a table.

"Hannah? Hannah! I could have sworn she was right here a second ago," a confused woman who looks a lot like Hannah says as she searches the room.

"I'm so sorry," Hannah whispers. "that's my family. Can you please do me a huge favor and keep Wyatt out of sight of them? Like, at all costs. I don't have time to explain now, but I promise I will as soon as possible. Pretty please?"

She grabs my hand and holds my gaze, but it's all I can do to gape at her. "I'm sorry. I have to go. Thank you. Sorry, sorry, sorry!"

She ducks out of the alcove and hustles over to an older couple who are weaving between some cocktail tables nearby.

I'm immobilized by confusion when my neck prickles with alarm. I don't know what the hell that was all about, but something tells me Hannah is hiding a major detail, and I don't like it. Across the room, Wyatt shifts awkwardly and kicks at the ground. I can't leave him hanging any longer. I feel bad for abandoning him as long as I have. The conversation with Hannah leaves me with a sense of impending doom, but I try to let it go and focus on my date. My feet unstick themselves, and I hurry back to Wyatt.

"Hey, I'm back." I sidle up next to him. "Sorry about that."

He immediately relaxes. "Hey, gorgeous. It's all good. You were distracting me from homing in on the flavors and making an impartial decision anyway."

"Oh, I'm a distraction, huh?"

He puts on an exaggerated frown. "A terrible one. And we couldn't have that with a drink menu at stake."

"It could have been disastrous," I agree.

I force a laugh, but my stomach twists. It had seemed like Hannah had the potential to become a friend, but now she's got my hackles raised. I didn't know what to expect from Wyatt, but doing what Hannah has asked feels wrong.

I don't want to hide anything from him, but she promised to explain soon. I'll try to give her the benefit of the doubt until the end of the night, but that's all she's getting.

Hannah and her parents walk past, heading toward a group

of her customer service colleagues. She points, keeping their attention faced the other way like a tour guide.

Swallowing another wave of guilt, I take Wyatt's arm. "Come on, let's take a look around so we can decide how quickly we want to get out of here. I don't know how long I can keep this dress on." I tug him in the opposite direction since he's frozen in place with his mouth agape.

Chapter 6
Wyatt

"What's your favorite game to deal?" I ask.

Warmth travels up my arm from where Moxie's hand rests near my elbow as I escort her around the room to scope out our options.

"I like the carnival games," she says.

I frown. I don't remember seeing darts and balloons, balls and cups, or rigged basketball hoops at a casino before.

She chuckles. "That's what we call table games other than blackjack. I like them because they're less math. The stakes are higher per hand. High risk, high reward."

"I can relate to all of that," I say, remembering Noah's confusing spreadsheets and the risk of our business venture altogether. "Sometimes risks are worth taking." I find her hand and give it a squeeze.

She flicks her eyes to the other side of the room, at what I'm not sure, and her mouth presses into a thin line. But then she settles her attention back on me, and her scarlet lips curve into a slow, seductive smile. "I think you might be right." She nuzzles next to me.

"What do you want to do next?" I truly mean at the party but my eyes keep returning to her mouth in anticipation of leaving the casino.

"Let's grab another drink, and those kabobs look yummy. Then I'll introduce you to some of my coworkers from the pit."

I trail on her heels as she sashays through the balloons and bright fluorescent lights. All this and the pounding beat thrumming through the speakers dazzle my senses. She introduces me to a bunch of other dealers whose names I immediately forget. We chat with what seems like a very friendly group of people. Moxie's conversation is a little stilted, and she seems tense, but when I rest a hand at the small of her back, she visibly relaxes.

"I see my bosses, Deshawn and Sally. Come on, I'm counting on you to help me impress the higher-ups." We walk over to them at a seating area to the left of the bar.

"Hi Moxie, are you enjoying the party?" Deshawn gets up and shakes our hands.

"Deshawn, Sally, this is my friend Wyatt."

I straighten with the reality check of being called a friend when I was imagining kissing every inch of her in a more than friendly way. "It's nice to meet you. This is an impressive event."

"Glad you're having fun. Moxie here is a very valuable member of our staff." Deshawn turns his attention toward my beautiful date.

A wave of pride rolls through me as I beam at Moxie. She's obviously well-liked by her bosses.

"Thanks. You both make it easy to come to work. We've got a great team." Moxie graciously spreads the compliment to include her coworkers.

"You're a big part of the reason it runs so smoothly. You're always calm in stressful situations. It's one of the many skills that make you a natural leader among the dealers. Don't think we haven't noticed." Sally gives Moxie's wrist a gentle squeeze.

"Thank you."

"You were offered a promotion in the past. Most people don't turn down a raise. Was there a reason why you didn't accept it?" Deshawn presses, a little too serious for a company party.

"Well, I really like my job, and it seemed like a promotion might not be right for me," she says.

"We see a lot of good things happening for you here." Sally winks.

"It was nice to meet you, Wyatt. Moxie, keep up the good work. You never know when good things are just around the corner," Deshawn says as another employee walks up to them.

We turn to walk away, and Moxie's steps are stiff as she breathes out a long, slow sigh. Her soft hand finds mine, and I give it a squeeze. Warmth springs from my chest and floods my senses. When I'd offered to be her anchor, I hadn't expected her to take me up on it. We float over to the game area in a bubble of silence as the cacophony of sights and smells swirls around us. Moxie seems absorbed in her thoughts, but a smile fights its way across her face.

"That went pretty well, huh?" she says.

I stop her progress and turn her toward me, glad she seems to have gotten past her nerves over the interaction and is able to take in the glowing compliments they had for her. "Can I give you a hug?"

Her eyes widen, but she nods. I pull her into my arms. She reaches around me and snuggles into my chest. When she pulls back, I take a moment to look into her glistening eyes and at her extra-pink cheeks. She doesn't say a word, but I swear she looks like she's trying not to cry.

"It must have been nice to hear those compliments," I say, gentlry prodding.

"Sorry, I'm a little flustered. I knew they were happy with my work, but I didn't expect them to actually say anything. Deshawn has only been here a few months. Come on, let's get something to eat." She shakes it off and grabs my hand as she heads to the food stands.

"Good, because the smell of those kebabs is calling to me."

We walk over to the stand, each thanking the server as we take our plates.

"Do you like the people you work with?" I grab a skewer with steak, onions, and peppers. The savory scent alone is so good my mouth waters. The sweet pepper and tangy onion, combined with the flavor of the tender juicy meat, is like a concert in my mouth. Out of respect, I should at least be sitting at a table to enjoy what I thought was going to be a snack on a stick.

"Oh, yeah. I mean, sometimes the pit bosses annoy me, and a few of the customers can be assholes when they lose too much, but it's a job, so whatever." Her eyes glaze over, and she stares across the room at an empty corner. She blinks a few times in rapid succession, pulling herself back to the moment.

"Is it something you always wanted to do?"

"No, not at all. I wanted to have an adventure. I needed to get out. My parents are fine, but I was frustrated. Right after I turned twenty-one, I moved to Colorado, because if you're looking for adventure, it seems like the place to go." A sad smile crosses her face.

"I get that. I love Colorado." I want so much to get that sparkle back in her eyes.

"When I heard about a job at the casino, I thought it sounded so cool. It was at first, but now it's turned into the same old, same old. Your job seems like you have fun every day. Half the time, I feel like I'm on autopilot."

Moxie's cheeks flush. The dejected way her eyes sink to the floor, pulling her shoulders down with them, guts me.

"Lately, things haven't been the best with my job either. The tours are a blast, but Noah has been trying to get me to spend more time going over his spreadsheets with mind-numbing detail. I'm not into analyzing every dollar as it comes in. He's good at finance, so for a numbers guy it's like a work of art. For me, it goes a little over my head. I know it's important, but I can't get myself to focus on it. The trips are great, though. The one with you was particularly enjoyable."

"Even though you dropped your favorite customer in the river?" She leans into my chest and sends an electric charge down my body as she shoves me.

"I think you mean even though I heroically rescued my favorite customer." I run my finger along her jawline and down her neck to the silky strap of her dress before I remember we're in her place of work.

"At least you agree I'm your favorite," she whispers.

"There was never any question of that."

"Come on, I need tacos." Moxie pulls me over to the cantina and we grab a couple spicy tacos to bring back to what has become our table.

"I think I'm ready for a full-sized Mango Margarita," I say. "Do you want one? I'm buying."

"How gallant of you to buy me a free margarita. Yes, I'd love one." We're almost to the back of the line when her eyebrows shoot up, and she tugs me in the other direction. "From the other bar. It looks like the line is shorter."

It technically is, but neither line is long, and by the time we walk all the way over there, they'd probably be about the same. "I think it would be just as fast to wait in this one."

"Maybe, but I want to say hi to that bartender." This seems even less plausible, given her general lack of desire to talk to any of her colleagues. I glance back the other direction, wondering if she's running from an ex or something, and I do a doubletake.

Standing around the game station are my former neighbor and short fling Hannah and her parents. There was a time where my first instinct would have been to say hi, but even though things with Hannah and me ended on good terms, the situation between our parents did not. The neighborhood still hasn't recovered. I prefer a positive vibe, so now my instinct is to avoid confrontation. I hurriedly follow Moxie. I was so hyped about her that I'd forgotten Hannah works here, too.

No sooner than I've sat down do they start heading my way. Hannah's parents talk animatedly to each other and don't look like they've noticed, but Hannah's eyes lock onto me, and she tries and fails to redirect them. They're heading straight for me, and there's no time to avoid being spotted. This could get ugly. I wanted to be Moxie's support system and help her look good in front of her colleagues. Instead, I'm going to be involved in some public family drama and Moxie will be embarrassed. I can't let this happen.

Fortunately, Moxie coughs and stands up so she's between the Nelsons and me. She takes her time straightening her dress. When she speaks, her voice is low and husky. A whole new Moxie has come out to play.

"I told you I can only deal with this dress for so long. I wanted to put in an appearance, and we've already talked to the bosses. We could hit a club, loosen that tie of yours, do a little dancing." She dips her head and runs her fingertip along the edge of her glass. As her eyes meet mine, there's no doubt that the moves she wants to see don't belong on the dance floor.

My tie suddenly feels tight at my throat, and I'm seconds from hoisting her over my shoulder and racing out of there. But even I know that isn't the way to get to a relationship. I'm trying to slow things down, and as great as racing to bed with her would be, it might hurt me in the long run. I need to prove to her I'm more than one-night-stand material, and being able to hold my own and support her among her colleagues seems like an important piece. If only I didn't have to steer clear of the Nelsons too. There's no time to waffle on the decision. We've got to get away from this area.

"It'll look weird to your bosses if you leave already. We just got here. Come on, let's play *Name That Tune*. I'll kick butt at it. We can refill our drinks and gather some of your coworkers."

I can't help but feel like I've just blown my shot like I always do. I *think* I made the right decision, but the rest of my body isn't in agreement with my brain. She sighs but walks with me toward the games. "Give me a minute. I'll see who I can wrangle into playing. Do you need a glass of water or something?"

I shake my head, and she runs her hands along the sides of her dress as she confidently walks away. Once she's out of earshot, I mutter, "I need a whole ice bucket."

Chapter 7
Moxie

The stress of trying to keep Wyatt away from Hannah's family gets to me, and the first thing my panicked brain can come up with is to hit on him and heavily imply I want to take him home. Good to see the old me hasn't completely disappeared.

"Hey Moxie, what can I get for you?" Kenji asks from behind the bar.

"Two of those Mango Margaritas and a water please."

Across the room, Wyatt fusses adorably with the tie that is clearly a foreign object to him. I like him. I want him. And I want to know why he has to stay away from Hannah's family because I'm convincing myself I'm being played.

After receiving our drinks, I search for safe people to wrangle into a game. Talk about gambling; we'll be playing a game Hannah could get dragged into at any moment. *It'll be fine*, I thought. *It's a big space! I'll keep him on the move and away from her.* Oh, Past Moxie, you, naïve, innocent child. I'm jumping through all these hoops, and I don't even know why. This is wildly outside my usual preference of no drama and especially no feelings.

I scan the room for Hannah to warn her that she needs to

avoid the games for whatever reason she's failed to bring me up to speed on. In fairness I didn't exactly tell her about my plan to bring him here either, but maybe I thought that with her "meet cute" or whatever out of the way, I didn't need micromanaging. How clearly wrong I was. A flash of twirling blonde curls catches the corner of my eye. There she is.

I throw a glance over my shoulder to make sure Wyatt is staying put. Then I weave around Cindy from the casino's snack shop. She clearly doesn't hold her alcohol well and is currently giggling up a storm while trying to talk several other staff members and their families into roaming the party Christmas caroling with her. Never mind that it's August. I hide behind Cindy so I can warn Hannah.

"You have to stay away from the games," I say without preamble.

"You realize that's an impossible ask, right?"

"I was planning to do it. It can be done," I say.

"It cannot be done. Everyone always thinks they don't want to play the games, until the liquor gets flowing. The next thing you know, you've discovered it was team Colonel Mustard in the slots with the roulette rake, and your arms are around that coworker you usually can't stand for a celebratory karaoke of *We are the Champions.*" Hannah takes a deep breath after her uninterrupted ramble and stares at me expectantly.

"I know. You don't play the games. The games play you." I glance at my shoes, admitting defeat.

Hannah nods in agreement.

"I think Wyatt saw you earlier."

"Maybe. That's alright, he's not the problem. It's my parents."

"Are you planning to tell me why we're keeping him away from them?"

"I know this is a mess. I planned to tell you before it became an issue, but I didn't expect you to bring him here. I'm super thrilled that you hit it off, and we need a serious debrief, but we don't have time now. Look I'm sorry, there is one teensy, little detail that I didn't tell you about, but I promise, it'll be fine. Trust me a little longer?"

"I don't like to be in the dark. It feels like I'm being played."

"Honest, if I'd known he was coming, I would have told you sooner," she pleads.

"You've got to give me something."

She sighs. "His parents and my parents are archnemeses in a big way. I know that sounds silly, but I promise you, if they see him, I can't predict what they'll do. I doubt it will be pretty, and neither of us needs that in our workplace. The whole thing is a long story, but that's the short of it."

"You realize this is ridiculous, right?"

"Try thinking of it as fun! It's like a continuation of Operation Meet Cute. You're like a secret agent in the name of love."

I roll my eyes. "Let's not push it too far with the L-word. Just try to stay away from the games. I've been gone too long, and your parents are wandering, too. Moxie, out." I zip back across the room.

"Hey." I draw out the word while I smoothly and nonchalantly nudge Wyatt to turn him back around.

"Did you find us teammates?" He takes a margarita from me. Right. Teammates.

"Yes! Oh, and here's a water, you looked like you needed to drink it or splash some on you when I left."

He doesn't buy it for a second. "What about whoever you were talking to?" He cranes his neck, and I steer him the other way again.

Cindy has made her way over to us, still looking for carolers. I grab her arm. "Cindy, you were saying you were going to join us for that game that involves singing, weren't you?"

"I was?" she asks.

"Singing, Cindy," I nudge. "*Singing*." Her eyes light up, and the others she'd been trying to cajole into caroling nod gratefully toward me. They'll be less grateful in a minute.

"Oh, yes! That'd be lovely. I'm a wonderful singer," she trails off in an unrecognizable and surely off-key stream of oohs and ahs.

Wyatt and I exchange a look.

"And you were coming too, right?" I pull out my best threatening teacher voice as I stare down Ned who works the table games.

"It's *Name That Tune*. I don't think—" Ned starts.

"I'm pretty sure I saw Aakesh playing," I say, having caught him majorly moon-eying Aakesh on more than one occasion. If Ned goes, his little flock of sheep here will too.

And so the game begins, and wouldn't you know it, Wyatt is super competitive.

"That's bullshit!" he shouts. "The title is 'Red Shoes,; We got that!"

"I'm sorry, but the title is, 'The Angels Wanna Wear My Red Shoes.'" The announcer isn't budging.

The red team, led by Vanessa, shouts out their joy as they high five each other. Our whole team is fired up. There's a small cheering squad that has gathered around the spectacle as we get a little too into the game.

Wyatt stands up to his full height. I should probably be concerned that he's ready to throw down at my work party, but the margaritas are doing their thing, and Wyatt being all cutthroat over corporate *Name That Tune* is working for me right now. I'm practically fanning myself. It's so weird that this is a turn on, but I'm here for it.

"The first part is in parentheses. 'Red Shoes' is totally the title," he insists.

"Yeah," I say. "Everyone knows that parentheticals are unnecessary."

"True though that may be, the point goes to the red team." The red team roars their approval. I can't help chuckling that the most competitive person on our team has no reason to care about winning.

"Damn it," Wyatt mutters.

My head is fizzy with alcohol and the competition has me all riled up. "That's a bunch of malarky! I shout."

Wyatt's head whips around, and he pulls out his phone. It's only as he answers a "call" that I realize I've accidentally said our code word, and like a sleeper agent freshly activated, Wyatt doesn't hesitate to leap into action. I doubt I've ever in my life said that word before tonight, but our conversation had it top of my mind, and alcohol does strange things.

"Wyatt, I didn't—" I say, but I don't get to finish the sentence.

"Oh no!" he shouts, heavily dramatic. "How terrible!"

Points for devotion, but I did not bank on his terrible acting skills drawing attention from the entire *Name That Tune* crowd and more. Like creepy glowing eyes in dark woods, the weight of everyone's gazes fall on us, startled by his loud outburst and intrigued by whatever drama might be unfolding.

I swipe my hand across my neck in a cut-it-out gesture, but he leans in and whispers, "I've got this." He pulls back and winks at me, then throws his hands in the air. Oh god, what have I done?

"What's happening?" someone I don't recognize asks.

Wyatt lets out an exaggerated gasp. "The horses have all escaped? Every single one? Of course, I'll come help. I'll bring my girl—I mean my Moxie. Er…"

"Oh my," Cindy says.

"Sounds like an all-hands-on-deck situation," another stranger adds.

Ned throws a glance at Aakesh and then rolls up his sleeves. "I'll come help too."

Wyatt hears this and his eyes bug out. He glances at me like *now what?*

I shrug at him in what I hope conveys, *I suggested saying you weren't feeling well. This is on you.* But his worried expression cracks into a smile when he catches me failing to hide a laugh.

The crowd around us grows, and I have to cover my mouth with my hand to hide my laughter.

"Oh, what's that? Some of them are walking right back into the stable?" he says, still far louder than necessary.

"Wow, how convenient," I mutter, egging him on quietly enough that probably only Wyatt can hear me.

He glares. *Are you kidding me?*

I bite my lip, holding back my laughter to see where else he's going to go with this.

"Are you sure, because I have lots of experience with horses. I'm happy to help," Ned says.

"Doesn't sound like that will be necessary. Sounds like they've got it covered," Wyatt says as an aside. "The rest are all coming back now, too? Perfect. I'll talk to—"

He stops in mid-sentence, his mouth agape. I spin to follow his gaze and spot Hannah waving frantically from behind her parents, who are following the crowd. Oh, for fuck's sake.

"But what about Geppetto, my favorite sheep?" I ask.

"Horse," Wyatt corrects.

"Right. My favorite horse. Is he back yet? I simply won't be able to enjoy myself unless I know he's safe and sound."

"Nope. Geppetto is definitely still missing. We'd better go!" Wyatt takes my hand, and we bolt, attempting to push through the crowd.

"I can still help," Ned says hopefully, really wanting to look like the hero.

"Nope. Only one horse missing. We've got it," Wyatt throws over his shoulder.

"But I—"

"Let it go, Ned!" I shout.

"Wyatt MacGregor, what are you doing here?" a woman screeches behind us.

Wyatt's body tenses as we skid to a stop, and a hush falls around the room.

"That's not good," he says.

"Did I mention I work with your ex, Hannah?" I say.

"We have some talking to do once we get through this," he whispers as we both turn to face our fate.

"And you don't think the sheep will work on her?" I whisper.

"Still not sheep. And no, we're screwed."

"Hannah! Did you know he was here? What's going on?" Ms. Nelson says.

Hannah fish mouths, fumbling for words.

"What do we do?" I ask Wyatt out of the corner of my mouth.

Hannah fidgets and finally throws her hands to the side as Wyatt says, "Run!"

He tugs at my hand, and I follow him. "Why am I leading? You're the one that works here!"

"I don't know, but the exit is behind them."

"You tell me this now?" he asks.

"Oh sorry, should I have said, 'No thank you. Actually I think we should go the other way' when you said 'run' and just took off?" I huff between breaths, stumbling forward in my heels, the tightness of my dress forcing me into more of a waddle.

"What do we do?"

"Storage room, over there! We can hide out until Hannah ditches them. If I go down, I'm so sending you my hospital bill."

He suddenly veers toward me, and I yelp as he scoops me up in his arms and keeps running without missing a beat.

"What are you doing?"

"My bank account called and didn't like the whole hospital bill thing, so I'm carrying, you. Is that alright?"

Laughing between breaths, we finally make it to the storage room on the far end of the vast ballroom. He sets me down, and we each free a chair for ourselves from the stacks of extras lined up along the wall.

"We kind of threw Hannah under the bus out there," I say once we're settled.

"She'll be alright. You know those parents that could watch their kid throw a rock at a window and somehow gaslight themselves into thinking it didn't happen because their child is a perfect angel?"

"I guess. How long did you date Hannah again? You both like weirdly specific metaphors."

He gives me a look and ignores my question. "Well, Hannah's parents are like that. She can do no wrong in their eyes, although she's always been close to perfect. She'll find a way to calm them down. We just need to give them a little time."

In another scenario, those words might have sent me spiraling, but the way he says them lacks the starry-eyed awe of someone still harboring feelings. Neither does it hold the grudging tone of being annoyed at someone always getting away with things. It's delivered as if it's simply fact with no emotion behind it.

"Was she annoying being that angelic?"

"Not really. I kind of thought of her as a challenge. I was always running around wild, and she would tell me I was going to get hurt or in trouble. I tried to drag her along on a lot of dumb schemes."

My innate skepticism has me running through and tossing aside all the disastrous ways these two could be playing me, but then Wyatt pulls a curl that's fallen loose from his ponytail back behind his ear. He fixes me with that wide grin of his that brings out his irresistible dimples and strong jaw, and it's so sweet that I want to trust him.

"I've gotten busted by Hannah's parents a lot in my life, but I didn't see this one coming." Wyatt looks me over as if he's considering whether I'm a shit show magnet.

The warm, fuzzy feeling dwindles under his evaluation. I've

also got my parents' voices in my ear telling me not to trust anyone. Every time something had to be sacrificed in favor of another necessity, I'd be reminded of how my "Aunt" Allison—my parent's friend and business partner—had gotten away with all their funds, and that mantra was driven into my mind a little deeper. Now, I'm not sure I can get rid of it, or if I even should.

Allison was one of those aunts that isn't related but is so close that you think of her as a member of the family. She made some sketchy deals, then cut and ran with my parents' money, effectively burning their business to the ground. Her name is now a curse word in our house.

"I'm guessing it's safe to say you know Hannah, and that she and I dated," he says.

I swallow and nod. While I'm dying to understand what's going on between their parents, the look on Wyatt's face tells me he's probably feeling just as worried about my intentions.

I owe him an explanation.

"Care to elaborate?" His tone is easy confidence, but there's a hint of worry in his eyes, and I want to take it away. I can't explain Hannah's motives, but I can explain mine.

I take a deep breath and start talking.

Chapter 8
Wyatt

I lose track of time as Moxie and I talk, but if I had to guess, about twenty minutes have gone by when Hannah pops her head around the door, and upon seeing us, pulls out a chair for herself.

Moxie explained the whole drunken logic for this dating fiasco. I'm a little hurt they didn't tell me about it from the beginning, but I understand Hannah not wanting to get my hopes up. She knows me well, and I don't have to do deep soul searching to admit that I'm a high-hopes kind of guy. I've been falling hard for Moxie since the moment I laid eyes on her, and her latest antics of teasingly letting me flounder with the horse story is no exception. The girl knows how to play and doesn't give me a free pass on my shit, and I'm into it.

"I'm sorry, I got rid of them as quickly as I could," Hannah says.

"It's alright. It gave us some time to catch up," I say.

"Oh good. What'd I miss?" Hannah asks.

"He knows we work together, obviously." Moxie waves at the room around us. "And I told him about the pact."

At that, Hannah's eyes widen. Maybe she'd planned to own

up to setting us up, but not that it was part of a pact. If it got me a shot with Moxie, the why of it doesn't bother me.

"He's basically up to speed. I, however, am not. Start talking, you two." She slumps back in her chair, clearly considering her role in this. Hannah and I look at each other, each willing the other to take the lead. On the other side of the wall, there's a roar of cheers when a popular line dance comes on. It's so strange that we're in our own little pod while outside this room the party rages on, our drama probably already forgotten.

Moxie taps an impatient foot. "Your parents hate each other," she prompts.

"Our parents are the Montagues and the Capulets. The Hatfields and the McCoys. In our neighborhood, their feud is legendary," Hannah says.

"Put them in a room together and they force everyone to start taking sides. I carefully time my visits to try and make sure I can slip into my parents' house without running into a member of a rival faction."

"Why do they hate each other?" Moxie asks. Hannah scoffs and throws her hands up. With each word, my gut churns. It feels like I've jumped off a cliff, realized my harness is disconnected, and am scrambling to grab onto the rope before my chance with Moxie splats onto the canyon floor. Now that I know there wasn't anything nefarious about this arrangement, I'm all in.

"Nobody seems to know. I don't think they even remember. They're just stubborn and have all decided to be enemies forever," I say.

"The origins have been lost, but they're constantly escalating with a never-ending barrage of pranks and targeted attacks via the HOA," Hannah says.

"Well, that's bound to get people heated. Nobody likes Homeowner Associations," Moxie says.

"But neither is willing to concede the neighborhood to the

other, so they still see each other constantly. They actually broke out tape and made a line on the carpet at Stitch 'N Bitch."

"You're joking," Moxie says, and her flat tone has my hackles up. I'm losing her. I have to salvage this, but all I can do is watch the train wreck continue.

"I wish. There was a brief hope a while back. I think they just got tired of fighting, and it fizzled out a bit. Wyatt and I grew up around each other and always thought the fight was ridiculous. We dated, and they..." Her wandering eyes search among the stacked chairs and folded tables for words before looking to me for help.

"Tolerated it," I say. They managed to be cordial while we dated. It was a great respite, even if it was short lived.

"Yep," Hannah agrees. "When we decided we were better as friends, we meant it." She looks to me for confirmation and bites her lip, as if afraid her life has been a lie, and I'll say it was completely one-sided.

"Absolutely. We're cool now, and we were cool then."

"But they were looking for a reason to stay mad. Like without the drama, they didn't know what to do. They convinced themselves that things had ended poorly, or that we'd only been in it to manipulate each other on our parents' behalf all along," Hannah says.

Moxie studies me, her bright eyes missing nothing, but there's not a shred of truth to what our parents believed. I only dated Hannah out of genuine interest, but the spark between us was always more friendly than romantic.

"So, the whole thing went kaboom, and the feud came back stronger than ever. If they see me and Hannah anywhere near each other, they lose their damn minds," I say. I don't add that our relationship lasted longer than it probably should have because Hannah was a better friend to me than I deserved at a time when I became miserable to be around. That's a story for another time.

"How'd you get them out of here?" Moxie asks.

"I told them the truth, that I had no idea he was going to be here. It took some convincing and distracting, but I sent them home with a promise to go over there tomorrow. My mom will put me to work with about a dozen half-finished crafty home renovation projects and hopefully forget about the whole incident."

Moxie's eyebrows fold in. I add it to the book of Moxie, my mental catalogue of all the looks on her beautifully expressive face.

"Alright, so your parents are a hot angsty mess, and you two are stuck in the middle of it. Sorry to sound unsympathetic, but I have to know. Were you trying to rope me into this, or am I collateral damage?"

I wish I knew her well enough to decode the meaning behind her question because there's clearly more to it than the words on the surface.

Oh hell, I thought I was the one being played, but maybe Hannah was playing Moxie. She's tough, but I swear I can see the cracks in her facade. Hannah better not break my potential girlfriend. I whip to face her with my full attention.

"I didn't want you to be caught up in the drama. Some of my exes really suck beyond us being incompatible. Wyatt was someone who wasn't a good match for me, but he's a good guy, and I knew he'd be great with the right person. I genuinely set you two up because I thought you'd hit it off," Hannah says.

I'd be more annoyed that I'm being talked about like I'm not here if she wasn't being complimentary. I flash her a grateful smile.

"Okay... I'm sensing a 'but,'" Moxie says. There's a lot of tension in the room, and it's strange with the music still thumping away at the party. I wish I could steal Moxie's phone and text someone an emergency ice breaking drink order delivery to the storage room.

"But, I also didn't think it would be terrible to do the whole two birds thing, minus the killing. I hate that expression. Why do we have to kill a bird? Totally barbaric, but you know what I mean," Hannah says.

"What was the other bird, Hannah?" Moxie sounds like she's trying very hard to be patient but is close to snapping. Whatever scenario she's concocted in her head, it isn't good. I subtly scoot closer to her in my chair. I'm not sure how casual of touchers we are, and I don't want to spook her, but she seems like she could use some comforting. I awkwardly hold my hand out and she takes it.

"I hoped that since our breakup escalated things, if they could see Wyatt and me both happy with other people, maybe we could mend the rift. Solving that problem was one teensy part of the reason I picked him for you. You two had chemistry the moment you met, so I thought once you got to know each other, the sparks would be visible from a mile away. I thought my parents would have to understand he was no longer a 'threat' toward me, and his parents would see that I was just a blip. I also hoped maybe I'd get lucky and hit it off with one of your exes."

"And so, a pact was born," I say dramatically.

Moxie shakes her head and laughs. Point, me. Her lips press inward, and she's for sure got her thinking face on. We sit in relative silence, aside from the muffled beats, while Hannah and I wait her out. Her fist taps on her bouncing knee, and then she lets go of my hand and stands up, pacing frantically about the room.

"I don't do this whole... talking thing, but I like you two idiots even though I'm sort of pissed right now. I feel like I need to do the talking thing, so I'm going to, but then you're going to forget I did, okay?"

"Of course," Hannah says, as if that was the most normal thing to say. I bob my head.

"I'm not great at trusting people, I have some family drama that I am not going into right now, but it drove home the lesson to always be wary. This whole thing made my don't-trust-them Spidey senses go berserk."

"I know it seems bad but—"

Moxie holds up her hand silencing Hannah in mid-sentence. "I've lost trust in you, but I'm reluctant to just end this." She wraps her arms around herself as she studies first me, then Hannah. "If I help you, and that's a big if, no more of this shit. I need you to be completely honest with me."

I'm itching to scream that I had no part in this, but her voice is shaking. This vulnerability is clearly hard for her. She doesn't need me being defensive right now. She'll figure it out later. Right now, she just needs support. I hold my hand up, thumb and pinky together. "Scout's honor."

"You would be a Boy Scout," Moxie mutters.

"You know it, baby. I can make a fire from sticks in forty seconds flat. I'd prove it too, but I try not to. Forest fires and all that." I'd be more than glad to show her my other Scouts-learned skills though. Tying knots has come in handy more than once, though usually not in the way the scouts intended.

We both look to Hannah. "Oh, right!" She fumbles to mimic my hand sign. "Me too. Not the Scout's thing. I missed out on that one. I just like the cookies. But only honesty, I promise."

"No half-truths either," Moxie says. "It's not enough to not lie. You didn't really lie before; you just kept things from me. If you want me to help, I have to be all in."

This, she seems to direct at Hannah, so I hope that means she isn't mad at me.

"I know. It was shitty to keep it from you, but the whole thing is so ridiculous. I didn't want to scare you away before you gave it a chance. But in the interest of total honesty, I need to add one more little, tiny, barely worth mentioning detail," Hannah says.

My head drops in my hands. "Here we go."

Hannah takes a deep breath. "My parents just told me tonight that they want to move in with me."

Moxie doesn't even know Hannah's parents, but her face scrunches into a grimace like she's bitten into a lemon.

Seeing this, Hannah points at her. "Yes, see? Big problem."

"What happened?" I ask, already knowing it's got my parents written all over it.

"The usual. They got into another spat over who knows what. She was still riled up from it when she saw you, so she said, 'That's it! I can't take it anymore. That woman follows me everywhere I go. I can't even get away from them at my own daughter's family day.'" Hannah mimics her mother's overly hysterical voice.

"You've really got the impression down," I say.

"Thanks, I've been working on it. Then she went on about how your parents are getting a 'fancy new hot tub that will have the whole neighborhood taking their side in everything.' I could go on and share the hours of complaints my mom has about all this, but we're at a party. As you can imagine, I'm now highly motivated to mend this feud, so I have to ask, are you still interested in helping?"

At that, Moxie looks to me, and suddenly I feel like I'm sitting on a shelf in some supermarket of bachelors. I straighten my tie and self-consciously shove my fist through my messy hair. While she scrutinizes me, I play back the conversation and don't love what I'm hearing. Somehow what started as us dating has morphed into her helping with the parents' situation. While I'd like that resolved, that was not my objective at all.

"I have some conditions." Yeah, that does not sound good.

"Name them," Hannah says in a tone that conveys that her highness the supreme ruler of the casino customer service desk has been greatly pleased and is confident in her ability and willingness to present Lady Moxie with any boon she might request. Sir Wyatt would very much like a word because this whole thing has gone off the rails.

"They're not yours to agree to," Moxie answers, then meets my eyes.

I'm still a part of this conversation then, and that's good at least. I think. "Hannah, can you give us a minute?"

She frowns but quickly catches herself and brings back her perky Hannah grin. "Sure thing. I'll be just out there."

She quickly pops her head back in, "Unless you want me to get some drinks or guard the door for a while."

"Hannah!" I shout at her.

When the door clicks shut behind her, Moxie sighs. "I'm sorry. I feel like you got blamed for this, but as I was talking, I realized you did nothing wrong. You just showed up to take me on a date.

I scratch at my jaw and throw her a grin. "I wasn't going to say anything."

"I'll work things out with Hannah, but I owe you an apology too. We didn't want to get your hopes up. I was going to tell you first thing tonight when we met her here, and then she freaked out about her parents. I truly didn't think we were up to anything nefarious. That's not how I operate."

"It's all good. I didn't get the vibe that you do. We cool?"

"Yeah. We're good, but I think we should redefine some para-meters. I agreed to this whole ex swap thing with Hannah because... fuck, I don't know. It was a weird night."

I consider this while she crinkles her nose, seemingly trying to work it out, and she puts Hannah's chair back on the stack. I envy her having something to do with her hands. My whole body is itching to move. "Do you really not know?"

She sighs. "Maybe? I mean, part of it was... well, you know Hannah. She's sweet, but she's also convincing, and she was so sad. I just wanted to cheer her up."

"I get that. But I'm sensing a 'but.'"

"Yeah. You ever feel a little bit like you're suffocating? Or you look around and wonder what the hell you're doing with your life?"

I take the time to think about my answer. The echo of the crack of a bat cranking a home run threatens to drag those desperate feelings back to the surface, but that is the past. Now I get to run a business with my best friend, and that business lets me be active, get out in nature, and do all the fun things that I love. Honestly, my life is kind of a dream, but it's a dream with a hole punched out where a life partner belongs. Do I ever feel suffocated? Honestly, no, but I have.

"Not lately. But I know what you're talking about. I always felt trapped in school. In particular, the last few months of high school, after I lost my baseball scholarship, were a special kind of hell. Suffocating is one way of describing how I felt."

"See? You get it. I came out here expecting something different. *More.* And I got in this rut doing the same thing, working the same job, and spending all my nights the same way, never even taking advantage of this incredible place we live. So, when Hannah insisted we trade dates, I agreed to her proposal because I needed to shake things up."

"Not to brag, but we were featured in the Tipton Gazette's Spring 2023 list of movers and shakers."

"Impressive." She laughs but then smooths her face into seriousness again. "This thing with the neighborhood. I want to help with this bananas situation you all have going on, so I'll put on a bit of a show for your families if you agree to take me on some adventures and help me out of my rut."

My mind runs with all the incredible places I want to take her hiking, kayaking, and exploring... Colorado and each other. "I can do that. I can adventure the hell out of this place with you. This will be dating like you've never had before."

She holds up her hand to stop me. "Hold on. I feel a little weird about exploring our feelings with an audience. For now, I think it's best if we stick to friends, and just put on a show in the hopes it resolves that ridiculous feud. In the meantime, we can still have fun hanging out together. What do you think?"

My heart sinks. I thought we had a connection. I was ready to slap a label on us. I guess she's ready for a label too; a nametag that reads "fake". She speaks about feelings as if they can be turned off or ignored. Trying not to show just how much I'm crumbling on the inside, I offer her a weak smile.

"Sure. Okay. If that's what you want."

Her body relaxes, and I hadn't realized just how tense she'd gotten while waiting for my answer. "It is."

I'm not good at sitting still to begin with, and this conversation has been a lot. I need to move. I stand up and shake my body out. "Then it's a plan. So, fake girlfriend, what do you say we head onto that dance floor and show these fools how to really bust a move?"

"I'm in," she says.

We collect Hannah and some of their other colleagues and shake it on the dance floor. Later, we absolutely demolish people in games as I keep my heart together with two things:

One, Carpe diem-ing the heck out of the evening, living in the moment and having fun.

Two, clinging onto two little words: "For now."

Chapter 9
Moxie

I pull into the parking lot and check myself in the mirror before getting out. *Why do you care what you look like? He's a fake boyfriend.* It's day two, and I'm already seeing him for reasons outside of our agreement. Stopping into his office is not exactly showing me adventure, and it's not doing anything to resolve parental rivalries, yet here I am.

I grab his suit jacket off my passenger seat and throw it over my shoulder so I can balance our coffees.

It's a great location. A small strip mall on the edge of town, visible enough to draw traffic but far enough out that it's probably convenient for their activities. Their brightly-colored signage is inviting, and had I known there was a bakery next to it that smells as heavenly as this one does, I would have gotten my coffee there.

I struggle with the door handle and my balanced coffees, and Wyatt's partner who drove us to the rafting excursion jogs from his desk to come grab the door for me.

"Oh, hey Moxie," he says. They must have dozens of new customers each week. I'm surprised he remembers my name, and I'm just the type of person to call him out on it.

"Either you've got an exceedingly good memory, or Wyatt's been talking about me."

His eyes widen and he laughs. "I plead the fifth."

"I'm going to take that as he's been talking your ear off. Sorry about that."

"No, no. All good things," he says.

"I'm sure. Can you remind me of your name? I'm sorry, I'm terrible with them."

"So am I," he admits, either just being nice or proving my point. "It's Noah."

"Ah yeah, that's right. Is Wyatt around?"

He opens the door wider and steps aside to let me through. "Yep, he's in the storage room. Wyatt! Someone's here to see you!" he shouts.

"I could have gone back," I say.

The door at the back of the office swings open, and Wyatt enters the room at a jog, skidding to a halt when he sees me. His face immediately lights up, wide smile, his dimples on full display. I get a little giddy at the knowledge it's my presence that lights him up.

"Hey! Good to see you."

I extend the cup of coffee I got him. "I didn't know how you take it, so I took a wild guess."

He takes a sip and smacks his lips. I'm pretty sure I could have filled that cup with mud, and he would have acted like it was delicious.

"To what do I owe the pleasure?" He does a goofy little bow that makes me giggle. Ugh. Giggling is not in my usual range of vocal expression. Blech, what is happening?

I hold up his jacket. "Someone *insisted* I hang onto his jacket, even for the very brief walk from the car door to my building after the party the other night. I'm not making any accusations, but that might be something one would do if they were trying to create an excuse to see someone again."

He presses a hand to his chest. "M'lady, I was merely

concerned you'd catch a cold from the evening air! Can't a guy look out for his girl's wellbeing?"

"Oh geez," Noah says with the kind of tone that manages to make his eyeroll audible. "I'm going to go... shine the carabiners. Or something. Anywhere else."

"Do carabiners work better when they are shiny?" I ask.

"Nope." Wyatt's grin widens. How is he cute and hot at the same time?

"Right. Anyway, lots to unpack there. One, what's with the bow and the m'lady?"

He shrugs. "I guess I'm just missing ren faires. Have you been to one of those?"

"Nope."

"That's an adventure for you. But it felt right. I was in the moment. Go with it."

"Sure m'lord. Whatever you say."

His eyebrows shoot upward. It sends a rush of heat through me, and not just a blush to my face.

"I like hearing you call me that."

I give him a shove. "Don't get carried away."

"Sorry, my bad. Carry on. You were listing things." He hops onto Noah's desk with the kind of effortful jump a toddler might have required, but when he settles, his feet still wind up touching the ground, courtesy of those long legs.

"Two, a guy can look out for his girl's wellbeing, but I suspect you had ulterior motives."

"You make it sound so sinister. Is it a crime to want to see your beautiful face?"

"Flattery will get you nowhere. I'm already your fake girlfriend. You do realize we were going to have to see each other again anyway, right?" I ask.

"Yeah, but you had a look about you that said, 'Maybe if I put this off, they'll forget about it,' and I wasn't going to let that happen."

My mouth falls slightly ajar before I snap it closed again. I hadn't expected him to be able to read me that well. I one-hundred percent thought that. There's a moment of silence while I recover, and he smirks at me like he's won whatever game we're playing.

"This wasn't one-sided. You promised me adventure. I'm not going to let you get out of it that easily."

The knowing way he tilts his head says he doesn't believe me for a second, but he doesn't argue further. "I haven't forgotten. I've got plans for you, baby."

"Which brings me to number three. I'm 'your girl' now, am I?"

"Caught that, huh?" he says.

"Indeed, I did." I'm keeping it light, but I need to remind him this isn't real. I'll gladly have fun with him, but I like Wyatt, and I don't want him having expectations for something I can't give.

"Well, yes. You're my girl, even if it's fake and temporary. My mother would have my hide if I didn't treat you right. Loaning you a jacket is the least I could do."

A sheepish grin creeps across my face. I despise that my bar is so low, that a man wanting to put in the effort and treat me right gets me going. The warmth that spreads through me to have another person care is a strange but wonderful feeling. Once again, I need to reign in these feelings of affection. Fake boyfriends don't cause flutters, and I'm going to have to be careful with this one if I'm going to stay unattached. He's too quick with his words. It's not easy to find someone who keeps me on my toes with banter, and I'm a sucker for it.

"Uh oh." I follow his gaze over my shoulder, where a woman I'd place in her sixties with bright purple hair and a scowl on her face marches across the parking lot. That doesn't look good. "Speaking of my mother... sorry about this."

He stands back up, and even though he's only been sitting for a minute, I blink at the sudden increase in height. It's jarring. He steps around me, placing himself between me and the Mama Bear headed our way.

"Wyatt Lucas MacGregor!" she shouts, and what is with all the shouty parents lately?

"Julie Eugenia MacGregor," he calmly replies. She halts in her tracks, apparently thrown by her own full name.

"Don't you middle-name me. You know I don't like people knowing my middle name." Honestly, I can relate to the name dislike, Mama MacGregor.

"Sorry. What's with the purple?"

She glares. "I don't want to go into it. Besides, you should compliment a lady, or if you have nothing nice to say, ignore it." Apparently, Wyatt was right that his mom would take him to task for any perceived mistreatment. Wyatt is still the poster boy for chill, but his resigned sigh tells me that maybe he'd appreciate a reprieve.

"I think it's a great look on you," I say.

She startles as if just noticing me. To be fair, Wyatt is a bit of a tower, so I was obscured from view.

"Thank you, dear. It's not staying. I grabbed the wrong box at the store. It'll be gone in five to eight washes. I was planning on staying inside until it was gone, but you forced my hand." She directs the last at her son.

How on earth she didn't notice bright purple on the box is baffling until Wyatt says, "I told you that you need to go get an eye exam."

"You know very well why I can't."

"Dr. Nelson isn't the only optometrist in town, Mom." A piece of the puzzle clicks into place. Hannah's mom is also their optometrist.

"No, but she's the best."

"But if you refuse to see her, a subpar optometrist is better than not being able to see. If you couldn't see the hair dye box, you probably shouldn't be driving."

"Mind your beeswax, son. You're getting me off-track. Speaking of the Nelsons, you haven't answered my calls. What were you doing at Hannah's place of work last night? I thought you agreed it's best to stay away from that girl."

He sighs and rubs at the back of his neck. "There's nothing wrong with Hannah."

Ms. MacGregor let's out a sob. "Don't tell me you're getting back with her. How could you betray us like that!"

"We're not getting back together. She's just a friend."

"As if that's any better! She broke your heart!"

I look to Wyatt for his reaction to this. Hannah gave the impression that though they've known each other for a long time, their relationship was brief and lacking chemistry. If that's not the case, this whole dynamic is about to get much weirder. But he seems unphased.

"No, she didn't. How did you even know I was there?"

"I was watching your location on my phone," she says nonchalantly, and my skin pricks in alarm. It could have just been poor word choice, but the distinction between "watching" versus "saw" seems important.

Wyatt's chest expands with a deep, steadying breath that is probably as close to worked up as this otherwise easy-going man gets. I'm not sure if I should run and hide or kick back with a bowl of popcorn.

"What? Why?" Wyatt asks between breaths, seemingly unable to string any more words together.

"Honey, I've had access to your location for years. It's a safety feature."

"I'm aware. I'm the one who shared it with you for convenience when I'm meeting you somewhere or if there was ever an accident on the mountain so you could notify the paramedics to save my life. Why were you looking at it yesterday?"

"Sometimes I like to watch your dot move. Like my own little Wyatt TV. When I saw you were at the casino, *where Hannah works*, I knew there was trouble a-brewin'."

Whew boy, I am in over my head, and Wyatt seems to notice. He glances nervously in my direction. I'm not quite ready to

throw out the man because of the mom, but this woman is...
a lot.

Up until now, even after seeing Hannah's mom's reaction at the party, I still hadn't quite believed that this feud was as terrible as they made it out to be. If Hannah's parents are anything like this woman, I can understand why the idea of them wanting to move in with her would have her bringing out the desperate measures. Wyatt's eyes are still on me, and I don't know him well enough to tell if they're pleading or commiserating.

I guess this is my cue, my part of the bargain. I hadn't come here expecting to have to play this role so soon. We've discussed zero ground rules for this arrangement, but I've always said in interviews that I'm capable of hitting the ground running.

I step forward and loop one arm around Wyatt's, my other hand out to her. "Hi, I'm Moxie."

She blinks, and my existence is once again all it takes to derail her. Manners win, and she shakes my hand. "Hello, I'm Julie."

"Nice to meet you. I've heard so much about you!" I don't add that none of it has been great, although despite being obviously sick of the feud, Wyatt seems to care about his parents.

"How lovely. I'm sorry I can't say the same." She tosses Wyatt a look.

"No worries. I'm not surprised. We're still new. I'm a dealer at the casino. Wyatt came as my date to our family night."

"Oh." The fight leaves her body, and her eyes go blank like they've shut off while her system recalibrates this new information. The moment passes, and she smiles. "A girlfriend! I can't believe you didn't tell me about this sweet young lady."

She tugs me over to one of the chairs in front of the desk Noah was at earlier. She sits in the other and immediately launches a barrage of questions at me without pausing for me to answer. I look up, bewildered, and catch a glimpse of Noah at the door. He spots Wyatt's mom and quietly reverses back through the door and out of sight. *Take me with you, Noah!*

Apparently in all those past job interviews when I said I could hit the ground running I was full of shit. I'm not equipped to be his fake girlfriend without preparation. I'm going to need a moment to adjust, and this woman in my face is making me feel like I can't breathe.

"I have to get to work," I blurt, even though I'm not due there for hours. I can't tug Wyatt into a storage room to hide again, and if I try to face this now with a severe lack of conversation between him and I, I'm going to say something that blows it all up.

Julie frowns, and Wyatt mouths, "I'm sorry" from behind her.

"I'll see you later?" he asks.

I'm in over my head. What have I gotten myself into? The words blare in my mind on repeat. I know my expression is dazed when it feels like fighting through fog to talk.

"Yeah. Maybe. Text me."

"Okay," he agrees.

"Nice to meet you," I say to his disappointed mother, whose questions I've answered precisely none of.

Then, I bolt out the door.

Chapter 10
Wyatt

I finally manage to shove my mom out the door, my eyes on Moxie's now-empty parking spot, certain the pavement must still be smoking from her hasty escape. From Moxie's point of view, my family must look like even the most extreme reality shows would turn us away for our distance from normalcy, but I try to convince myself that she caught us on a bad day.

The watching my location thing is legitimately stalkerish, and it's a huge boundary issue I'm going to have to deal with, but as a kid, I might have ditched school periodically and given Mom a few reasons to question my common sense. It isn't surprising she has the urge to keep an eye on me.

Once we started Shred and Tread, it made sense for someone to be able to find me in case I ended up dangling from a cliff and couldn't be found. Even so, that location sharing is revoked just as soon as I get my hands on her phone. Outside of that, she's generally a reasonable person and has always been an amazing mom. I love her, but when it involves the Nelsons, all rationale goes right out the window, and both my parents and Hannah's become different people.

Unfortunately, Moxie has only seen them at their worst. My overbearing mother may have just cost me something that could have been truly special. My ideal person looked like she feared for her life on her way out.

I stomp around the office, rearranging kayak paddles until I accidentally knock over the display of reusable water bottles. "Shit!"

I have to salvage this. I whip out my phone and take a deep breath. I've never groveled in a text before.

Me: *Would you believe me if I said we're trying out a new interactive theater called 'Stalker Parents, they never give up.'*

Five minutes of silence. It's amazing how long each minute lasts when you're disheartened and waiting for an answer.

Me: *Listen, I know we have an agreement, but I won't hold you to it. If you don't want to deal with the whole parents fiasco after what you just witnessed, I get it, but let me take you out. You decide what and where, or I can surprise you. Please let me make it up to you.*

No typing ellipses, nothing. There may as well be crickets chirping. It's the sound of loneliness. Guilt stabs me. She didn't sign up for this. I mean, she did, but there's no way she understood. I wouldn't blame her if she decides to ghost me. I angrily restack the water bottles. As I stand up, my breath goes out in a woosh.

Me: *I owe you a grand adventure. The best adventure. An adventure that has you lying in bed reliving the moments that warmed your heart, tickled your funny bone, and awakened your curiosity.*

I return to my desk and beat my head against it.

Noah peeks around the corner. "Is it safe?"

"Define safe," I mutter.

"Free of mothers who've lost their grip on reality, and of disgustingly cute flirtation?"

"Then yes. No chance I'll be on the receiving end of flirtations any time soon." I flop my head into my arms.

"Maybe I should have also asked if it was free of emo business partners."

I glance up and give him a sarcastic smile.

"There's my guy. What the hell was all that about?"

An Ex-citing Proposition

When I walked in this morning, I didn't have a chance to debrief him about the party. He was already nose-deep in spreadsheets, scowling at the screen, and telling me we needed to cut costs. He started spitting out numbers, and my head roiled, so I went to deal with the equipment. That's where I'm in my element, where I'm comfortable and know what I'm doing.

"Turns out Hannah set us up," I say.

Noah let's out a low whistle. "No way."

"Yeah way."

Noah sinks into his roller chair and spins it to face me. "I didn't peg Hannah as vindictive."

I shake my head. "It's not like that."

I spill the whole story, telling him about the party, the pact, and everything that just happened, though he could hear most of it from the warehouse.

"Dude," he says.

I nod, because what else is there to say?

"That's messed up."

"Which part?" I ask.

"All of it. I take it Moxie panicked and fled the scene."

"She looked like she was confronting aliens eying her for research. She's going to ghost me. I can feel it."

"Let's not catastrophize. Do you have plans to see her?"

"I asked if I'd see her later, and all I got was a maybe. She's going to cut and run, and I can't even blame her for it. I know I just met her, but it felt like fate right after I told you I'm ready to settle down and then she lands in my boat. I'm going to lose everything again."

"Woah, buddy. Let's have some perspective here. Maybe she'll ghost you, maybe she won't, but what's everything?"

I glare at him. I know I'm being a dick, but I'm feeling panicky and don't have it in me to care. "Her, for starters."

"You just met her. You've been out with her once," he says. Someone take a vote because now I'm pretty sure he's the asshole.

I pace around the office and finally end up with my hands on his desk, glaring at him.

"When you met Mindy, did it feel different?" I ask.

He at least does me the courtesy of thinking about it before he answers, and when he does, it's reluctant. "Yes."

I fold my arms in response, knowing I've just won my argument.

"Alright, so she's special?" he asks.

"Yes. I can't put my finger on what it is, but I feel fucking great when I'm around her. She's fun. She makes every minute feel like a game, in a good way. She agreed to this ridiculous arrangement, and she's gorgeous, and I don't know. It feels right."

I know I just met her. I know I went into it with my mind set on falling in love, but I also know that those conditions don't mean it can't be right. I felt it. It's more than just a physical attraction. Something clicked.

I look at my best friend who pulled me back together when I was falling apart, the best friend who put all his faith in me to build a business together. We've been through it all, and I silently beg him to understand me on this.

"Okay. I get that. Today was not great, but that doesn't mean she's gone."

"You don't get it," I whine. "This isn't three strikes and you're out. You get one shot, and it's not even in your hands. Then that rug gets pulled out from under you, and you're done."

He stares at me and takes a deep breath. "Are we still talking about Moxie?"

"What is that supposed to mean?" I ask.

He hesitates, and his next words come out quieter. "I'm just saying that Moxie isn't baseball. And just because something didn't pan out once, that doesn't mean nothing ever will."

A lump forms in my throat, and I shake my head in disbelief that he'd go there. He knows what college was like, when I was supposed to be out on a field, and instead was in a classroom with my arm in a sling. He knows how hard that was for me.

"Wow." I need space. I stand to retreat to the warehouse, my eyes watering. I was raised knowing there's nothing wrong with showing my emotions, but I'm pissed, and I don't want Noah to know just how much he's gotten under my skin. "I got hurt and my chance was gone. I lost my dream. You think I can just forget that?"

"No, but you found a new dream. We did. And you're happy, aren't you?" he asks. Noah's face reddens as he stands. He looks like he's reached the end of his rope and I'm not sure if he's going to shout at me or give up.

That defuses my frustration and I turn back to him. "I am. I love what we do, and I'm so lucky I get to do it with you."

"I'm glad to hear that, and if it doesn't work out with Moxie —which I'm not saying it won't—but if it doesn't, you're not going to end up alone. The right person will come around. I'll hope for your sake that it's Moxie, but if it isn't, there are other women out there that would fall for those dopey dimples of yours."

"I've got it bad for her. I'm all torn up. She's calling me her fake boyfriend and says she wants to keep emotions out of it. That doesn't sound like someone who wants to be in a relationship," I say.

"Yeah, that worries me a bit. You're not really a no-emotions kind of guy. But as much as I give you a hard time, you're a catch and I'm never going to tell you that again or your head won't fit through the door. Do the fake date thing if that's what she wants and be cool about it. She'll come around."

"That's what I'm hoping." It's more than hope. I'm counting on it. If a month from now we somehow manage to resolve the feud, and she decides she's done with me, I'm going to be a mess.

"My fingers are crossed for you. Now, you've got a horseback ride coming up. Even better, it's a full group. You've got ten people signed up. You ready for it?"

There's excitement in his voice. We always get people on our tours, but he's been stressing that they're often only half full. I know it'd be better to get more, but I like smaller groups, too.

"What'd the horse say when it fell over?" I ask.

Noah laughs, and I know that we're back to normal, that he won't hold my dickish attitude from earlier against me. "I don't know. What?"

"I've fallen and I can't giddy up."

"Yep. You're ready. Now get out there and get a bunch of five-star reviews. We could really use them. Here's the sign-up list." He hands it over.

"You worry too much, my friend, but I'll make sure they have a great time." I leave him to his work and head back to the warehouse to grab the equipment I'll need.

My watch vibrates, and I trip over myself in my rush to check the notification, hoping it's Moxie. The text isn't overly reassuring, but at least she isn't ghosting me. This is like being up to bat with two strikes and then hitting a foul ball. It's not the homer I was hoping for, but I'm not out yet.

Moxie: *I don't bail on my commitments.*

Chapter 11
Moxie

The buzzer for the front door to my apartment sounds. I glance at the clock as though the time matters. It doesn't. No matter what time it is, I wasn't expecting company. I'd prefer to shut off all the lights and hide behind the couch until whomever it is goes away so that I don't have to people. Unfortunately, since my window is open, the TV is loud enough that I'm not fooling anyone. With a sigh, I pause it and press the button for the speaker.

"Who is it?" I growl.

"Your new bestie!" a cheery voice announces. I frown at the speaker and reluctantly buzz her in. I give the apartment a quick scan, decide it's presentable enough, then open the door to a widely grinning Hannah.

I'm bowled over as she charges past me. Hannah, who usually doesn't have so much as a strand of her wavy locks out of place, has a mysterious orange glob on her forehead, and her shirt actually has wrinkles. I think she's one of those unicorn people who still irons their clothes. I don't even own an iron.

"Are you okay? You look a bit… frazzled." I nod at her hair poking out at odd angles from her ponytail. Her eyes cross as if she's trying to look at herself, and failing that, she pats her head.

She catches a loose strand, and after a feeble attempt to fix it, motions for me to follow her to the couch.

"Never mind about my hair. There was an incident involving knitting needles and jello."

She's been here for two seconds, and this conversation is already giving me a headache. Hair smoothed, she fusses with her shirt and straightens out her clothes.

I shut the door behind her as she marches to the living room with her giant purse and a vice grip on a grocery bag full of wine. Maybe this won't be so bad. She waves dismissively. "It's a whole thing." She finally pauses in her haste and takes a deep breath. "Sorry. That was a lot. Hi."

"Hello." I draw out the word, feeling a bit like I've had way too many drinks and woke up having blacked out our entire conversation. "Did I forget plans?"

"Nope. You'd have to respond to have plans." The words imply irritation, but her tone is bright and unbothered. I guiltily remember a handful of unanswered texts that either came in while I was busy or that I didn't know how to respond to. It ought to be so easy, but sometimes a simple response feels like a momentous task.

"Right. Sorry."

"Not a problem." Hannah hums to herself as she holds out one of the wine bottles, and I hurry to get out two glasses. "Lucky for you, I'm undeterred by your antisocial tendencies and ready to smother you with my friendship."

I wave a hand in the air in front of me.

"What was that?" she asked.

"Nothing," I mutter. *Just me trying to figure out if I'm dreaming.* I can't remember the last time I had a friend. Thanks to my parents' business issues, I got so caught up in not being overly trusting of anyone that I kind of missed out on friendships altogether. I spend my free time on hookups and dreaming up elaborate vacations based on travel magazines and TikToks, that I never actually go on.

This sudden effort at friendship from Hannah is putting me off balance.

"Okay, weirdo."

"You showed up unannounced with jello on your forehead, but I'm the weirdo?" I hand her a napkin.

She frowns. "Mirror?"

"Bathroom's on the left." I point down the short hall of my small apartment. While she's gone dealing with the glob, I dazedly pour us each a glass of wine, still coming to terms with the fact that she's here.

"Thanks." She takes my offered glass as she walks into the room with her hair perfectly coifed and her face free of debris.

"So, what do you want to do? I've got a deck of cards, or we can watch something. I've got some adult coloring books in here, too." She rummages through her bag.

"Easy there, Mary Poppins. I'm not doing anything until the knitting needles incident is explained."

She sighs. "I was hoping you'd breeze on past that."

"It wasn't a very breeze past-able statement, especially if it managed to get you frazzled." I fold my arms.

"Yeah, but I don't think it's going to do me any favors."

Now she's definitely not getting away without telling me. I narrow my eyes at her.

"Alright, alright. So, my mom dragged me to Stitch 'N Bitch, and Wyatt's mom showed. That's not unusual—they just stay on opposite sides of the house and drag people into their drama— but my mom said something about his mom's knitted kitten looking more like a mouse. She said my mom's scarves weren't color coordinated, and a gasp went up around the room, and needles were brandished. I threw myself in the middle so nobody would get stabbed, and then someone flung Jello, and then I heard things like 'you crusty pumpernickel loaf' and 'you soggy toe waffle' and I bolted before the name calling could get Shakespearian, right as a full on food fight started."

If my own experience with their parents hadn't already

convinced me that this absurd feud needed to end, this proves it. "So, you left them there without supervision? You might go home to a crime scene."

"I know! I panicked. What happened to my wine?"

"You drank it." I pour her a fresh glass. "At least it wasn't just the two of them. Surely some of the others will step in."

"Right. Yes. I'm sure they will." Nothing has ever sounded more like "they won't." Hannah tries to smile but her grin has a little too much teeth and is less than convincing. My heart thumps away anxiously in my chest, and I flick a longing glance toward the antacid in my medicine cabinet. My new maybe-friend is giving me heartburn.

"Assuming they all come out of knitting club alive, what are we going to do about it?" I ask.

"We?" Her question is meek, but her doe eyes are full of hope.

"I already agreed to this. I'm doing it."

"I know you did, but I honestly thought you might bail when you realized—"

"Stop," I snap, interrupting her. What is it with everyone questioning my commitment? "Even for something as ridiculous as this, I get that the average person probably would not have agreed to it in the first place, and maybe I shouldn't have. But I did. I've gone out of my way to avoid friendships, but your challenge came when I was weak with boredom. In spite of this being as weird as French fries and ice cream, I'm going to do it. You and Wyatt both need to stop doubting me and let me help."

Hannah shrinks back at my tone but nods. "Well, now I just want to go out and get ice cream and French fries because it's delicious. I really did come over here just to hang out, but if we're doing this, I guess we should dive in." She pulls out a notebook, three different colored markers, and a ruler, which she carefully spreads out in front of her like my couch is her new office.

She didn't come over here to do this, my ass. I do a double

take at her oversized binder. It's mostly poop-brown, mottled with other colors that look like it's trying to be camo but can't quite pull it off. It is without a doubt the ugliest notebook I've ever seen.

"That is the most un-Hannah looking notebook of all the notebooks that ever notebooked."

She giggles but holds her precious office supply as if it were a close friend.

"Seriously, what the hell is that?"

"Allow me to introduce you to Alfred."

She brought her notebook. Her motives may not be nefarious, but there are motives nonetheless. We're back in familiar territory. If she's here because I'm being used and not because she wanted to spend time with me, the world makes sense again.

"That thing is your notebook? I can't imagine you strolling through Target with an entire aisle of options and settling on that."

Her eyes light up. "Oh, I know! Isn't it hideous?"

"Yes. Why on Earth do you have it?"

She leans in and lowers her voice, secret-telling mode activated. "I have this thing where I collect notebooks. My bookshelf has like fifteen beautiful notebooks that I can't bring myself to write in. So now, I make it my mission to search for the ugliest ones I can find so I'm not afraid to use them. This one might be the best."

I bite back a laugh at the complete sincerity in her tone. While this sounds absurd to me, she conveyed it like she was imparting the secrets of the universe.

"Normally with conflict resolution, I would suggest we get to the root of the problem. You can see here in Section A, I've detailed the history of the feud."

This is more like the Hannah I'm used to. I know I'm supposed to take it seriously, but she has an entire novel here on her parents bickering with their neighbors. My cheek muscles ache from fighting the smile. My lip quirks, and she catches it.

"You're laughing at me!" She shuts the poopy journal. "It's fine. We don't have to do this."

"Oh, don't be so sensitive. I'm sorry. I'm not laughing at you; I'm laughing at the situation. Carry on."

She reluctantly opens it back up. "Since we don't know the origin, the closest we've got is the escalation point: the breakup between me and Wyatt. We've tried proving we're friends before to no avail. That's where you come in. They have to believe you two are smitten."

"When tips are on the line, I can convince tourists every day that they're the most fun table I've ever had. Getting some parents to believe that I've fallen for their gorgeous and goofy son shouldn't be a problem."

"I'm sure you can do it." Her smirk puts me on alert.

"What?" I ask.

"Do you really think it's going to take that much acting?" she asks. "I've seen the looks on your faces when you're together."

Adrenaline floods my body, and my whole system says, *Defensive mode, activate!* "I don't know what you're talking about." I take a sip of my wine to hide whatever my mouth is doing.

"Even when you're trying to get tips, I rarely see you smile at work, and Wyatt makes you *giggle.* You can't tell me you don't like him at least a little bit."

Damn. I'd hoped no one else had noticed that. But this was all too messy to begin with. Combine that with the fact that I don't do relationships, and there's no way we'd work. Emotions have no place here. "He's alright. I don't mind his company, and I'm sure we'll have a good time while we convince the parents." My nonchalance is just as much a reminder to myself as it is to convince Hannah.

"Whatever you say. So, we have to get you two together in front of both sets of parents. I think if I'm there too, clearly unbothered by it, maybe that will do the trick."

For someone who's been dealing with this nonsense for years, she seems far too optimistic.

"I've written down a list of ideas on where and how we might be able to do this, but first, if it's going to be believable, you two should spend time together where you're not in the spotlight."

"He's promised me adventures, so we planned on time together anyway. That shouldn't be a problem," I say.

Hannah scratches her head, and her eyes wander around the room. Whatever she's about to say, she doesn't want to say it. I grip the couch cushion to brace myself. "Yes, but if the idea is for you two to be believably smitten, you should probably... you know," she trails off.

I think I know where she's going with this, but I'll be damned if I let her get away with not saying it. "No. I do not know. We should probably what?"

She holds up her phone and my TV remote and taps them together, like she's six and making two dolls smash faces.

"Oh. Right," I say, though it's admittedly exactly where I thought she was going, maybe with words instead of a technology puppet show. I allow myself to envision this. Wyatt and me on various excursions, making out. Wyatt deftly removing his shirt and running his hand down my spine.

I shake the thought before my imagination gets too pornographic with Hannah here bearing witness. I've never had trouble keeping emotions out of sex before, so I don't see why it'd be any problem now. At the very least, I could enjoy making out with Wyatt.

Hannah's toothy grimace is back as she awaits my response. "Yeah, I don't think that'll be a problem either. Does that sacred notebook have a minute-by-minute schedule of how my cell phone and his remote are going to get together?" I ask her, half joking, half concerned that she might.

"Nope, just the suggested locations. We don't want to over-think it," she says.

"Yes, we wouldn't want to do that," I shoot the binder a pointed look. "You realize you're a walking contradiction, right?"

"Just keeping you on your toes. So, has he reached out, or are you going to make a move?"

"I don't know. I wasn't sure what I should be doing. There's no guidebook to follow."

Hannah hoists her binder and opens her mouth to speak before I cut her off. "I meant that this isn't a typical dating scenario. I understand you've written a literal guidebook."

"Step One: Moxie texts Wyatt to schedule first date." She taps the page and claps excitedly. Hannah's timing in coming here tonight was perfect. I had been frustratedly scrolling through Netflix, uninterested in any of the options, wanting to do something but feeling like I had no one to call.

My life has gone stale, and I'm constantly bored to tears. Her company is nice, and I'm looking forward to whatever activities Wyatt conjures up. And yet, there's a tinge of disappointment there too, that planning really seems to be her sole reason for being here. It's expected and comfortable, but sometimes I wish she was actually my friend so I could call her up to hang out. My loneliness is a choice, but sometimes it gets... well, lonely.

Setting aside my dismay, I focus on the task at hand. "Alright."

Hannah flips through tabbed sections. "What do you want to do on your date? I have info on bowling, miniature golf, rock climbing..."

"You would go rock climbing on a date?"

"Of course not, but I thought since you're more of a daredevil than me that it might be an option."

"Let's see if he has any ideas. After all, he's the one who promised me some real adventures. I want to see what he can think up."

Hannah looks like she showed up for a party on the wrong night.

"I'm sorry. We can use Alfred. Show me what you think he will like."

"No, you're right. He hinted that he had some exciting activities for you, so text him and let's see what he's got."

Never has my communication with a man been so planned out. Hannah leans over so she can watch in real time as if she wants to record this life-changing event. As my thumb hovers over his name on my phone, my heart rate kicks up a notch. I can't wait to see him again, which is another thing that takes me by surprise. I rarely want a second date. It must be because we haven't so much as kissed that has me itching to see him so soon.

"What do I say?" I ask, suddenly a little nervous and over-thinking it. He's expecting to hear from me, so this shouldn't have the pressure that a real date has.

"Keep it simple," she says.

Me: *Hey, it's Moxie.*

I show her the text, and she nods with a gravity wholly unwarranted for the simple text. I take a deep, steadying breath and tap send.

"And now we wait," she says.

"Now we wait," I agree.

"And eat gummy bears." She pulls a bag from the counter, but before we can even crack it open, my phone vibrates. Hannah squeals.

Wyatt: *I was hoping I'd hear from you.*

I like the image of him sitting by the phone, awaiting my text. I doubt that was actually the case, but it doesn't hurt to dream it that way.

I show it to Hannah.

"Well?" I ask.

"My brain is screaming at me to give you an entire script, but I'm not going to do that. I got you through the door. You two lovebirds can handle it from here."

"We're fake dating, remember? Your families are way too complicated to give this a real shot."

"Either way, you've got this." She tears open the bag of gummy bears and pops a few in her mouth before pulling out her phone and scrolling away to give me some privacy.

I guess I'm on my own.

Me: *Antsy, were you?*

Wyatt: *Strictly business reasons, of course. Someone wanted to keep this professional. And I had to check in on your sore feet. You threatened to toss your heels into the hottest flames in the depths of hell about ninety-two times towards the end of the party, and I didn't get a chance to ask at the office how your feet were doing.*

Gorgeous and concerned about me. If it weren't for this pact, I might have given him the multi-date treatment anyway. I smile to myself. Hannah notices and grins as well.

Me: *Glad to know my health is a high priority.*

Wyatt: *The highest.*

Me: *My feet are doing much better. My shoes survived my burn threats but are in a time-out.*

Wyatt: *Good. Show them who's boss.*

Me: *When are we starting this fake dating thing? Someone owes me an adventure.*

The text window remains stagnant for several minutes. My eyes keep flicking to the phone screen, waiting for the familiar glow of a notification. Did I lose him? I usually rely on body language to figure out where I stand and then hit them with a sultry look, but even I know a spontaneous video call would be an etiquette breech, no matter how good my fuck-me eyes are. Hannah sitting next to me would be a bit weird too.

"Maybe he changed his mind." I sink back into the couch cushion, closing my eyes.

"Give it a minute. He didn't change his mind. Trust me." Damn, doesn't she know those are the hardest two words in the English language? The couch shifts. "Movie?" she asks.

I crack an eye open to find her settling into her side of the couch, and I search the room for answers. I'd half expected her to get up and bail on me now that the date-my-ex protocol is reestablished. Apparently, she's staying, and we're doing friend things.

"I—okay."

We choose *Game Night*. Actually, Hannah chooses it as the self-proclaimed movie expert. As the opening credits roll and my phone screen remains dark, my fingers start drumming. Before I can stop myself or overthink anything, I tap out another quick text.

Me: *Unless you changed your mind.*

Nothing, not even an ellipsis. Shit. I suck at dating. Even fake dating. I shouldn't care about this. One-night stands are much easier. You show up at a bar and pick someone out. There's none of this text analysis.

"Watch the movie," Hannah sing-songs as she tosses a gummy bear at me.

Reluctantly, I settle in to watch. Finally, my phone buzzes on the table.

"It sounds like he's in. He said he has some ideas what to do and asked when I'm free," my voice pitches higher.

"That's great!" She holds up her hand for a high-five.

Me: *Does Wednesday night work? I could be ready around six.*

Feeling more confident, I take a sip of some water and resume watching.

Wyatt: *Text me your address and plan on wearing hiking shoes. See you then, gorgeous.*

I hug my phone to my chest and immediately realize that it may be the least Moxie thing I've ever done before chucking it onto the table like it bit me. Hannah raises her eyebrow at me, but I pointedly ignore her and fix my gaze on the screen.

Hannah wrestles my phone from me. "Sounds like he's bringing you to the mountains. Don't get naked on the trail. I don't want you crying that your butt itches because you were doing it in a patch of poison ivy."

I throw a pillow at Hannah. "I'm not promising that we won't be doing it, but I'm not getting naked in the wild. With my luck a bear would find us, and I'm not running naked through the woods screaming at the top of my lungs."

She almost falls off the couch laughing. "Make sure you ask Wyatt what to do if you encounter a bear because I know you are definitely not supposed to run. That would be an awesome first date story to share with the kids someday."

"Kids!" I feel the sweat breaking out on my forehead. "Fake dating, remember?"

I get up and pace around the room.

"Relax. I was only kidding. Besides, what happens if you really like him? It could happen. Never say never. But if you're a child-free-by-choice kind of gal, I totally support that." Hannah pats the couch cushion for me to sit back down.

"Alright, but let's not even joke about that. I think I'd rather face the bear."

Chapter 12
Wyatt

Torrential rain beats against the window, ruining my perfect hiking date with Moxie. She told me she came to Colorado for adventure, so I was ready to get her out there to enjoy the wilderness. I planned to impress the pants off this girl, figuratively. Okay, I wouldn't object to literally. Once again, a force in the cosmos has interfered with my ideal date in the form of shitty weather.

"Bella's, how can I help you?" a woman's voice interrupts the instrumental Italian hold music. I will not be defeated. I have a backup plan. Hopefully they still have an opening.

"Hi, do you still have space for two in your cooking class tonight?" I ask.

"You're in luck. I just got a cancellation."

Jackpot. After making the reservation, I pull my hair up. The man-bun isn't my usual style, but if we're going to a cooking class, the last thing I want is to get a stray hair in our food. I'm no chef, generally doing just enough mixing and seasoning to keep me from starving. Attempting culinary skills will be a challenge, but the idea of standing close to her and watching her hands work sounds enticing. If that wasn't enough to worry about, I have to follow the take-it-slow method and pretend I'm cool with this fake dating plan when I want so much more.

On my way out, I pass Ms. Lieberman from next door with an armful of groceries.

"I can help you with those Ms. L," I say.

"Such a good boy." She hands over the grocery bag, and I carry them into the house and set them on the counter for her. "Got yourself a hot date?" she asks.

"Something like that," I say, not wanting to tell her too much in case I go down in flames tonight.

"Don't get yourself into trouble now."

"I'll try." I wink. "Have a good night."

As I pull up to the restaurant, I'm suddenly anxious. I quickly call Noah.

"Hey man, what's up? I thought you had a date tonight." I've clearly caught him in the middle of dinner. He chews in my ear.

"I'm about to go into Bella's, but I don't know if I can do it, man."

"What do you mean?"

"The whole fake dating thing. Maybe you were right, I'm a feelings guy."

"Yeah, but tonight's just you and her. This has nothing to do with the parents, right?"

"Yes." I put the phone on speaker and rub sweaty palms on my pant legs.

"Then, now is a good opportunity. Have fun on the date but play it cool. She's calling it fake for now, but if you treat it like a real date, maybe she'll eventually see it that way. You don't want to rush it anyway, right?" Noah says.

I take a few deep breaths, and he patiently waits on the other end of the line. "You're probably right."

"I know I am," he says, which gets a smile out of me.

"You're such an ass."

Noah coughs and his voice gets quieter. "I hate to bring up work, but let's get together tomorrow. I've got some concerns."

"Concerns?" I ask. Anxiety presses on my chest and I flash back to meeting doctors and physical therapists telling me my baseball career was over before it even began.

"Forget it. Now's not the time. Don't keep the lady waiting. Go have fun."

Right. As if I can forget ominous words like that.

"It sounds like this is more than the usual worries."

Noah sighs. "I know you think I exaggerate the concerns. You always say, 'Don't worry. We're paying the bills,' but I think this time it's a little more serious. Shit, I didn't mean to bring this up now. Seriously, go have fun. We'll talk next time you're in the office."

"Aye, aye. Don't stress, I'll come in tomorrow and you can show me. I've got to go. I don't want to be late."

I walk into Bella's Ristorante and see Moxie bathed in the orange glow of the stained-glass lamps, chatting with the hostess. My eyes lock on every contour and curve of her body in a black and white dress, straight down her toned legs to a pair of ruby red heels.

I finally notice she's watching me check her out. I move closer, trying to calm my nerves. "I never would have suggested hiking if I knew about this dress. You have a lot of faith in me not to spill something on it," I joke.

"I told you, I'm a risk taker. Don't totally ditch the hiking idea because that sounds fun too." Moxie turns away from the hostess and squeezes my hand. Warmth radiates from where our palms meet, sending an electric current all through me.

"Sorry about the last-minute change in plans. I know this wasn't what you were expecting." I'm confident the class will be fun. It's only been a few times, but I don't think I'm capable of not enjoying myself when I'm around her. Still, I'm a little self-conscious about the fact that she probably wouldn't classify cooking at a restaurant as an adventure.

"How dare you not control the weather," she teases, and

when she smiles, I swear the restaurant warms up about ten degrees.

I throw my hands out as if casting a spell. "I tried, but I'm a little rusty, so this will have to do."

"Really, it's not a big deal. Are you a good cook?"

"I can grill burgers and scramble some eggs. I wouldn't say good, but I'm ready to learn something new. What about you?"

"Oh, I can cook, sauté, and sizzle, but I like learning new techniques and recipes." Her intense gaze, the deep brown of a mountain path after a cool rain, sends a shock wave that pulls down my jaw. I might not survive this class without stepping into the commercial freezer to cool down.

She entwines her arm in mine. It's the second time she's casually touched me already, and it's messing with my head. She wants to keep feelings out of it and just have fun, but these touches tug at my emotions. If she keeps this up, taking it slow is going to be off the table and her ass will be on it.

A chipper woman in an official looking chef's outfit walks up to us, along with two other couples who must also be there for the class.

"Hello, I'm Michelle, and I'll be your lead chef this evening. I hope you're ready to have fun and make some delicious food. If you follow me, we can move to the back room where we have stations set up for you. Grab an apron on your way." She points to a coat tree with white aprons with *Bella's* in red script across the front.

I grab one off the tree and hand it to Moxie. "I'd be happy to tie those strings for you."

"Why, thank you. Such a perfect gentleman." She turns around and my fingers brush against her back as I admire the silky skin of her neck.

They've got optional chefs' hats as well. Moxie and I both put on the towering white hats, and I pull out my phone to take a selfie of us. When we lean together for the picture, the tips of the hats bump together, and hers falls to the ground. She snorts with laughter, then tries to clap her hand over her mouth to cover it. My right hand fumbles to grab my hat, and the left tenses up on the photo button, resulting in a burst of shots.

"I have to see those pictures!" She laughs and puts the hat back on the rack.

Her shoulder presses against mine as I scroll through the shots. They start with a cute and goofy pose and devolve into chaos. Her eyes and smile are bright with her laughter. It might be my favorite set of photos I've ever taken.

"Will you send me those?" she asks.

"Depends. You're not going to go selling this handsome face, are you?"

"Not sure I'm desperate enough for the pennies that'd bring in." She sticks her tongue out at me.

"Ouch." I clutch my chest.

"Personal use only," she sighs.

My eyes widen.

"Oh, not like that!" Her eyebrows shoot up, but then her face morphs into a wicked smirk. "Well, maybe a little like that."

There's a mental image that will be hard to shake: her legs spread, her fingers between them, her eyes on my photo. I can't deal with the mixed signals coming from this woman. Chef Michelle returns and guides us toward the kitchen. The restaurant has high open ceilings and old-world charm. I follow Moxie over to our station as her red heels click on the dark wood floor of a room that feels like a television set for a cooking competition.

While the front of the restaurant is crowded, the back is open with five long, white, counter-height tables with lots of room to move around them. Three are set out with mixing bowls, pans, and rolling pins. Next to the equipment is a tray with pre-measured seasoning, flour, cheese, spinach, and other spices.

She hands each of us a recipe. "It's nice to meet all of you. The idea of the class is to have fun, hopefully become comfortable with cooking techniques, and enjoy a delicious meal that you've made yourself. So, wash up while I get some of our ingredients from the refrigerator and we'll get started." She disappears into the walk-in cooler.

I splash Moxie with water as I wash my hands, and she gives me a gentle shove. "You're going to give me flashbacks of my plunge."

"Too soon?" I ask.

"Way too soon." Her expression falls flat and stoic, but then she cups the water in her hands and completely douses me.

It's the kind of banter I saw in my parents' kitchen all the time growing up. *Don't overthink it, just have fun.* The nervous atoms bouncing around inside of me quiet, leaving me in the kind of relaxed state I chase after a good adrenaline rush on the mountain. It's not something I expected for our date-that's-not-a-date. I'm pretty laid back when I go out, but inside I'm analyzing every action and word, waiting for a spark to ignite. Even when the match doesn't strike, I convince myself there is something there. Tonight, there's small flames bursting to life all over the place, and I'm trying to ignore their existence because that's what she wants to do.

Moxie looks up from familiarizing herself with the utensils and gives me a once-over.

"I'm a little annoyed at how well you pull off this ridiculous hat." She looks me up and down as if she's a fashion blogger.

"Oh?" I strut between the counters and spin.

"Yeah, and dammit you rock that apron," she admits.

"It's a gift. Looking good in a variety of outfits is one of the skills that has gotten me through life." I demonstrate a few magazine-worthy poses before Michelle clears her throat to begin the class.

"Tonight, we're making spinach and ricotta ravioli," Michelle explains. "I've divided your recipe into sections. We'll start with making the dough, then we'll make the filling, and then we'll cook the ravioli. Let's get started with putting your flour into the mixing bowl and adding seasoning and the egg."

An Ex-citing Proposition

Moxie and I banter about who cracks the eggs more cleanly, and she only gloats a little when I have to fish out some shell.

"Next we're going to knead the dough," Michelle calls out to the class.

We both reach for the dough at the same time.

"Trying to hold my hand?" She turns to me and I'm suddenly conscious of how close our lips are. The air stills as I linger, bent close to her.

"Not yet. After you." I take a step back.

A knowing smile slinks across her face when she catches me staring at her hands as she works the dough. My neck burns, and I tug at my collar. *Go slow. This isn't a real date.*

The time it takes to accomplish each step allows us to talk in between listening to instructions. As we work, we chat about the weather, our town, and our families. For a while, we focus on cooking and get things done without bumping into each other.

At first it seems like there's a magnetic field around her that pulls me into her orbit as we try to negotiate the small cooking area, but eventually we ease into a rhythm working side by side as we move on to mixing the pre-steamed spinach, ricotta, lemon zest, salt, and nutmeg.

Michelle comes by and assesses our progress. "Everything is looking good, but let's try to roll that dough thinner."

Moxie takes over when I press too hard, tearing the dough.

"Be honest, what'd you think when I suggested a cooking class?" I ask.

She tilts her head in thought for a moment, then grins her wicked grin. "You were ordering everyone around on the river, so I thought it would be fun to see if you can take it as well as dish it out. How does the captain do in the passenger seat?"

"I think you'll find that I don't care which seat I'm in, as long as I'm along for the ride." I'm having so much fun that any concerns have left my brain like my four years of high school Spanish.

Moxie rolls the dough as if she's done it for years. Soon there are four strips of perfectly even, super-thin dough.

"Moxie, that looks great," Michelle comments as she evaluates our work.

"Why do I get the feeling I've been hustled?" I ask.

"I told you I can cook! It's only fair after my plunge in the water that we do something I'm better at than you. I'm sure you'll balance it out next time when the weather is more cooperative and we can get outside."

Next time. It's at least gone well enough that she wants to continue this, even if it's only for the sake of the pact.

"Okay cooks, let's focus now. It's time to put the ravioli in the boiling water, so I want to make sure the wine glasses are set down and everyone is working together." Everyone dramatically moves their wine glasses away from the cooktop.

"They should take about five minutes to cook, at which point you should remove them to the pan with butter and sauce. If you want, you can put them into the oven for ten minutes to get crispy."

We concentrate on cooking while the ravioli boil. I put them on the pan and am again distracted as I watch Moxie bend down to put them in the oven.

"Tell me about your business. You're one of the owners, right?" Moxie asks and grabs her wine glass.

"You remember Noah? He and I started Shred and Tread a couple of years ago. It's great working with him and doing the things we love every day. He sometimes helps with transport like you saw, but most of the time he handles the books and everything in the office, while I handle the actual tours." I love the business, and if I'm not careful, I'll go on talking about it for hours and bore her to tears. I force myself to keep it short.

"Wow, that works for you? It must take a lot of trust." She frowns and chews on her lip.

"I guess, but it's Noah." I shrug and search for the right words to explain the simple fact that he's my guy. I trust him. It feels as natural as breathing fresh mountain air. "If anyone should be worried, it would be him. I'm more of a loose cannon, but if I'm screwing up, he usually tells me." Thinking about this reminds me that Noah said he needed to talk to me about something. I feel a twinge of guilt that we haven't had that conversation yet, and that I haven't checked in with him for a while.

The timer goes off, so I put on the oven mitts as Moxie opens the door to the chimes of the other two groups' timers going off.

"Those look good." Moxie eyes the ravioli, dusting her hands off on her apron and getting the plates. "You okay?"

"Yeah, why?" I snap out of my worrying, resolving to talk to Noah tomorrow.

"You've got a look on your face like I dealt you sixteen against a ten at the blackjack table." Moxie's brow furrows.

"Sorry. There's something at work I need to take care of." One solid look at her deep brown eyes and she reels me back in.

"I'm sure it's a big commitment." Moxie visibly quivers, as if a spider was crawling on the back of her neck.

"It was scary at first, borrowing so much money. Noah got married right after we opened, so a lot was going on, but we work well together and I never had a doubt we'd be a great team." I guess I've never said this out loud before, but it's true. I've never doubted Noah. I need to make sure he feels the same way about me.

Moxie gives me a curious look, "I admire people who are willing to take risks, but I don't know if I could trust anyone with my money and my job. I mean if they screw up, I'm the one who will have to pay."

She turns back to the pan and starts plating the ravioli.

Suddenly the room feels darker. Her tone implies a story there, but it doesn't feel right to pry.

"I guess it has to be the right person. I trust Noah with my life. But enough about me, tell me what it's like working at the casino."

She shrugs a bit dismissively. "It's a job." She turns to scope out the other groups' ravioli.

I loosen up as we enjoy a little wine and chat with the other couples while Michelle brings in a salad and garlic bread to round out our meal. Moxie cracks us up as she reenacts an early waitressing fiasco that got her fired from her first job.

A hint of golden-brown color forms on the ravioli in its short time in the oven. The dough is plump with filling, and our sauce is chunky and brilliant red. It looks delicious and smells even better due more to Moxie's efforts than mine. She hands me a plate as Michelle goes from table to table complimenting everyone's meals.

"I'm not trying this alone. If I go down from poisoning, you're coming with me," I tease.

"I think as the true adventurer between us, you should go first." Moxie's lips mesmerize me, and I find myself leaning closer. She lowers the glass and tilts her head a tiny bit, exposing her neck.

Without conscious thought, my feet inch forward. Heat radiates from her. "I swear you told me you were always up for adventure." I bring my mouth mere inches from her bright red lips. This is the opposite of taking it slow. This is not how a fake date should feel. I have to break this somehow before I'm head-over-heels for her while she still sees me as just fun.

As she leans in for a kiss, I move a fork full of ravioli to her mouth. I give her my most mischievous smile and she laughs around her mouthful.

"Mmmm, this is so good," she purrs, making me wish I went for the kiss. She steals the plate away from me.

"You're still standing, so I guess it's safe for me to try." My fingertips brush her waist as I reach for the plate.

"Oh no, I don't think I want to share. You were too chicken, so I think I'm going to enjoy all this myself." Moxie takes another bite and pulls the plate behind her back.

"Don't tease me like that." I lean into her. I couldn't give a shit about the ravioli.

"You want a taste of this?" She does a slow spin and when she's facing me again, she has a ravioli on her fork and eases it to my mouth. An explosion of rich flavors hits my tongue, velvety and sweet. I stare at her smoky eyes, and she slowly smiles.

"Well, do you like it?" Her voice drops to a husky timbre.

"Oh yeah, I really like it." It's enough that I'm calculating the sturdiness of the table and struggling to remember that we're in a very public place. I clear my throat and step back to regain my composure.

Michelle interrupts our moment. "What does everyone think? Is this something you could recreate on your own at home?"

Everyone agrees it's a winning recipe. Moxie and I rejoin the class and behave for the rest of dinner. All the while, I'm cautiously amazed at how comfortable this feels. With my new resolve to take things slow and not force feelings where they don't exist, there's an underlying itch to review the mental game footage, making sure that what I'm feeling is real. Stronger than that is the desire to be in the moment with her and not worry at all. Maybe that's my answer.

I help slip her sweater over her shoulders before we walk out to the parking lot.

"This was a lot of fun, even though I must bow to your superior chef skills. I'm not in your league." I lean in to give her a chaste hug before we part. Surely fake daters can hug.

When she leans closer, the light of the moon catches her skin, bathing her in a magical glow. I should back up, but it feels like her hand is glued to my chest. If I step away, I'm sure my heart will stop.

"You know, if we're going to really sell this to your parents, we should be prepared," she whispers.

"How so?" If she's going where I think she's going, I'm in trouble. Because I don't have it in me to say no to something I desperately want.

"We'll have to be at ease with each other. At some point we might have to kiss in front of them, and they'll probably be able to tell if it looks awkward."

I swallow against the lump in my throat. All I can do is nod.

"Good. I'm going to kiss you now," she says, and the remains of my resolve are whisked away in the current. I want this. "That alright?" she asks.

"Hell yes."

Her confidence is both intimidating and sexy as hell.

"Good." She closes the narrow gap between us and presses her soft lips onto mine. She tastes sweet, like the wine we had with our dinner. It's like there's a string connecting my mouth and my chest, and it tugs insistently with each movement. Her tongue glides over my lip, then she teases me with a gentle bite, and my head goes fuzzy. My hands find the curve of her hips and I pull her close.

I lose myself in her until she pulls back the tiniest bit, gently caressing my chest.

"Wow. Yeah. I think they'll believe that," she says. It snaps me back to reality in an instant, with the reminder this is all for show, even though I can feel myself falling for her more with every passing minute.

"Totally believable," I manage to say, when I really want to clutch at my chest and try to hold my heart together.

"You know, just because we're keeping feelings out of this doesn't mean we can't have some fun. Do you want to come back to my place?"

The fire in her eyes leaves zero doubt as to what type of fun she's referring to. I'm dizzy with desire for her, fighting against the fog to remember why this would be bad. I'm not a one-night stand kind of guy. Sex would not be just sex for me.

It takes all my will power to pull back. *Take it slow so you know it's real, and so she can grow to want more.* I take in a deep breath.

"I should head home. I have an early-morning hike." I

grimace as I say it because I want to punch myself in the face for turning her down.

Moxie jerks back so suddenly I almost fall over. Her lips purse and her muscles tense. "Maybe some other time." She heads to her car as if it might leave without her.

"I'll text you," I call out. My head spins. Damn. Of course I want to go back to her place and have her for dessert. I growl as I run my hand across my forehead. It feels like we were connecting, but I can't be confident in that with my dating history. Now I know what it feels like to be dropped in the ice-cold river.

Chapter 13
Moxie

"I had a flush until you stole my heart," one of my regular players, Simon, says as he sits down at my table.

I roll my eyes, but it's a relief to have the talkative goof at my table. He's a welcome distraction from my disappointment from Wyatt's rejection.

"You do realize you're playing blackjack, right?"

"Yes, ma'am."

"And that there's no such thing as a flush in blackjack? I feel like you probably should have a basic grasp on the game by now. You've been coming here for three months."

I still can't believe he didn't want to go home with me. It's his prerogative—I wasn't about to force him—but I can't understand what I did wrong or how I so badly misread the signs. Years of nothing but one-night stands, and the moment I give a guy more time with me, I wind up home alone.

"You're right." He hangs his head in shame, but he's got that mischievous twinkle in his eyes before they briefly dip out of sight. It's a twinkle I know all too well. Been there, done that. Simon has a line in my little black book. He's a nice guy, but he fell to the one-and-done rule. Somehow Wyatt wormed his way in. He's the only one I want right now, even if whatever we're doing is just for fun.

"Remind me, what are these little clover things called again?" He looks back up and winks at me.

"I'm pretty sure they're called dinglehoppers," I say.

"You've been watching too much *Little Mermaid*," he responds.

Simon *would* use a Disney reference. The one time I went back to his place, I could see evidence of his many fandoms on his shelves and overflowing from boxes.

"In all seriousness, you've got to get yourself some better lines if you're going to find yourself a girl out here."

"That's why I keep practicing them on you."

"Glad to be your test subject," I deadpan. I don't mind it, though. He's a good guy, and I know he comes here because it gives him a sense of stability. He misses his D&D and bowling leagues from his old neighborhood, and I guess hanging with his favorite dealers and the other regulars gives him a similar vibe, at least until he finds his niche here. Hannah keeps insisting she's not ready to take up her dating end of our bargain, but when she is, I'll keep Simon in mind.

Jin, the evening's relief dealer, walks up behind me. "You're up."

I perform the changing of the guard's hand jive for the cameras, then wave to Simon. "You think up another one for me. I'm off to lunch."

I snag a bag of chips from my locker, plop down at one of the five small round tables in our break room, and pull out my phone. One missed text.

Wyatt: *No one warned me that flour was like sand, and that I'd be finding it everywhere for days.*

I grin, then scowl when I remember that I'm annoyed with him. I thought our fake date was headed for a very real, very steamy night of passion, but he blew me off. Getting shot down for sex is not something I'm accustomed to. I'm not sure where I went wrong. We shared a perfectly good night, but somehow, I got left with only my vibrator for company. Two days later he wants to reach out with a joke about flour as if nothing happened.

He's fully entitled to say no if he's not interested. I know I don't have a right to be mad, but it caught me by surprise. I've analyzed the night in my head a dozen times, and I swear he was flirting with me all night. I'm fully prepared to continue ghosting him when I remember they need me, and even if I'm annoyed, I won't back out of a commitment.

I glance around at the small break room that smells vaguely of dirty socks mixed with popcorn, and I sigh. If I'm going to be used as a fake date, I may as well be getting something out of it. I'm still owed some damn adventures.

Me: *Probably because I don't think that's true.*

Wyatt: *Are you calling me a liar?*

Me: *Are you one?*

The text feels unnecessarily aggressive as soon as I hit send. Hopefully he reads it as flirtatious instead. I'm moody and going to mess this up. I wish I had supervision for these texts. This whole pseudo-relationship is so strange. I don't ever feel like I know how to proceed without guidance. I blame Hannah and Albert the notebook.

Wyatt: *Not at all. What're you up to?*

Me: *Work. I'm on break. I've only got a few minutes.*

Wyatt: *Bummer. Would you be interested in a little adventure?*

That doesn't sound at all like someone who wants to end evenings early. I should be able to handle this conversation, but now I'm feeling paranoid. What's a day at work without a little unnecessary stress? I scarf a handful of chips and bolt out the door to the customer service desk.

"Oh, hey!" Hannah says, her usual chipper self.

"Can you take your break now?"

She frowns. "Oh, sure, let me—"

"She'll be back in twenty, bye!" I grab her arm and tug her

along, power-walking to the break room. Why does the damn casino floor have to be so big? "I've only got twelve more minutes."

"Then start talking," Hannah says.

"It's Wyatt."

"That much I guessed," she teases.

My steps falter, and I blink at her. "Where'd that snark come from?"

"I guess you're rubbing off on me." She grins. "Hurry up, Miss Antsy Pants. What happened?"

Eleven minutes.

"He texted me about flour." I throw as much gravity into my voice as possible.

Hannah squints at me. "I think I'm missing context."

"No, that was pretty much it," I say.

We bust through the door to the break room, and I pull her over to the table I'd previously vacated.

"What the hell, Toby? Those are my chips," I say to the bartender who took the bag of chips I temporarily abandoned while I went to fetch Hannah.

"Nobody was eating them," he says.

"Who just starts eating someone else's chips?"

"I didn't know they were someone else's chips," he says.

"Were they *your* chips?" I ask, incredulously. He frowns as though giving this deep thought.

"Don't you have like, nine more minutes?" Hannah asks.

Right. Fuck the chips. We abandon Toby the snack thief and sit at another table. I whip out my phone and hand it to her. She does a quick skim and shrugs. Clearly, she's not grasping the problem.

"He's messaging me like nothing happened," I say.

"And did something happen?"

I bite my lip. The problem is that something *didn't* happen. And now that the time has come to explain myself, I'm not sure I want to detail my sex life in front of my coworkers. I lower my voice to keep Toby out of my business. "I asked him to come home with me, and he said no."

Hannah's lips quirk in contemplation. "I thought you wanted to keep emotions out of it."

I give her a look.

"Right, we're very different creatures. Sex doesn't always equate to emotion for you. I'm caught up. Maybe he wasn't ready for that."

I sigh. "Maybe. And that's fair."

"But you're still feeling..." she trails off waiting for me to fill in the blank.

"Annoyed. And like I'm losing the game."

"The game?" Hannah asks.

"Yeah, cat and mouse."

"Are you the cat or the mouse?" She crinkles her brows in confusion.

"The cat. No, the mouse. Both?"

Hannah folds her arms and stares at me as two more people on break head for the vending machine. "Let's rewind a bit. You think it's fair that he didn't want to take that step, but you still seem a little hot about it. What's really bugging you?"

It's a reasonable question. Why the heck *am* I so upset? I can't stop thinking about his dimpled smile and how he made me laugh the entire night. I genuinely enjoyed myself. Nothing felt like the rehearsed enjoyment I usually force when trying to take someone home. Knowing it's only for show takes the pressure out of it, and the conversation flowed like we had been friends forever.

I've ghosted him for two days, but weirdly, I've kind of missed him. That's not how fake relationships work.

I rub my chest. "This is all so confusing. I don't feel so good."

"Chip to settle your stomach?" Toby asks.

"Why are you offering me *my* chips?" I yelp.

"I was trying to be nice," he says.

I put my head between my knees until the feeling passes, and

Hannah rubs my back. "Your head doesn't want more than a fake relationship with him, but your heart is maybe telling you something different. Is that why you're upset?"

I shake my head. "I'm just a little confused."

"Okay." She holds up her hands, but it's clear she doesn't believe me.

"Then there's you. I like having you as a friend, but you and Wyatt are friends. If this all goes poorly and he wants nothing to do with me, then…" I let my sentence hang, while in the back of my mind, I'm also screaming, *and then you won't have any reason to hang out with me!*

At some point in my rant, I leap to my feet and start doing anxious laps around the tables. Staff enter the room and gape at me while Toby pops another chip in his mouth. So much for flying under the radar at work.

I halt in my pacing. "Do none of you have anything better to do?"

They all make to look busy, and I throw myself back into the seat beside my one and only friend.

Hannah places a hand over her heart. "Moxie, are you worried about losing me as a friend?"

Yes. "No, I don't think so."

"I'm touched, but I'm the one who forced my friendship on you, remember? You're not getting rid of me that easily."

While this is a relief, I still worry that my invitation and Wyatt's refusal put us in an awkward place. Instead of accomplishing our goal of getting comfortable with each other, we're going to come across more awkward than ever.

"You don't think I screwed it all up by pushing him too fast, do you?"

"No, I don't think so." She bites her lip and looks concerned.

"Oh no, you do."

"No, it's not that," she rushes to reassure me.

"Then what aren't you saying?" I ask.

"It *is* a little surprising he turned you down. There's so much chemistry between you two, and he's not exactly known for taking it slow. On the contrary, he's more of a 'Seize the day' kind of guy. I heard his last girlfriend dumped him because he took her over to his parents' house on their second date."

I open my mouth to speak, and she holds up a hand.

"Text him back. Don't overthink it. Let's figure out how to get you two in front of the parents. I think it's best if we focus on the fake dating right now and you get your lady bits under control," she says.

"It would be easier if he wasn't so damn hot."

Me: *I'm with Hannah right now, and we wanted to set up a first attempt with the parents. Thoughts?*

I tap send, skating right on past the offer for adventure and keeping it to business. Straight to the point. If we both ignore the issue from the other night, it's like it never happened.

Wyatt: *I just so happen to know where both our moms will be Saturday morning. You in?*

I show the screen to Hannah.

"I've got work in the afternoon, but I can do morning," she says.

"I've got the night shift, so I'll be tired but free."

Me: *We're in.*

Wyatt: *Excellent. How do you feel about farm animals?*

Chapter 14
Wyatt

"I can't believe I let you talk me into this." I hoist the strap for my yoga mat over my shoulder and shut the door on my truck.

"Oh yes, twisted your arm, didn't I? If memory serves, I made a suggestion, and you jumped right on board." Mom, whose hair has faded to a much lighter shade of purple, hops down from her seat, water bottle and mat in tow. She's right, but I normally wouldn't have agreed without some pushing. If I'm going to sell this, I'd better do some complaining now.

We make our way across the field to the fenced-in area next to a faded red barn. Then again, if I wasn't here to mediate, who knows what trouble Marge would have gotten into. She needs supervision.

"Remember, Mom. Please don't start anything today. Moxie is going to be here. Don't scare off my girlfriend."

"I'm not the one who starts it," she says, which is only accurate about 50 percent of the time.

"Even if she starts something, don't take the bait. Be civil to her for one day. Don't you want her to see your son happy with another girl? Treat it like a secret mission."

"A mission, huh? I like that, but these pants are way too

bright for sleuthing. Ah, look who it is! Hello Moxie, dear." She waves her hand around like a magician who needs a hell of a lot more practice with their distraction techniques. "Go get your girl. I'll busy myself over here."

I pinch the bridge of my nose and take a steadying breath. She lets herself in the gate, calling out greetings to her friends and doling out hugs. Across the parking lot, Moxie strolls over with a yoga mat bouncing off her swaying hips.

"You made it," I say.

"Fitness this early should be illegal. Being awake this early should be illegal."

I chuckle. "Right, you're a dealer. Probably more of a night owl."

She yawns. "Definitely."

I lean in and whisper, "Can I kiss your cheek?" She nods, and I press my lips to her soft skin in what I hope is a believable greeting for a new couple.

"Here, let me take that for you." I throw her mat over my shoulder. The rolled-up foam is light, but at least I can feel like I'm being useful.

I set us up in the back corner. I know better than to down-ward dog in front of this collection of cougars.

"Marge is here!" One of the women exclaims. "Oh, and she brought Hannah!"

"Here we go," Moxie mutters as Hannah holds open the gate for her mom, politely accepting the group's overwhelming greet-ings. Marge's hair, usually gray, is hot pink. Behind her, strolling across the field from the parking lot, her posse is a rainbow of brilliantly dyed hair too.

There's no age limit on fun hair colors, but I've never once seen any of these women rocking anything but natural colors until Mom's dye incident. My eyes snap to Mom. Her jaw tenses, and I can practically hear her teeth grinding even from far away. Leave it to them to somehow turn hair dye into a competition.

I glare at Mom, willing her to keep it together. She winks and performs a series of complicated hand gestures as if baseball coach is her side hustle. I don't know what any of her gesticulations mean.

The opposite of subtle, Mom's movement quickly catches Hannah's attention. She sees Moxie and me and makes her way over. The field goes silent as everyone watches with such rapt attention it's like they think she's about to slap me.

She winks at us as she draws near, then loudly says, "Moxie! Wyatt! I didn't know you two were going to be here." She gives us each a hug. Marge's eyes look like they're about to pop right out of her head, and my mom's mouth hangs open. If nothing else, our friendly show has distracted them from duking it out over dye.

When Hannah pulls away and sets up her mat in an open spot nearby, whispers erupt all around us. There's not an ounce of subtlety to be found in this field. The drama is interrupted when a young woman enters the gate.

"Hi everyone! I'm Chelsea and I'll be teaching today's class. Find a spot to set up your mat. I think we have one or two more people coming. For those of you who are new to our class, thank you for coming. This is just like regular yoga classes except we have our young goats joining us. Being with animals has been shown to help reduce stress levels. Don't be surprised if they wander around, and they might even climb on top of you while you are in a pose. Once we're all settled, I'll get our four-legged friends. Remember to stay calm; sudden movements could startle the goats, and we don't want goats or humans getting hurt."

At Chelsea's words, the rest of the class disperses. A couple of the women in this group are notorious flirts, especially with younger men. The mostly older women scramble like a bunch of overgrown preschoolers in a very intense game of musical chairs. They fill in every spot except for the one next to me. I sneak a quick pit check. Mountain fresh; that's not the problem.

Maybe having a girlfriend with me acts as a deterrent, or

maybe they're just trying to stay out of the blast zone should Hannah and I erupt.

Chelsea returns to the gate with four goats at her side. A tiny goat with black and white patches hops over to a woman up front, who laughs and pets it. Two average-size goats split up, weaving between mats and along the fence sides, testing the enclosure's edges. A larger white goat bleats and stamps a hoof. Its glassy eye seems to be set in my direction.

"Is that goat staring at me?" I ask.

"Yes," Moxie answers, leaning away.

"Should I be concerned?"

"Maybe?" Hannah's voice rises to a nervous squeak.

The goat charges, and I leap to my feet, ready to run. It's got horns that I'm not keen to interact with. Yep, time to go. I spin, covering the few feet between me and the wire fence in two long strides, and I leap. I get an unexpected boost over the fence when the goat head butts me, ramming a horn straight at my ass. The pain makes me instinctively ball up, and I topple to the grass.

"Wyatt!" Moxie, Mom, and Hannah shriek in unison.

"You're not supposed to run," Chelsea says with what feels like an inadequate level of concern for what the situation warrants.

My butt is throbbing.

"That would have been a helpful tidbit about thirty seconds ago," I grumble. I'm supposed to know those rules for bears and mountain lions. Not evil goats.

"I said stay calm." Chelsea shrugs.

After realizing I'm not in any mortal peril, I'm surrounded by mouths pressed tight into thin lines, trying not to laugh. It hurts like hell, but with a few seconds of hindsight, I can see the humor in it. My laugh grants the rest of the group permission. Being laughed at by a large group of predominately older women, an ex, and the woman I'm currently fake dating, was not how I planned on spending my morning.

An Ex-citing Proposition

I limp back to the fence and extend a hand to the goat, who sniffs it and walks away disinterested. I watch him for a few more seconds to make sure he doesn't change his mind. Mom scurries over and extends an entirely useless hand to "help" me back over.

"What are you doing?" she whispers. "We're in enemy territory, and you've got a girlfriend to impress. Stop wasting time playing with goats."

My jaw drops. "Are you kidding? That thing attacked me."

"Nonsense. Look how cute he is."

I glare at the goat. The goat glares back.

"I'm sorry I wasn't prepared for it to charge me."

"Think on your feet! Does the river tell you when it's going to send you a wave?" She returns to her mat. There's no point arguing with her, so I do the same.

"Sorry about that," Chelsea says. "He's never done that before. He's usually very friendly."

"I guess I'm just lucky, huh?" I wink, and Moxie shakes her head next to me. "If your ass needs care, we are not at that level. The extent of my fake girlfriendly duties will be driving you to urgent care."

"Thanks for the heads up, but I think I'll be alright."

Chelsea moves to the front and begins the class. The goats roaming around make for a much more casual atmosphere than a regular yoga class, and whispered conversations continue while everyone follows the positions Chelsea demonstrates.

The first few poses are far less comfortable than usual with the pain in my rear end.

"That's great everyone. Now let's do some partner stretches." Suddenly I'm very grateful for the pain. It might be the only thing that saves me from a prominent erection if I'm doing partner poses with Moxie. Since we're here to show everyone just how smitten we are, there's really no choice other than to do them with her.

"Are you okay with this?" I ask.

"Yes, are you?" she whispers.

"Yeah, I'm good."

"First we'll do seated grounding pose," Chelsea says, then demonstrates the back-to-back cross-legged pose with Helena as her partner.

I rest my back against Moxie, and we clasp our palms together, out from our sides. Every point of contact between our bodies, of which there are currently many, is electrified. Though we're supposed to be relaxing into the stretch, I'm doing my very best to focus on the pain. It's hard when I can feel Moxie's breath quickening as her chest expands and contracts against my back.

"Great job, everyone. Now let's tilt into seated crescent," Chelsea says.

We tilt together, her fingertips dusting along my wrist before settling back into place. It sends a tingling sensation up my arm. I didn't think about interacting so closely with Moxie while my mom and her posse watch.

"Now let's move to a seated twist. Place your hand on your partner's inner thigh like this, and I want you to really feel that stretch."

I swallow in anticipation, then slowly twist. The deliberate movement with her body shifting in sync with mine feels far more erotic than even our shared kiss the other night. I tentatively place my hand on her thigh, and her leg twitches.

"You sure you're alright? You seem a little jumpy," I whisper.

"I'm good. You're good. Sorry." She heaves in a deep breath, and I find myself matching my breathing to hers until, as instructed, she places her hand on my thigh too. *Pain. Literal pain in the ass. Remember the pain.*

Chelsea walks us through a few more stretches, and my skin feels scalding with arousal. I'm doing my best to keep my dick under control, but honestly, who could blame me in a situation like this? Finally, she calls an end to the partner stretches and instructs everyone to get some water before we return to solo poses.

An Ex-citing Proposition

I glance over at Moxie, whose face is flushed. "You know that thing we practiced?" she whispers.

I dig my nails into my palm, trying to calm myself. "Yes."

"Everyone's watching us. Maybe we should... you know."

I glance around. We do have a few spectators, but the goats are diverting most people's attention. She's right that we should kiss again if we're trying to show everyone we're head over heels for each other, but I think she's so turned on, she wants a kiss to alleviate it.

I lean in, wanting to scoop her into my arms, but my mom is watching. She leans in too, and our lips collide. It serves to scratch the itch of the desperate desire that was building between us throughout the stretches, but the relief is short lived, as her taste and the feel of her mouth on mine sends me into overdrive and feeds my desperation.

"Moxie," I breathe, forcing a break in the kiss and rolling away from her to wrestle myself back under control.

"Sorry, I needed to," she says, before guzzling her water. I nod, because I know exactly how she felt.

"Well done, you two. They're buying it!" Hannah whispers. I look up, and now every eye in the field is on us. It didn't feel the slightest bit like an act, but if our goal was to show the moms that my interest is in Moxie, we've certainly succeeded at that. Hannah plays her part well too, smiling in a completely unbothered way.

Moxie and Hannah chat during the break as if they're on stage for the crowd.

The class resumes, and one of the medium-sized goats steals the show, having the time of his life squeezing underneath the arched bodies of everyone in the class, one at a time. I manage to calm myself and carry on with the poses, even though my mind is taking me elsewhere and scolding me for turning her down the other night.

Moxie crashes to her mat from her perfect tiger pose, startling me from my thoughts.

"Hey, I think that goat is watching you again," she says.

I quickly zero in on him, and those beady eyes are staring me down hard. I've never seen anything so menacing. *Be cool.*

Chelsea guides us toward a wide-legged forward bend, which feels awfully exposed with an evil goat staring me down.

"Easy, buddy," I whisper, as I enter the pose without taking my eyes off him.

He cockily saunters over as if he knows I'm terrified of him.

"Nice goat." I try to become one of those alpha creatures that have the entire animal kingdom respecting their authority, but I think this damn goat smells my sweat.

He bends his head toward my groin, and my life flashes before my eyes. I cringe, covering my junk with my hand, and brace for impact. There's a tugging at my shorts, and I peek a one-eyed glance to see the goat nibbling at my pocket. I bat him away, but he keeps nibbling.

"Shoo, goat," Moxie says, half-heartedly.

"So helpful," I mutter.

She laughs as she twists herself into the next pose. "Come on, it's a little funny."

"You're not the one who was gored."

"We've changed poses. See if you can switch to cat pose, everyone," Chelsea says, and a quick look around reveals that I've fallen behind and that she's talking to me. Everyone else is smoothly moving to more vulnerable positions.

The goat continues to tug at my shorts, and they slide precariously lower on my waist. I'm not about to have this goat cause me to flash everyone here. I tug my shorts back up and try again to nudge the goat away, but he persists, nipping at my clothes. I grunt in frustration, desperately holding my shorts up, but my battle has attracted some attention. I give the goat one more gentle nudge, and he steps away. Before I can feel any sense of relief, Marge gasps.

"Oh my God, I think he's going to mount Wyatt!"

My eyes widen, as mental images well beyond the Kama Sutra assault my brain.

"His name is Napoleon," Chelsea says, and I glare at her for her lack of helpful interference.

"As in the conqueror?" My voice shakes.

"Yep," she says, and it's safe to say Chelsea is not going to be receiving a positive review.

"I do not consent to be mounted, Napoleon," I whisper, trying to keep my voice soothing.

"I feel like I should do something, but I don't know what." Moxie abandons her pose and puts her hands up in front of her like maybe she can just give him a little shove.

I'm about to stand back up and take my chances with a second attempt at running away, when my hands are slammed back into the ground. The goat has leapt onto my back, where he returns to nipping at my shorts. That's when I remember I stashed half a muffin in my pocket. Anyone who lives near the mountains knows better than to have accessible food around lest they attract wild animals. I should have known better than to have a pocketful of treats around the goats. Rookie maneuver. The belated realization comes as the fabric tears free and muffin crumbs go flying in all directions.

The field erupts into chaos as the other goats rush toward the food. It's a miniature stampede and I'm at the center. The two little ones bleat loudly as they search the ground for crumbs. The other large one frames up on Napoleon, who has a chunk of my shorts and a bright turquoise patch of fabric with dancing yellow bananas printed on it hanging from its teeth. Goat number two lunges and gets a hold of the fabric, and the whole class stares agape as the goat tug-of-war over my boxers commences.

In a moment of poor decision making, I yell, "Give me back my shorts, you thief!"

The yell attracts their attention, and they both turn on me. I hurriedly back up, knocking over an elderly woman in cat's pose. I spin in time to watch in horror as the domino effect of squeals and falling yoga poses tumbles yogi after yogi to the ground.

Still unsatisfied with the chaos he has unleashed, Napoleon charges after me again. I sprint in circles around the edges of the class, vaguely recalling Chelsea's advice against running but unable to think of a better option in the moment.

I finally leap the fence once more and collapse into an exhausted heap.

"I think we'll call it for today," Chelsea says as she rushes to wrangle the goats.

"At least I still got a workout in," I mutter. Moxie helps me up while I hold the large gap in my shorts together.

Across the field, Marge is tugging Hannah out the gate, but her eyes are on my mom. Mom's eyes are on Moxie and me, smiling at us arm in arm. Somehow this managed to be both a disaster of epic proportions and a great success.

"You alright?" Moxie asks me.

"Mostly just wounded pride. You good?"

She bites her lip as she considers. "Yeah, but that was a lot." Between the palpable hostility between the two sides and the sexual tension between Moxie and me, I have to agree. I'm wound up tight and ready to snap.

"When did you say you have to work?" I ask her.

"Not until tonight. You?"

"I've got three back-to-back tours tomorrow, but today I'm free as a bird. What do you say to relieving some of this stress?"

Her eyes ignite, and I realize the implied innuendo, which is probably cruel given I recently turned down her invitation.

"What did you have in mind?" she asks.

"How are you with an axe?"

Chapter 15
Moxie

"Alright, Mr. Outdoorsman," I say, eyeing Wyatt. He's still wearing the bright orange shirt he had on for yoga, hugged tight against his muscles, and thankfully a new pair of shorts. "Show me what you've got."

He hesitates, then grins. "Ladies first."

I don't have a clue what I'm doing and don't want to make an ass out of myself, but I'm not about to let that on. "Scared?"

"Of course not." Confident words, but his voice lacks conviction.

"You know how when you're driving and someone says watch out for that mailbox and you end up pointing right toward it?" I ask. "I think that same thing is happening with your dayglow orange shirt. You better watch your back."

"I don't think that's actually something that happens. I think you just may be a crappy driver," he says.

"It's a thing," I say confidently.

"*Now* who's the one with the weird metaphors." He's got me there.

He retrieves the axe from where it hangs on the side wall of our lane, takes his stance, swings, and throws. The axe spins toward the target in a graceful arc, where it promptly bounces off with a loud bang and clatters to the ground halfway down the lane.

We both jump at the bang, and he turns around to face me with wide eyes. I stifle a laugh.

"It slipped," he says.

"Mhhmm." I click to mark his throw as a miss.

"Alright hotshot, let's see you do better." Wyatt folds his arms across his chest, so certain that I'll also fail that he appears to have a mocking chuckle cued up.

I intentionally graze arms with him as we trade places. I can feel his eyes on me as I take a controlled breath, pull my arm back, and launch the axe.

"Oh shit!" I yelp, ducking behind the wall for cover.

It ricochets so hard it almost makes it all the way back to me. Maybe this isn't going to come as naturally as we thought. Wyatt is so shocked he forgets to laugh.

"Not so easy, is it?" he teases with an adorable grin that makes me weak in the knees.

I'm familiar with lust, and I'd like to chalk it up as just that, but I'm not sure I can. I want him in a physical way, yes, but I'm generally content to hump 'em and dump 'em with no desire for further interaction. Even if he hadn't promised me adventures as part of our pact, I'd be cool with spending time with him.

My mind repeats *I like him* in a mantra that makes my head go fizzy. That grin kills me. I want his lips on mine so badly, I can't help myself. Fuck it, it's practice for our showmance. I glide to him and pull him into a kiss. Wyatt responds quickly, tugging me closer with one hand at the hip while cupping my face in the other.

He eases back, his eyes taking a moment to focus and shake off the dazed expression. "I'm not complaining, but what was that for?"

"You smiled, and I... had to. I figured a little more practice wouldn't hurt."

He raises an eyebrow, and the dimples are back on his cheeks. "Is that all I have to do?" he asks, ignoring my comment about practice. He massages his cheeks. "I've gotta get these bad boys warmed up." He's teasing, but I'm serious. Much more of those dimples, and I'm not sure how long I'll be able to stay away.

We alternate throws, cheering each other on as we try out different tactics and struggle to get the damn thing to stick. Whipping it only earns us glares when the axe crashes to the ground. On his fourth try, Wyatt finally lands it firmly in the cork wall.

"I think I've got it now. You want me to help you?" he asks, as if he's suddenly a pro.

"No, I'll get it. I think it was close last time."

"Okay, but loser buys snacks."

"Seriously? I need a few rounds to loosen up and get a feel for things," I pout.

Two tries later, I finally get the hang of it, and it feels good. Between confusing feelings for Wyatt and the weird anxiety of putting on a show at yoga, it's just the stress relief I need. The axe flies toward the zombies projected on the wall and, *thunk*, it crushes the skull of the projected undead. My arms go up in celebration.

Wyatt's eyes light up in admiration. "You're the first person I'm seeking out in the zombie apocalypse. I've never seen anyone crush a skull so enthusiastically."

"It's weirdly satisfying, isn't it?" I ask. Part of it was practice and getting into a groove, but the larger part is that I got out of my head and allowed myself to just be with him.

We switch over to a classic bullseye, and after another couple of rounds, we retreat to the bar for some pizza.

I collapse into my chair, laughing. "Every time I go out with you, I have such a good time that it becomes my new favorite day." As soon as the words are out, I'm shocked that I've said them, but I can't deny their honesty.

He tips an imaginary hat, and that bubbly feeling fills my chest.

"What was your favorite day before?" he asks.

I shrug. "It's hard to choose just one day."

"Okay, but pick one."

I pause to think for a moment, distracted by the distant clunk of axes and nearby buzz of bar patrons, but a memory comes into focus. Suddenly, the long-ago day is crystal clear in my mind. I can feel the crisp cold water hitting my skin and hear the birds chirping.

"A family friend had a cottage on a lake they let us use for the weekend. It was my parents and me, and I was maybe twelve years old—young enough that I wasn't too cool to hang with my parents, and the three of us had the best time. There was a rope swing hanging from a tree that we could use to swing out over the water, and my dad and I went out on it again and again until our hands had calluses. We spent the whole day outside and picnicked on the sand."

"That sounds like one kickass day," he says.

I chuckle. "Yeah, it was. What about you?"

"I'm living the dream. Every day I get to go up in the mountains is the best day ever," he says.

"That's cheating. You have to pick one."

He holds up his hands. "Alright, you got me. The day we opened up Shred and Tread. Starting a business would be a big deal for anyone, but it wasn't always my dream."

"No? What was?"

"When I was in high school, I was a pitcher, and I was good. Scouts came from all over to watch me play, and I was on track to make it big. I had a scholarship to play ball, and it was going to be everything I ever wanted."

My heart drops as he talks, knowing this is probably going to take a bad turn. I lean forward, hanging on his every word. "What happened?"

"I tore my rotator cuff which sucked, but usually surgery and a little recovery time gets you right back in the game. There were complications with the surgery that delayed my recovery and when I finally did come back, I couldn't throw like before. It never felt right again and if I'm honest, I couldn't get the injury out of my head. It's mostly better now, but I'll never be able to throw like I used to. My scholarship went out the window, and nobody was willing to give me another shot after that. I learned quickly that your dreams can be taken away from you in an instant. I might be impulsive sometimes, but it's because I know you only get one chance at things, and I don't ever want to miss an opportunity again."

"I'm so sorry that happened to you." I put my hand over his, and he flips his over to hold mine.

"That was my dream, and it was gone. I thought I was done, but then I met Noah. He was the friend I needed at the exact right time, and together we found a life dream with Shred and Tread. It took so much work to get everything ready, and when we opened our doors it was World-Series-level satisfaction. We had like ten customers that day, and they were all family and friends, but it didn't matter because we were putting ourselves out there and doing it." I'm in complete awe. I can't even bring myself to leave the job I hate for something I might enjoy more, let alone take the huge risk of starting a business.

"I admire that." My breathing slows and my lungs expand as a fog rolls in over my good humor.

Wyatt seems to sense the change in my mood. He eyes me cautiously as he dishes out a slice for each of us and hands me my plate. My logical brain is screaming at me to eat my pizza and continue enjoying the afternoon, but my heart is ordering me to talk to him. I'm completely baffled to find that I'm close to caving to my heart.

"Everything alright?" he finally asks, and the question opens the floodgates.

"I know a big part of why I'm enjoying myself so much lately is you."

He smiles, his eyes locked on me, encouraging me to go on.

"You get out there and do things. You've made a career out of it. I don't know why I haven't taken advantage of living in the mountains when adventure was my whole reason for moving out here."

"I wouldn't have met you if you hadn't signed up for the rafting trip."

My stomach rumbles, and I take a bite of pizza to settle it while I think. My skin crawls with the discomfort of unloading my truth to him, but I've already started. "No, I've been doing all the same things. If it wasn't for Hannah trying to get me to meet you, I wouldn't have gone rafting. I said I wanted adventure, but really I came here because my family life was kind of a mess."

Wyatt puts down his pizza, his attention focused as he waits for me to go on. While I pull my thoughts together and try to decide what I want to share with him, a comfortable silence settles between us. It's that comfort and the gentle look in his eyes that makes exposing my feelings a little less scary.

"The short story is that my parents bought and ran a wedding barn venue and event planning business with their friend Allison. They trusted her completely, and in the end, she wound up betraying them. They were destroyed financially and emotionally. They'd loved working with couples to make their dream day special. Allison embezzled funds, didn't pay bills, and took deposits from people when she knew they were double-booked. The business ended up being forcibly shut down, and my parents' reputation was ruined. They were heartbroken. When that was taken from them, they'd lost such a core piece of who they were, it took them a long time to find themselves again. The lesson that no one could be trusted was the mantra in our house, so it became clear that the only person I could count on was myself, and that the only way to keep myself safe was to keep moving and never get attached to anyone or anything."

"What a horrible experience for your family."

I shrug because I try not to think about her and the whole shitty situation, but lately, as I've become less satisfied with work, it's been on my mind.

"I came out here with that same burning need to stay moving, and in my search for something new, I somehow did the opposite. I don't know where I went wrong."

"Nothing in your life is set in stone. You can change with the wind."

"I'm not just bored with my job. I hate it," I blurt, surprised because I haven't shared this with anyone. I wait for the usual, nobody-loves-every-second-of-their-job platitudes, but then I remember I'm talking to Wyatt, and he spends his days doing exactly what he's made for. I can tell from his furrowed brows that it doesn't compute.

"How come?"

"I don't know. When you're young, you can't go to casinos, so they carry a certain mystique that made them seem like the most exciting thing in the world. But the days are all the same, and I'm locked in a room with no windows for hours on end. I feel like I'm drowning."

"Fortunately, I've got experience pulling you out of the water." He gives my hand a squeeze, and we each take a few bites. "How can I help?"

My gut reaction is to wave him off, so I do.

"No, seriously. I know you're not actually my girlfriend, but you're stuck with me for a while. We might as well be friends, and friends help each other. I'm really asking if something I can do would improve things for you. I don't have magic powers, but I'll sure as hell try.

Another friend gained in these last few wild weeks. Letting people in still makes my skin crawl, but maybe, just maybe I can get used to it. Friends don't have to be complicated.

Wyatt patiently watches me as he waits for a plea for help. I consider the question. Maybe accepting help from someone wouldn't lead to the end of my world, but I don't know where to begin. "I don't know, but it feels like you already are. Just keep being you. That's enough, I think."

He smiles his beautiful smile.

"That I can do." Wyatt takes another bite of pizza.

"And you?" I ask him.

"What about me?" he asks.

"Are you happy?" He certainly seems like it. I want him to be happy. I want him to love every second of life. In this moment when I feel so vulnerable, I want him to open up to me a bit too, not just about his past, but about now.

"With my job?" he asks.

"In general," I say.

"Yeah, I think I am."

I glance at the table and pick at the crust on my slice, trying not to frown. It's twisted that I'm disappointed to hear that he's happy, and I kind of hate myself for it.

"Most of the time," he adds, and my head shoots up.

"When are you not?" I say each word with caution.

"I don't know. Sometimes I see my parents, and I see Noah with Mindy, and that's a different kind of happy. I love my life, my friends, and my family, but sometimes I look around my quiet house and my life seems empty. I get a little jealous."

My heart thumps away in my chest. "Oh," I say densely.

He catches sight of my expression, and his own eyes widen. I can practically see him on the bicycle frantically backpedaling.

"That came out wrong. I didn't mean that I have any expectations for us. I know that's not what you're looking for. I just meant when we're done with this, that's what I'd like to find."

I force a smile while my brain does somersaults. I should be worried that despite what he says, he might be harboring hopes for us that I can't give him. Instead, I'm trying to understand why the idea of him moving on from our fake relationship to find something real with someone else is making me jealous.

"I know. Don't worry about it. I get what you meant," I say.

"We good?" he cautiously asks.

"We're good," I say, but on the inside I'm far from good. My anxiety is through the roof. The jealousy hit me out of nowhere, and it isn't even fair of me to feel because I'm not looking for anything long-term. Giving my heart to someone despite knowing what humans are capable of doing to one another is not something I ever see myself doing.

We pay our bill, and he offers me his arm as we walk down the hallway. We're nearing the exit when an area of the facility we haven't been to yet catches my eye.

"Have you ever tried the rage room?" I hastily ask.

"No..." Wyatt draws out the "o." I'm clinging to his arm with a death grip. It had never crossed my mind to do the rage room before, but now that it has, it feels like a lifeboat to the Moxie flailing around on an ocean of nerves inside me. He glances down at my arm, and like a light switch he flips into charm mode and smirks.

"It's just an empty room that holds all the garage sale leftovers that no one wants. They outfit you with safety gear and give you a big hammer or a bat and you get to whack it all to pieces. It's surprisingly therapeutic."

"Do you have a lot of pent-up aggression that I should be worried about?"

"Maybe a little bit," I say wryly.

"I never imagined such violent tendencies would be wrapped in such a pretty package." Wyatt eyes the sinister neon graffiti covered rage room with trepidation.

"Don't knock it until you try it. I think we should give it a go." I silently beg him to go with me on this.

"Okay, let's do it." Wyatt wastes no time tugging me up to the desk in front of the small rage room. "You go first. I want to see you attack that room."

"Okay, but you're doing it too." I sign the waiver and head into the room.

Heavy metal blasts through the speakers as I put on safety gloves and safety goggles, and I pick up a hefty sledgehammer.

Confusion swirls in my brain, and the pressure is heavy on my chest. My heart thunders, and my breaths come fast and shallow.

I need to channel this. Like a yoga exercise, I start with my toes and picture all the nervous energy leaving each part of my body and working its way down my arms. Then, I start swinging. Shrapnel flies in every direction as I destroy pottery, bottles, and an old television as if it had personally offended me. About halfway through my time, a guttural scream escapes me.

The freedom this unfettered rage fest allows me is like an orgasm. I'm no longer in control of my faculties. What's coming out of me is pure instinct.

I take a deep breath and set down my weapon of destruction and personality-changing goggles, and I return to a wide-eyed Wyatt. He silently hands me my drink.

After a quiet moment he says, "Holy shit, you were like a Tasmanian devil in there. I will try my best not to make you mad." One side of his mouth curves up in a smirk.

"Did I scare you?"

"Maybe a little." He winks at me.

"Well, it's your turn now. Get in there and beat the shit out of lots of obsolete junk. You'll love it." I push him toward the room.

"Stand back. I'm going to bust that up."

Once the door closes, Wyatt grabs the sledgehammer and circles a television and printer like he's a lion on the hunt.

He starts swinging and tearing things apart, but his heart isn't in it yet. I want him to have the same cathartic moment I did. We both got a lot off our chests, and now it's time to shake off the lingering heaviness.

He glances over at me and I nod. He tosses the hammer from one hand to the other and meets my eyes once more. *That's it. Feel it.*

When he swings again, the printer erupts into a spray of tiny pieces, and he lets out a howl of satisfaction. After a few minutes of thrashing around, he exits the room, breathing hard and grinning from ear to ear.

I hand him his beer and ask, "Well, what do you think?" I can tell by the bright look in his eyes that he enjoyed it.

"I'm kind of disappointed that I wasn't mad when I came here because swinging that sledgehammer is incredibly satisfying."

"Do you want me to make you mad?" I lean into that solid chest in a playful challenge, and I swear I've lost all control over anything I do. *Get a grip, Moxie. Stop flirting with him.*

"I don't think you could make me mad." He drinks me in with mushy eyes, and I've got to get out of here before I say or do anything else to lead him, or myself, on.

"Oh please, I can be as annoying as the next person. But you're right, I'm too tired to get you riled up." Heart-to-hearts and destructive stress relief take it out of a person. "I should probably get going. I want to have some time to freshen up at home before work."

When we part ways, I'm left feeling more confused than ever.

Chapter 16
Wyatt

I pull into my parents' neighborhood armed with muffins from Penny's. I wave to folks I've known since I was a kid. Thankfully, they either have short memories or hold no grudge against me for possibly being involved in some childish law-bending activities. Everyone, that is, except for Hannah's parents, who live right next to Mom and Dad.

They are bent in their yard, surrounded by an assortment of gardening equipment. A few feet away, on the other side of a half-built fence, are some blindingly-bright tiger-striped spandex pants that make my mom impossible to miss. She surveys a complex grid of string that has taken over the back yard.

The fence is a saga in and of itself. Years ago when the feud was raging, Dad and Mr. Nelson got into an argument over who-knows-what that it ended with an epic Easy Cheese versus Whipped Cream battle.

Mr. Nelson started building the fence, and Dad stormed out with a pie tin full of whipped cream aimed at Mr. Nelson, who immediately ran inside and armed himself with a can of Easy Cheese. He charged the fence while shooting a line of cheese at Dad. As a result, Dad slipped, staining his new pair of sneakers and pieing himself, and Mr. Nelson laughed so damn hard he tweaked his back. Dad gave him a ride to the doctor, and for a brief period of time, there was a lull in their arguments. The partially-built fence remained.

They could have taken it down or finished it, but then they wouldn't have something to argue about with the homeowners association. I'm not about to encourage them to take care of it, either, because they could use the common enemy to keep them off each other's backs.

"Hey, Mr. and Dr. Nelson. Good to see you," I call out as I cut across the grass toward my mom. Ever since the breakup with Hannah they usually ignore me, so I don't really expect an answer.

Dr. Nelson stops digging in the dirt and stands up with her arms folded. "From what I saw at yoga, it looks like you have yourself a new girlfriend."

I stop in my tracks. Either hell has frozen over or maybe we've made some progress. Last I'd heard, Dr. Nelson was still threatening to move in with her panicked daughter. "Yes, Ma'am. Her name is Moxie, and she's friends with Hannah. It's still new, but she's nice." Damn, I should have talked to Hannah about this possibility. Being the queen of contingency plans, she would have known the best way to handle it.

"How nice for you," Dr. Nelson says without sounding happy for me at all. On second thought, maybe we only stoked the fires of hell.

"Marge, let's just drop this." Mr. Nelson prefers a cold war to active aggression. Maybe he's worried he'll end up with another back injury.

I take the hint and say my goodbyes before it gets ugly.

I lean over to give my mom a one-armed hug. "It looks like things are progressing with the hot tub."

"You were supposed to help talk him out of this."

"I tried, but like you said, I think he was hot-tub-or-die from day one." She was kidding herself if she thought I wasn't pro-hot-tub from the beginning, too.

Mom rolls her eyes. "I'm sure you tried really hard." She puts air quotes around "really hard."

I can't help but laugh. "Mom, it's a hot tub. It'll be awesome."

"Well, thanks to all your help, your dad and a couple of his buddies are at the pool store checking out options right now. As you can see, he spent most of the morning measuring out his elaborate plans for his backyard oasis." Mom shakes her head.

"It won't be so bad. Maybe you can change your parties from Stitch 'N Bitch to bubble and whine. Think of having all your friends in the tub, soaking in that mountain view while you discuss your favorite books or the latest gossip about Ms. Kowalski's nephew. Your friends will love it."

She eyes me and studies the backyard. "When you put it that way, it doesn't sound so bad at all. How's that girlfriend of yours?"

Mom grabs my arm and pulls me to the patio table.

"She's great. I like her a lot, but we've only gone out a couple times, so don't get your hopes up too high." There's also the slight problem of her wanting to avoid feelings and deciding the dates aren't real, but that's not something I'll be sharing. I'm still clinging to the hope that she'll change her mind.

Mom leans closer and whispers, "It was nice that you came to yoga so Marge could see that you've moved on. It's been… what, five years since you and Hannah dated?"

I shake my head. "It's been like ten years Mom, more than enough time for all of you to move on because Hannah and I have. We keep trying to tell you guys that it was no big deal. We were better as friends than dating. It just happened at a bad time that summer after my shoulder."

"I always liked Hannah, but I think she should have stayed with you. You were in a dark place after all of that." My mom's body droops as she remembers.

I guess I didn't really think about how difficult that time must have been for her and my dad.

"No, she shouldn't have. I wasn't in any shape to be dating

anyone then. I needed to figure out my life." I was a miserable person to be around, but Hannah called or visited every week just to check on me, even when I told her to get out. Then sophomore year I met Noah, and together he and Hannah reminded me there was more to life than baseball. Once Hannah saw I was going to be okay, she moved on.

"But it was a challenge for so long," Mom pleads.

"None of that was Hannah's fault, and if things hadn't worked out the way they did, I'd never have opened up Shred and Tread with Noah. Please don't blame Hannah for any of that. You couldn't ask for a sweeter person."

Mom sighs, "I know she is. It was a bad time, but we're all past that now, aren't we?" She gives me a hug.

"Yes we are, but the feud is still alive and well. Don't you remember when you guys were good friends with the Nelsons? All those happy hours, weekend barbecues, and helping each other out? They drove me to a fair amount of baseball practices when I was little. Wouldn't it be nice to get back to that?" I plead with her.

"It isn't just me, honey. They refuse to give in. They think you broke Hannah's heart, but it's beyond that. They're always annoyed with every little thing we do. I know this hot tub is going to be a problem for them."

"Hannah is fine. You saw her at yoga. She, Moxie, and I all get along. I think you should try to mend the fences, so to speak. Maybe have them over as soon as the hot tub is up and running."

My suggestion is met with silence. I shoot her a pleading look and she scowls.

"What do you care anyway?"

"Moxie and Hannah are friends. You wouldn't want a fight with the Nelsons to cause me to lose my girlfriend, would you? What if she's the one?" The manipulation of it turns my gut sour. I can't lose her when I don't even have her. Though she did open up yesterday and even kissed me out of the blue. Maybe my hope isn't entirely unfounded.

"Promise me you'll think about it and talk it over with Dad. I've got to get going."

Mom hugs me goodbye and I grasp at a growing belief that she might try to talk to Marge.

On my way out I hear arguing from next door.

"I thought Hannah told you she was fine with Wyatt dating someone else." Mr. Nelson sounds exasperated.

"Well of course she *said* she was fine; she doesn't want us feeling sorry for her. But they were at the class looking so happy together. You should have seen them. Hannah was chatting with Moxie, but you know how friendly she tries to be. I don't believe it. I'm worried she was crying inside. Wyatt and this girl were the picture of young love." Dr. Nelson's anger comes in clear over the fence.

I thought I had been playing it cool with Moxie, but even Dr. Nelson could tell that I'm falling for her. I can only hope I'm less transparent to Moxie.

I climb in my car and call Hannah.

"Hi, Wyatt. What's up?"

"Hey, I was just at the old homestead. I saw your parents, and I don't think goat yoga helped calm the situation."

"Donkey donuts. My mom left me a message earlier, but I was at work. She wants to know the scoop about you and Moxie."

"I think the whole thing just made her mad, like I went there to show off that I had a girlfriend."

"I'm calling Moxie. I think we need an emergency strategy session. Why don't you get some pizza and come over to my place in an hour? We need to plan."

"You're just excited for a chance to use your whiteboard."

"Maybe, but you have to admit this is the perfect situation."

"I guess, but I'm bringing some beer. That's the only way I can face all your graphs and flowcharts." Between her and Noah, everyone in my life is pushing spreadsheets on me. It's like high school algebra all over again.

"Trust me, it will help. Hey, as long as I have you on the line, what do you think of Moxie?" Hannah asks.

Now I feel like I need one of her charts to get me through this conversation. One wrong comment and I'll be in poison ivy. I want to thank Hannah for the introduction, but Moxie's mixed signals have my head spinning.

"I like her."

"Is that it? You like her with no enthusiasm at all? Are you trying to tell me you don't think she's the best thing since ice cream-covered brownies?"

I sigh heavily. "I've been having fun with her, but she's made a point of this being just for the pact. It's complicated. My mom flipped out after the casino party. You can imagine her in full mama bear mode. It was over the top, and Moxie saw it all. I know she wanted to hightail it out of there and never look back. I'm on very thin ice with her. I appreciate you introducing us, but I feel like I fell into this pretend affair when what I want is something real."

I hear a gasp from my phone. "Oh, Wyatt."

"Noah suggested I take it slow, so I'm trying to change up my usual game, but there's no third base coach to help me on this one. Sometimes I think she's coming around, and others I think she's going to bolt at any minute."

A high-pitched squeal comes through my phone so loud I'm surprised it doesn't blow the speaker.

"I knew it! I'm a master matchmaker. I just knew you would like her. This is fantastic! You have a coach. It's me!"

"Chill. You can't tell Moxie this or she'll run. You have to act like we're all just friends and that's it. We are just friends. Didn't you hear what I said? She wants this to be fake."

"Don't worry. I won't say a thing about it. Go get a pizza and get your love-struck butt over here. I'll get Moxie here and we'll come up with a master plan to get our parents together before your wedding."

"Hannah!"

Her laughter echoes in the background before she hangs up.

I run my hand through my hair. I should not have admitted that. Hannah can't play poker to save her life.

I shut Hannah's front gate behind me, a pizza balanced in one arm.

"Wyatt's here!" Hannah says while holding the door open. She throws me an exaggerated wink.

"Anyone care to fill me in on why we're here?" Moxie asks, coolly leaning against the kitchen counter.

"Hannah didn't tell you?" I ask.

"She texted me SOS and politely suggested I bring a dessert."

"Did you?" I ask.

"She brought brownies and ice cream!" Hannah takes the pizza from me and sets it on the counter next to a stack of red plates and cloth napkins with hearts on them. "Wyatt, why don't you fill her in while I turn on some music."

My eyes roll back in my head as I ponder how Hannah got out all her Valentine decor in the hour since I talked to her on the phone. She's amazingly productive but not the least bit subtle.

"I'm all ears," Moxie says.

"It sounds like our attempt to show that you two are dating wasn't received as well as we'd hoped," Hannah calls from across the room.

"I thought I was telling the story." I fold my arms across my chest.

"Oops." Hannah mimes zipping her mouth shut, then busies

herself with lighting a candle and carefully placing it on the table.

I glare at her.

She mouths, "What?"

I quickly recap my visit with Mom and my run-in with the Nelsons while we each grab our plates and move to the romantic kitchen table.

"Long story short, they're not about to let this thing die, and we may have only stoked the flames."

"Now that everyone is up to speed, let's press pause while we eat so I don't get my markers greasy," Hannah says.

"We wouldn't want that," Moxie teases.

We talk about TV and books and laugh about the goats while we eat. When we're all finished, Hannah disappears to her room.

"Have you been here before?" I ask Moxie.

"Nope, first time. What is she getting?"

"You'll see."

Moxie raises her eyebrows at me, but I don't want to ruin the surprise of just how extra her new friend is. I've been experiencing the phenomenon of Hannah Nelson for a long time.

There's the sound of wheels rolling on hardwood as Hannah guides a classroom-sized whiteboard into the room.

"Wow. That's... a lot," Moxie says.

"I know. Isn't she a beaut?" Hannah's voice is full of awe.

Moxie meets my eyes, and I shrug. She clears her throat. "Yep, 'she' is sure something."

Hannah uncaps a purple marker and writes "Problem" and "Solutions" in big bold letters across the top of the board.

"Okay, what's our problem?" Hannah asks, her marker poised to write.

"Our parents are worse than kindergartners and won't get along," I say.

She points at me with the marker, really getting into her teacher role. "Excellent, Wyatt. But that's been going on for years. What is the current problem. Moxie?"

Moxie straightens in her seat, and I chuckle. "They aren't convinced that either of you is happy, and they think you both screwed each other over."

"Yes." Hannah writes, "Not sold on happiness" on the board, and Moxie shoots me a look that says, *Ha look at me! I'm the teacher's pet.* Under normal circumstances this might strike a sore spot for me, but she's cute taking Hannah's absurdity so seriously and getting competitive about it.

"How do we fix it?" Hannah asks.

"We could keep going on dates in front of them," Moxie suggests, her eyebrows dance as she grins at me.

I'm all for this, because I want to win Moxie over even more than I want to convince our parents, but for the sake of playing devil's advocate, I add, "But if what I heard today is any sign, that could make things worse".

"An adverse effect is likely, but we're in brainstorm mode, so there are no wrong answers. I'll add it to the list." Hannah writes this on the board.

"I changed my mind. I'm getting another slice. Does anyone else want one?" Moxie asks.

"Sure, thanks," I say.

Hannah taps the back of the marker on her chin. "If they're not taking you two seriously enough, we could do something to show you're really serious."

If she's going where I think she is, this is very dangerous territory. I glance at Moxie, who doesn't seem to have heard in her single-minded focus on more pizza. I don't blame her. I find cheese distracting too.

"What do you mean?" I ask.

"Well, you could temporarily move in together," Hannah says.

There's a strangled sound behind me, followed by the plop of a pizza slice hitting the floor and sauce splattering everywhere. Moxie is frozen like a deer in the headlights.

Seeing her panic, Hannah backtracks. "Or not! We're just

brainstorming. You have to have terrible ideas to get to the good ones."

I frown as I pick up the downed slice and wipe up the sauce from the floor. I don't know if I'd call moving in with me a *terrible* idea. I can't be that bad.

Moxie jumpstarts herself, having forgotten about our slices as she sits back down. "Yeah, let's keep thinking."

I grab myself a slice and pass one to Moxie, who stares at it bewildered. I think we've broken Moxie's brain.

"The funny thing with them is that none of this fighting actually stops them from spending time together. They go to neighborhood parties, Stitch 'N Bitch, and more just to glare at each other across the room," Hannah says.

Frustration swells within me. Hannah may have just scared off the ever-skittish Moxie, and we're no closer to resolving this. I throw my hands in the air. "Here's an idea. The three of us can go over there and tell them we're all cool with each other and that they don't have to stick their noses in our business anymore."

"You know they won't listen. We've been saying that since we were in college. They don't believe it."

The three of us sit in silence. The only sounds in the room are occasional chewing, and the quiet hum of Hannah's air conditioner.

"There is one other solution," Moxie says tentatively.

Hannah and I both turn to her, Hannah's marker at the ready.

"The pact," Moxie says.

Hannah writes the words down, but hesitates on the 't.' "Wait, what about the pact?"

"Our pact was to date each other's exes, so we need to get you a date." Moxie folds her arms and leans back in her chair as if she's just explained the means to bringing about world peace —or at least *neighborhood* peace. She may be confident in this solution, but I see lots of holes.

"I wasn't there when you made the pact, but Hannah's been

dating since we split, so I don't know if having her go on a date will do it." I look to Hannah and she nods.

"I agree. Besides, I told you that I'm not quite ready to get back out there yet. There must be another option."

"You said you haven't gone on many second dates, so to them, it looks like you're still broken-hearted while Wyatt is happily moving on." Moxie persists.

"Okay, harsh," Hannah says.

"Sorry. *I* don't think that. But in their minds that's what's happening. But if we all went out together someplace public near the neighborhood, they wouldn't be able to deny it anymore. If what you tell me about the gossip channels are true, they'll definitely hear about it."

I don't particularly love the idea of meeting someone else Moxie's been with, but I push that insecure thinking out of my mind. She sees me around Hannah all the time without it bothering her.

"That might work. I'm sure I could subtly plant a seed within the neighborhood to make sure word gets back to both our parents," I say.

"I'm not ready for something serious, though. I'm a mess," Hannah protests.

"Neither am I, but here we are," Moxie says, and I'd be lying if I said that didn't sting a little. "I can set you up with someone horrible so you don't have to feel bad if he's not the one. You just have to smile through an evening."

"I don't know that we need to jump straight to horrible," Hannah says.

Moxie waves a hand. "Middle of the road then."

Hannah groans. "Fine."

"So we all agree?" I ask.

"We do. I'll set it up for like a week from now. In the meantime, I didn't see any more rain in the forecast." Moxie turns toward me and it feels like Hannah, her board, and all of her planning fall away.

"Blue skies for days." I grin. I finally get to take her out to the mountains, and I know just the place. Two more planned times to spend time with Moxie. Two more chances to win her heart.

"Adventure tomorrow? I believe you promised a date I'll never forget," she teases. Behind her, Hannah gives me a thumbs up.

"It's a date," I say.

Moxie bites her lip but doesn't argue. Hope lives to see another day.

Chapter 17
Moxie

The buzzer to my apartment sounds, and I check myself in the mirror one last time before darting to answer it.

"I'll be down in just a sec!"

I snag my keys off the counter and run to meet him. The weather is finally cooperating, and after the chaos of debuting our fake relationship to the moms at yoga, I want this date more than I want to admit. I have no idea what I'm in for, only that it's outdoors.

"I see you listened to my clothing recommendation. Good call on the jeans. You look fantastic."

"Are you going to tell me what we're doing and why I need jeans?"

"They are generally the recommended attire, but nope." He tips his cowboy hat because of course he's wearing a cowboy hat. Something about the combination of the cap tip and the accompanying smile and wink makes my knees nearly buckle. Maybe we should stay here...

"You ready?" he asks.

Every time I'm with him, he throws me off balance. I never spend this much time with a man without winding up in the bedroom, and no matter how much I tell my body to chill, it wants him. But sex doesn't equate to feelings, so maybe today is the day I stop fighting it. Date first, but that's one cowboy I have every intention of riding before the night is through.

"You really aren't going to tell me?" I ask as we walk out to his truck.

"And ruin the surprise?" Wyatt holds his hand to his chest in apparent shock that I would even consider it.

I guess I can roll with that.

"Just be glad I didn't make you wear a blindfold for the drive there."

"What if I'm into that?" I ask.

Wyatt swerves and nearly jumps the curb, scaring some pedestrians. He's so easy to rile up.

"You're a hazard with this thing. Are you sure you don't want me to drive?" I tease.

He laughs, having regained control. "What do you expect when you say things like that?"

"For you to file it in the bank for future reference," I say, smooth as silk.

Wyatt only shakes his head, eyebrows raised.

Between the clue with the jeans and the fact that we're heading toward the mountains, I'm giddy but not surprised when we pull up to a stable. I've been living here for ten years and have never ridden a horse.

My hand brushes Wyatt, and I'm not sure who made it happen, but the next thing I know we're walking hand in hand, sending a flutter to my stomach. These small casual gestures are a new unexplored territory for me, and yet with him they feel natural. I could take my hand away, and I'm confident he'd be gentlemanly enough not to let it phase him, but why bother? Even though there's no one around to see, holding hands always feels like a declaration. *Mine.* I've always kept people at such a distance, so for once it feels nice to be claimed.

We enter a large red barn where the scent of sawdust and a tinge of ammonia fill the air. Used to the busy noises of the city, I expected the barn to be quiet, but it's filled with its own kind of peaceful noise. Tails swish and flies buzz, mixing with the occasional stamp of a horse's foot or chewing sound.

The stable consists of ten stalls. Each has a bed of straw on the ground, a water bucket, and some even have toys in them. One of the gray horses nibbles on a hanging apple snack.

"We have an arrangement with them for our tours," Wyatt says as a woman with her gray hair pulled into a loose braid approaches us.

"Hello." She smiles at Wyatt before turning to me. "You must be Moxie. It's a pleasure to meet you. I'm Luna."

"Nice to meet you." I extend my hand to shake hers. "Thank you for having us here."

"Of course. Wyatt always takes good care of my babies." She runs a gentle hand down a horse's neck, then directs her attention back to Wyatt. "Sonny hasn't been eating well, so I'm going to get him checked out. Otherwise feel free to take out whomever you'd like."

"You're the best, Luna," he says, and she wanders out of the barn with a bucket in-hand.

"This is Storm," he says. "I usually ride him. Now tell me the truth this time. Have you ever been riding before?"

"Do those ponies that go around in a circle count?" I ask.

"No, I don't think so." Wyatt laughs. "Well, at least we can steer clear of water so we don't have to worry about you getting swept downstream this time."

"I'll fall off and get trampled by a giant beast instead." I flash him a bright grin and say it with as much sarcastic pep as I can muster.

"That's the spirit!" Wyatt says. "Okay, so we'll go with Molasses. She's nice and low-key and will be an easy ride."

After looking ridiculous on the rafting trip, the last thing I want is to try to show off and get myself in over my head again, but Molasses looks like she's ready to retire and enjoy her remaining days grazing in the sun. I'm not sure she's even moved since we've come in here. I stare at her, still as a statue. I finally catch her shifting a fraction of an inch. If I'd blinked, I would have missed it.

"She's so slow her name is literally Molasses. Come on, I don't want the wildest one, but surely there's got to be a middle ground," I say.

"All right, how about Porcupine?" he asks.

I wince. "Depends on if she has quills."

"I think Luna's niece named that one and thought it was funny."

"Porcupine it is," I say.

Luna returns to the barn. "Did you figure out who you're taking out?"

"We're going with Storm and Porcupine," he says.

"Good choices. I'll help you saddle them up."

Luna works on saddling Storm.

"Do you want to do it with me?" Wyatt asks as we approach Porcupine.

"Sure," I say with more confidence than I feel. I stick close to his side, cautiously approaching her.

"First, let's just take a minute to let her get to know you."

"Hey, girl. I'm Moxie. Nice to meet you." I keep my voice soothing. I pet her smooth neck, and then he shows me how to carefully brush her. Once Porcupine and I are more comfortable with each other, we put the pad high on her back and slide it back to ensure the hair underneath lays flat.

"Perfect," he says, then guides me through the rest of the process until both horses are ready to go. I hang on his every word. Competence is so sexy. Before we climb up, he adds a small pack from his car to a saddlebag.

"A little surprise for later, and don't even try to weasel it out of me, because I'm not telling you."

"But Wyatt," I lean over, squeezing my arms together in just the right way for optimal cleavage.

"I won't be tempted by your seductions." Wyatt turns away

so he can't even accidentally look at me. "I suggest you get on your horse and try not to fall off or you might never find out what the surprise is."

Porcupine is a beautiful chestnut with kind, calm eyes. At least, that's what I hope I see in them. Storm is shiny and black; he exemplifies speed. He looks like he just needs Wyatt to put on some brightly-colored jockey pants and goggles and he'll take off.

"One foot in the stirrup, hand on the horn, then stand up on that leg and swing the other over."

I step up next to Porcupine and follow his instructions. My stomach jumps as I prepare to swing myself onto her back, but I suck in a breath and go for it.

"Ha!" I laugh. "I did it! Did you see that?"

Wyatt laughs too. "Great job."

He talks me through some last-minute steering basics and walks alongside us. I wobble a bit and take a minute to stop tilting from side to side with each step. This isn't so bad. I can do this without making a fool of myself. We complete our loop without me losing my balance, so Wyatt mounts Storm and we're off.

Beneath me, this wondrous creature moves us forward, clip-clopping on the dirt behind Storm and Wyatt. I duck a branch as we move up a narrow path between trees before the forest gives way to open terrain. The path widens so we can ride side by side. A rippled field of patchy grass with sporadic trees extends out on either side. Before us, the mountain peaks are visible over the woods.

With each stride, my comfort and confidence grow. I'm getting the hang of it and guide Porcupine around turns, stops, and starts with ease. I smile, enjoying the sway of the horse through the wildflowers. I catch Wyatt watching me.

"What?" I ask.

He shakes his head and blinks. "What do you mean?"

I laugh. "You were staring."

"Right. Sorry. You look like you're having fun. You want to try going a little faster?"

Do I want to get bucked off my horse? No, but this is what I've been craving: bold, yet peaceful. A gust of wind whips across the field, brushing across my face and tugging the flowers so that they bend like they're trying to Limbo. I briefly close my eyes and turn my face toward the sun, letting its rays warm my skin. In a matter of ten minutes, I'm already loving every second of this, and I can't believe I've missed out on experiencing this all these years. Instead, I've spent my time wrangling drunks at the blackjack table and riding a bunch of one-night stands. I take a deep breath of crisp, pine-scented air and feel my grin widening.

"Hell yeah, I do." I sit up a little straighter and lightly squeeze my calves like Wyatt instructed, and she immediately responds, lengthening her stride and picking up the pace. The wind whips the strands of my short hair, and I'm flooded with euphoria. I press a little more and Porcupine takes off. My heart rate jumps, thudding away in my chest and matching the thunderous beat of her hooves. I grip the horn so tight it's a wonder it doesn't crumble to dust in my hands. The crash of each hoof resounds in my ears, and it's the only thing I hear. I'm alive.

"Woohoo!" I yell.

Alongside me, Storm snorts, and Wyatt hollers too. We shout at nothing, and our own exclamations echo back at us, reverberating off the mountain cliffs that frame this sanctuary.

The two horses near each other, and as if rising to the challenge, Porcupine's strides quicken. I yelp in surprise before adjusting my grip on the reigns and laughing at the adrenaline rush.

Eventually the path narrows, and we slow the horses. A small stream trickles alongside the trail.

"Let's stop and let them have a drink." Wyatt hops off Storm. Bowlegged, he saunters over and offers me his hand.

"I could use a drink, too." I take his hand, the usual static electricity of his nearness melding with my waning adrenaline and sending flutters through my body.

"I can help with that." He unlatches his saddle bag and retrieves a four-pack of margaritas.

I raise my eyebrows in surprise, and he pulls out two water bottles next.

"Gotta stay hydrated, too."

"You thought of everything."

Wyatt twists the cap off my margarita, handing it to me with a smile. "You were awesome. I'd never have known you hadn't ridden before if I hadn't seen you back at the stable. You're a natural."

"I was pretty good, wasn't I?" It doesn't feel like a time for modesty. It's never been one of my strengths. I'm proud of the way I rode, and I'm owning that shit.

Wyatt ties the horses to a tree and offers me his hand. I don't want to lead him on, but sometimes my body acts before my thoughts can catch up. Soon we're holding hands and walking through the small patch of forest we've stopped in. It feels good.

"Close your eyes," he says.

My muscles tense as I start to panic. Margaritas, a beautiful setting, and closed eyes. This is starting to feel all too much like the kind of surprise I want nothing to do with. I've taken this too far, and this is becoming real, and we're only going to let each other down.

Wyatt laughs at my expression. "Did a bear walk up behind me or something?"

"No, I. Wyatt—"

"Hey, relax. No big deal. Don't close your eyes, then, but you're totally missing out on the surprise. Trust me, it's the best damn view you've ever seen."

He tugs at my hand, pulling me forward. I follow without argument, but my feet are leaden underneath me and my throat feels tight. I like him too much for this to be ruined by pushing for a commitment that I can't agree to right now.

An Ex-citing Proposition

We step free of the trees and I gasp. Even without the big, eye-opening reveal, the scenery is stunning. We're in an open valley of brilliant purple and yellow blossoms amid tall grasses that extend far and wide before abruptly giving way to the rocky faces of the distant mountaintops dusted in snow.

"Oh," I breathe.

"Pretty great, huh?"

I squeeze his hand and find myself leaning on him, thrown completely off balance despite the worry still festering inside me. I take a moment to feel the beauty around me. It's a full-body experience with the sweet smell of the flowers and pine and the soft dirt beneath my feet. I turn around to soak in the dazzling sun.

"It's breathtaking." I release his hand to walk through my own path and spin around, Julie Andrews style, minus the singing. Wyatt stays in place, watching me with his hands tucked into the pockets of his jeans and his hat pulled low. He's clearly relishing watching me, and even with fear that he'll push me for commitment, I allow myself to soak in his appreciation. I throw my arms up and spin again because it's what the environment is tempting me to do. All the while, I feel his eyes blazing a trail over my body.

He steps forward, and my heart skips a beat. Shit. This is the moment he's going to do it. He's going to ask me for something I can't give and ruin everything. Then he throws his arms up the same way I had and prances around.

"Am I doing this right?" he asks. My whole body shivers in relief, and my heart swells with gratitude that he's joined me in my ridiculousness without expecting anything more.

"You need a little more skip in your step." I demonstrate.

Our dancing through the field eventually circles in, and we fall into each other's arms and collapse onto the grass. I lay my head on his stomach and watch the clouds, a little amazed at how much I can enjoy a moment.

We laugh as we search for shapes in the clouds, enjoying each other's company as they change from rhinos to ships and even angels above. Never before have I felt so in tune with another person. I keep expecting the inevitable to happen, but it doesn't.

Wyatt twists his fingers through my hair. "Tell me about your dreams, Moxie."

I huff out a short laugh. "Going right for the hard-hitting stuff, huh?"

"You bet," he says.

We relax into a quiet moment, staring at a pillowy cloud drifting by. I've never been asked this by a man before, but if I had, I'm sure my answer would have been snarky. Whatever is growing between us, I don't want to deflect this time.

"I don't know," I whisper, and I shrink against him, feeling vulnerable.

"You don't know what your dreams are?" he asks, incredulous.

I roll, resting my chin on his chest, and meeting his eyes. "I don't. Is that incredibly pathetic?"

He stares into my eyes, considering. "Not pathetic. A little sad, maybe." He runs a gentle hand down my back.

"Following dreams was not a mantra strongly encouraged in my house growing up."

"Because your parents had theirs stolen from them," he says, remembering our previous conversation.

I nod. "It's not that they didn't encourage me. They still cheered on my wins when I got a good grade or got a prize in art for a painting I did, but if it required risk? Forget about it." I don't want his pity. What's done is done. I knew it was what made it hard for me to get close to people, but I guess I hadn't considered that it had held me back in other ways too. What *do* I want?

"I'm sorry. I know exactly what that's like. Sometimes I still go up to the high school baseball field when it's empty and sit on the bleachers to remember what it was like, and I always end up wishing I could have that back. But then Noah and I dreamt up

Shred and Tread. Your life isn't over. I hope you can figure out your dream too," he says.

I run my hand over the grass, not ready to take that conversation any deeper for today. I sit up and lean on one hand, my legs stretched out beside me. Wyatt pulls himself up, too, our faces mere inches apart.

He holds up a crown of purple flowers he's been fiddling with. "My lady," he says dramatically, and I duck to let him place the flowers on my head. I smile up at him, peering flirtatiously through my lashes. "The purple looks good against the blue in your hair," he says.

"Thanks," I whisper. In this pure moment, I finally let the last of my fears dissolve. This is Wyatt, the impulsive adventurer. This is safe, and I'm done holding back. Riding the adrenaline high from before and the inspiring romantic scene around us, I push for what I've been longing for since I met him.

"Kiss me," I say. Bold, because it's all I know how to be.

Wyatt straightens in surprise. He blinks, and I think I catch a faint flicker of hesitation. Maybe I imagined it, though, because the next thing I know, his hand comes up to my face. His thumb gently brushes across my jaw and his eyes devour my mouth before his lips even get close.

"You're so beautiful. I could kiss you all day." His words come out in a husky whisper as he moves in closer. I grab a fistful of his shirt and tug him closer as his gentle lips kiss mine. I can taste the faint tang of margarita. His hand finds its way to my back and presses into me, pulling me gently but firmly against him. I arch my back and tilt my head, deepening the kiss. He shifts over me, and I fall back onto the grass.

The heat of passion curls through me like wisps of smoke, grazing each of my nerve endings and setting them alight as they pass. Tendrils of plants tickle the heightened senses in my arms, and I gasp. My curves press against his hard muscles. Our kisses explore each other like it's newly discovered territory. A taste of him isn't enough. I crave more. I run my fingers through his wavy curls and down his strong back. He's as gorgeous as the field we lay in. I'm about to reach down to traverse more of him when an insistent braying interrupts. I laugh against his lips.

"I think the horses are getting bored," I say.

"Too bad," he says. I laugh again but give him a gentle shove, and he groans before rolling off me. "All right, fine," he sighs.

We mount up, and ride side by side. When we reach the narrowed part of the path, Wyatt and Storm take the lead, their cowboy-hatted, grayish silhouette outlined against the sun as it begins to sink on the horizon. My heart flutters, and free of his glance, my fingertips trace the edges of my blissfully swollen lips. I wasn't ready for that to stop, and there's no way I'm letting our day end there.

Chapter 18
Moxie

The truck screeches and putters out on something like Wyatt's thirtieth failed attempt to start it.

"I'm so sorry," Wyatt says, his hands in his face. A concerned Luna watches on.

"It's no big deal. Should we call a tow truck?" I ask. I wouldn't mind—shit happens—but this is really putting a damper on my plans to take Wyatt home and stake my claim on every inch of him.

He takes his phone out, and I breathe in deep, willing my body to settle. It's clear my plans have been foiled and that I'm not getting lucky any time soon.

Wyatt taps his phone and looks up with a grimace. "They're busy. They can't come get it for a few hours."

Luna glances at the sky where the colors are shifting from the pinks and oranges of sunset to the darker blue of early night. "Why don't you just tell them to come get it tomorrow after I've opened up. I can give you a ride home now."

Wyatt conveys this into the phone. The car situation sucks, but I can always bring him wherever he needs to be to get it sorted tomorrow. I might just be able to get Wyatt out of those jeans yet. After hanging up he says, "You don't need to do that. We're way out of your way."

I've already got my phone out checking for a rideshare. "I'll book us a ride. There's one just a few minutes out."

"If you're sure," Luna says before reluctantly leaving us to our own devices while she closes the barn.

Her exit acts like triggering a magnet and I snap to his side needing to kiss him. This time there's no hesitation as he kisses me back.

"So, this car," he says, catching his breath. "Is it taking us to one place, or two?"

I could cry with relief. "One. Definitely one. Mine, and I can drop you off in the morning."

"Good plan." He leans in and nibbles my lip just as a car turns onto the dirt road leading to the stable.

We climb in, and it's a challenge not to tell the driver to step on it. He turns up the radio from barely audible to a more moderate level.

Every cell in my body is alive and straining to touch Wyatt. Like a flower reaching for the sun, I crave him. I need to feel his skin against me, his tongue on mine, his lips roving all over. I ache to feel him inside me, to wrap my legs around his back to pull him in deeper.

The car bumps over a pothole, and I'm already so turned on from our mountain top make-out session that when it tugs at my jeans the slightest bit, sending sensation to my core, I nearly moan.

The darkness of the car against the soft glow of the moon gives a sense of privacy that I logically know not to trust, but that has me feeling daring. My hand wanders across the seat, and my fingers graze the fabric of his jeans.

That tiniest connection sends nerves prickling down my neck, and another pulse of need dances through my core.

Wyatt glances over and flashes me a grin. Oof, those dimples do something to me.

An Ex-citing Proposition

We ease around a corner and the force has me tilting against him. Wyatt uses the excuse to wrap an arm around me, and when the car straightens out, rather than returning upright, I lean into him. The pressure is nowhere near enough to satisfy the ache of need that has turned from a flame to a raging inferno. It's like scratching a bug bite; there's temporary relief, but when that subsides, the itch that only Wyatt can reach comes back ten times stronger.

I tip my head, deliberately letting a soft breath catch his neck before whispering, "This guy is driving too slow. I need you."

Wyatt shifts and pulls my legs over his lap. Out of sight, his hand slides along the underside of my thigh, higher and higher, closer and closer to where my body is pulsating for him. I may have dressed appropriately for the horses, but I'm cursing the jeans now and wishing for a skirt.

I press my lips together and fight a moan as his fingers rub against me through the fabric in the most delicious of ways.

"Wyatt," I breathe.

He leans to whisper, "We're almost there. Hang on, baby."

It comes out like a command, and my need becomes so overwhelming I have to cross my legs tightly to ease it. I force myself to slow my breathing.

"Good girl." Wyatt's voice drops to a sensual tenor.

Fuck, I need a recording of him saying that to get me from zero to sixty whenever I want.

We pull onto my street and he shifts again, easing my legs off of him and sitting up.

The second the car stops, we both bolt with barely murmured thanks. My body is in almost complete control. My mind, rapidly losing its grip, holds onto the reins just long enough to remind me that tackling him now might get my lips on his sooner but would only delay anything beyond that.

I fumble with my keys, bobbling them like a hot potato thanks to my jitters, before finally landing them in the lock and cranking the door open.

We crash into each other in the doorway, both in such a hurry that it might bruise later.

"Sorry," we mutter simultaneously, our hands coming together again in the dark. I don't bother with the light switch, and Wyatt doesn't look away from me long enough to find a light switch if he wanted to. I fling my wallet and keys toward the counter. I hear them slide and tumble to the floor. I turn my head in time to see them cruise under the fridge.

"Damn it," I mutter.

Wyatt chuckles, running his hands over my shoulders and down my arms. "The hell with it. I'll help you look for them later."

"Not now?" I feign innocence and bat my lashes at him as I kick off my shoes.

"No, I can only think about one thing right now. Let's get these clothes off you." He pulls my chin up, and I lean into the kiss, nipping at his lips and gliding my tongue over his. His erection pushes against my leg, sending a fresh jolt of arousal through me. I lift away from the counter and press into him. He groans and his fingers tighten in my hair, tugging lightly at my scalp. I gasp and kiss him harder.

"Fuck." He lifts my legs up around his waist, hoisting me by my ass with one hand and pulling me into him with his other hand on my lower back. He spins us toward the hall and loses balance, toppling us into the wall, which we both push off to regain balance.

A stream of laughter from both of us interrupts our kisses, turning them into hurried pecks between exhaled laughs. "I don't even know where I'm going. Where's your fucking bed?" he asks.

"In the bedroom," I tease.

"In a bratty mood, are we? Are you looking for punishment?" he growls, and I tug at his lower lip with my teeth. His eyes fall closed and his mouth drops open.

"End of the hall, on the right," I breathe.

An Ex-citing Proposition

He carries me, swaying and nearly losing his balance again but managing to get us there. We fall together onto the bed and he braces himself on all fours above me. My fingers fumble with the button on his pants as he tugs off his shirt, revealing that chiseled and tanned upper body that short circuits my brain.

I tug his pants down and his erection springs free. I catch myself licking my lips as soon as I have him in my sights. Damn. My hands find his cock, gripping him and beginning a slow exploration. He quivers at the contact. I kiss him again, which snaps him back to the moment, and I pause in my ministrations to help him remove my clothing.

His pupils dilate and his jaw goes slack as he takes me in. I love the way he drinks my image, how the effect is visible. Knowing what seeing me naked does to him makes me feel fucking powerful, and my head rushes with the thrill of it.

"I so badly want to take my time with you, to taste every inch of you and enjoy you the way you ought to be enjoyed, but—"

"I know," I interrupt. "Me too. Next time. I need you now."

My body spasms to emphasize this need, and I grind against his hand, whimpering when it grazes against my clit. Fireworks erupt behind my eyes.

Wyatt reacts, circling his thumb over the spot and teasing my entrance with his fingers.

"Like this?" he asks, his throaty voice further evidence of my effect on him.

"Yes, just like that."

Pressure builds in my abdomen, and I cry out, pumping my hand over him.

"Now," I repeat, commanding.

He raises an eyebrow at me.

"Please," I whimper.

He pulls out of my grip temporarily, his hands roving around the bed to the sides of us. "Where'd my pants go? Condom."

"Floor." My body shudders in protest at his absence, and he presses against me in response.

He bends backward, fingers straining toward the ground and he fumbles for his pants.

"Oh, for fuck's sake," I yell and scurry backward, flinging open the bedside drawer. My collection of toys rolls, and I shove them aside to get to a condom.

"We're exploring that drawer next time too," he says.

I tear into a condom wrapper and hurriedly scoot back. When I roll it over him, he releases another pleasured sigh.

His fingers dance again over my clit, bringing back the building sensations before he pushes his fingers in and out of me. My muscles tense and relax, pulling at him.

"Moxie, you're so fucking wet and ready for me."

"Now," I repeat, and he plunges into me, burying himself deep inside. I clench around him, and he leans in close, our bodies pressing together. Every centimeter of my skin is hyper aware and tingling at the contact.

He moves inside me, hitting all the right places. I moan and whimper as I buck my hips up to meet his, desperate for all of him that I can get. As my breathing becomes more ragged and the pressure inside me builds, his pace quickens, and his fingers move between us, finding my clit and matching our rhythm. The pressure I'd thought was near its maximum somehow pushes higher, past what feels like ought to be possible. I'm gasping and panting as he thrusts deep inside me again and again, and spots flash in brilliant colors on my eyelids.

I'm going to fall to pieces, I'm going to combust. I can't... I... I... I erupt. My body spasms and I scream as the orgasm quakes over me, wild and untamed. Wyatt pumps into me with a few final hurried thrusts, grunting as he comes. He collapses onto me, and on either side of him my legs shudder. Tears of pure, unfettered bliss leak out the corners of my eyes and fall down my cheeks as my body quivers with the final aftershocks of my release.

"Holy hell. Why did we wait so long to do that?" I ask.

"Because we have questionable judgment," he says.

I laugh and roll onto him. Indulging my hands in running over his chest one more time, I kiss him. Then, I head for the bathroom to clean up and can't help it if I strut a little. My hips swing with each step, brimming with the confidence and satisfaction of the ecstasy I brought to his face. I toss a glance over my shoulder. "Guess we'll have to make up for lost time."

Chapter 19
Wyatt

Today might be the first day since starting Shred and Tread that I don't want to go to work. Looking at Moxie asleep this morning, I want to make her breakfast and spend the day together as if she were my real girlfriend. It sure as hell feels like she is after everything we did last night, but it's not a question I'm about to ask her in case it sends her running.

I know Hannah's suggestion that Moxie and I move in together wasn't serious, but it hasn't scared me. I'd do it without hesitation if Moxie were comfortable with it, but she's miles from there. Light years, probably.

I gave Noah my word that I'd be in today to do inventory. Since he's been wound as tight as a stripped screw lately, I sadly left Moxie dreaming with a note on her nightstand and took a rideshare to work.

As I step on the sidewalk, I'm hit with the dizzying aromas of cinnamon and blueberry that instantly get my mouth watering from Penny's bakery.

"Hey, Wyatt. Nice to see you this morning. You want some muffins?" Penny is God's gift to my sweet tooth. She opened the most popular bakery in our city of Tufton about the same time we opened Shred and Tread. I confess, I'm hooked.

"Absolutely. I'll take a blueberry muffin and a cinnamon roll for Noah." I follow her into her store. "It seems like you're busier than ever."

"It's been going great. I've had to hire a couple extra people to work the counter."

"That's terrific. You've earned this. Your food is fantastic." I'm proud of her success.

"It's actually becoming a problem because I'm running out of room. I have to keep more supplies on hand and we're adding another display case. I think we're going to need a new refrigerator and… I don't know. It's happening so fast," she says with an anxious smile.

"It's a good problem to have, right?" Noah would love this kind of issue.

"I just don't want to have to move. I like this location. I'd miss you and Noah." As she hands me my purchase, two people come in. "Here you go, have a good day!" I don't want her to move either. I can't imagine the street without her and her bakery.

"Thanks. Hang in there."

I walk next door to our much quieter storefront, grinning at the sign and feeling pride every day in everything we've accomplished.

Noah gives me a nod while holding up his finger as he talks on his phone. I take my muffin out of the bag and put his cinnamon roll on his desk.

He shakes his head in exasperation as his focus returns to the caller. He spins his chair and scratches the back of his head. "Yes, sir. I understand. We'll take care of that by the end of the month. Thanks again for working with us on this."

He hangs up, sags into his chair, and rubs his face.

"I got your favorite." I'm glad he deals with the day-to-day office headaches and I get to do the tours.

"Thanks. This is just what I need. Penny's got skills." His mood improves as he bites into his breakfast.

"I know. She says she's running out of space next door. She's afraid she might have to move to a bigger space."

"Can you imagine? I'd be back to granola bars for breakfast." Noah's tone is joking, but he's got worry lines etched across his face.

"Is everything okay? You seem stressed." It's been a little while since I've spent a day at the office, and I notice that Noah's desk is unusually messy. Dark circles ring his eyes.

"I haven't been sleeping great. There's a lot going on at home, and I'm kind of worried about things here." Noah paces around the storefront, running his hands along the stacks of t-shirts.

I study him, "You said Mindy had a honey-do list; I can come over and help you knock some of them out if you want."

Noah shakes his head. "I appreciate that. I just want to make sure business stays busy and everything."

I get up and grab the stress ball off his desk. "You put too much pressure on yourself. You said you had some concerns, so let's talk about it. My gut is that you're stressing too much, but show me what you've got. I'm here for you, man. You know that, right?"

Noah gives me a half smile that almost looks sad. "Yeah, yeah. We're a team. You said you're going to do the inventory today, and then I think we need to go over some of the numbers here."

I hate numbers. Noah seems to live for them and puts them in these elaborate spreadsheets with percentages, ROIs, expenses, and all the things that make my head spin. I think a shudder actually runs through me.

"You know you tend to overanalyze every tiny detail, so try to chill. Maybe you and Mindy need a date night and to get yourself laid. Look at me. Do I look stressed?" I spread my arms and spin.

Noah rolls his eyes. "I take it you and Moxie hooked up?"

I plop down in a chair next to his desk, images of last night rolling through my head.

Noah interrupts me, "Uh, oh." He sits down in his chair and eyes me.

"Even with everything she's witnessed with my parents, she's still giving me a chance. You know my parents, that's saying a lot. She's the best." My heart is shouting that she could be the one, but I'm not about to say that. He'd give me so much shit.

"It's only been a couple weeks. You've been on two dates, but you already know she's perfect?"

I glare at him. "When you know, you know."

Noah shakes his head, holding his hands up. "I'm happy for you, but don't move too quickly. I don't want you to scare her off before you really get to know her. I can't afford to have you check out because you're heart-broken."

"I have no choice but to move slowly. Remember, she thinks we're fake dating. Hannah was trying to use this dating situation to end the feud with our parents." I let out a heavy sigh in frustration.

"I forgot about Hannah's eternal optimism. How's it going?" he asks.

"Not great."

"I thought it was ambitious."

"I thought so too, but I had ulterior motives to try and make it work. You saw my mom flip out about going to the casino, and they're already revving up to have the great hot tub war of Tifton. Then the three of us show up to our moms' goat yoga class hoping Hannah's mom would see we were all cool with this hoping they would let it all go."

Noah stops what he's doing and looks at me quizzically. "It's kind of amazing that Hollywood hasn't found your parents and their friends yet. If a director set up cameras in their neighborhood, they'd have a hit reality show." Noah laughs and bounces the basketball that we keep back here for sanity breaks.

"Don't ever tell them that. It'd go to their heads."

An hour later, I'm tired but the inventory is done. I pull up a chair next to Noah and toss the completed storage log on his desk. "What's going on with those fancy spreadsheets of yours?"

I look at his screen and do my best to pay attention while he walks through it, but I'm not sure I grasp the whole picture. Numbers tend to jumble together on the page for me, and he has this worksheet with columns of numbers that appear to have dire implications to Noah but just seem like innocent digits to me.

"Do you see why I'm concerned?" Noah sounds nervous but I honestly don't get it.

"I see the numbers in this section look a bit lower, but it doesn't seem too terrible. I told you I was thinking about an overnight hike. I think there would be a lot of interest in something like that. It could help bring in more customers."

My phone chirps with an incoming text. I don't want to look at it because Noah is clearly stressed out, but eagerness to hear from Moxie wins out. Damn, it's not even from her.

My thoughts are interrupted by a heavy sigh as Noah plops in his chair. "Let me guess. That's a text from her." He doesn't look happy, and I'm momentarily confused.

"Uh, no. Sorry." I smile sheepishly.

"Look, an overnight hike isn't the answer. I thought the Expo was going to boost our numbers, but we didn't get as much of a spike in bookings as I hoped."

I shove my hand through my hair while my other hand grasps my phone. My eyes cross as I take in the chart that Noah has on the page. I want to understand, but the more I try to focus, the more my head spins. "I need a little time for this to sink in."

"Okay, I can see I've lost you for today, but we need to have a real conversation about the business at some point." He waves his hand at his color-coded graph. "Until then, focus on cutting costs and increasing revenue. We can't spend money on tents and cooking supplies for an overnight hike right now. Don't even consider any hikes, camps, or new trips. I need your word, Wyatt."

"You've got it, boss. We're going to be okay, right?" My stomach roils as I expose a little of my fear to my best friend. I may not understand everything that the numbers translate to, and he does tend to stress too much, but I don't want him to worry.

His smile slides off his face as he studies me. All joking aside, he seriously considers my question. A patient smile eases on his face as he tosses his stress ball to me once again.

"It isn't going to be easy, but it seems like we're heading in the right direction. Now get out there and get us a few more customers. And remember, nothing new until our rafts are full."

Chapter 20
Moxie

The parking lot at Fork and Spoon is completely full. After circling several times, I give up and pull into a neighboring lot, conveniently at the same time as Hannah.

"What on Earth? I should have made reservations." We both stare at the line that extends out the restaurant door and well into the parking lot.

"They must have a special event going on, maybe trivia or something. We might have to switch to another restaurant."

I pull out my phone to text the guys a change in plan and find a text from Wyatt already waiting for me.

Wyatt: *I got here early to get a table. I'm in the middle of the room. You can't miss it.*

"Oh. Never mind, we're good. Wyatt is already seated."

"Excuse me!" A frantic young woman sprints past us while tying a serving apron around her waist.

"They must have called in more staff to handle the crowd," I say. It's unusual to see a packed house here ever, but especially on a Thursday night.

Hannah's pace slows as she inspects the line. "See those two couples? They're from Eagle's Landing, my parent's neighborhood."

"That's perfect. Now we don't have to count on your parents seeing the posted pictures because we'll have witnesses."

"Yeah, I guess that's a good thing." Hannah doesn't sound so sure as we approach the neighbors. "Hi everyone," she says with cautious politeness.

An older woman with frizzy brown hair and glasses reaches over to shake Hannah's hand. "Good to see you, dear."

A blonde woman with the classic may-I-speak-to-the-manager haircut jumps in. "I was worried we were late, but you're just getting here too."

The whole group giggles.

"Is there trivia here tonight?" Hannah asks.

The foursome breaks out in laughter. "No, but I think there will be a show of sorts."

I look to Hannah, but she looks as perplexed as I feel.

"We're going to head in. I hope you have a good dinner," Hannah says.

"I'm sure we will. See you inside."

We take a couple of steps in silence, and as soon as we're out of earshot, I ask, "Have you ever seen any of those movies where a whole town has been taken over by aliens?"

"It was weird, right?" she whispers in a rush, her hand clamping onto my arm.

Just as we approach the door, Hannah points out three more people from the neighborhood.

"Hi, Mr. and Ms. Wong, Ms. Hayworth."

"Hello there Hannah. Is this your girlfriend?" Ms. Wong asks.

"No Lin, that's Wyatt's new girlfriend. We saw her at yoga."

"Oh, that's right. It's nice to see you two."

Mr. Wong smiles at us both but looks like he'd rather be at home in sweatpants watching TV.

"Enjoy your dinner," I say and pull Hannah inside before any further conversation with the folks from her parents' neighborhood can give me more extraterrestrial vibes.

"There are so many people I know here," she hisses. Hannah

looks not exactly like she's going to vomit but like her stomach is considering its options. She wasn't thrilled about this date to begin with, despite having Wyatt and me as buffers. Now, with all these people she knows here, I'm afraid she might bolt.

"This is just a weird coincidence. Let's get to the table and everything will be fine.

As if on cue, heads swivel and fingers point in our direction. A panicky feeling builds in my chest as people lean in to whisper to their companions all around us, and I swear I hear Hannah's name whispered down the line.

We push past the crowd, and I don't think I'm imagining that all eyes are on us. The hostess brightens when she sees us approach her stand.

"I went to high school with her. Hopefully she knows what's going on," Hannah mutters.

"Hannah! It's so good to see you, and on your special night! I can take you to your table. We put the guests of honor right in the middle of the room so everyone can see!"

So everyone can see what? My stress level builds. I'd be catastrophizing right now if I had a clue what I should be panicking about.

"Stacia, what's going on? Why are all these people here?"

The hostess shrugs. "I was kind of hoping you could tell me. Your assistant called about an hour ago saying you and Wyatt needed a table for four tonight and that she needed a table for six nearby."

Hannah blinks. "You know I don't have an assistant."

Stacia goes on as if she hasn't said anything. "I was like, cool, I hadn't seen you or Wyatt in a few years. Your assistant then got very chatty and said that it was going to be a big night for you guys so could we set you up with a special table, preferably in the middle of the restaurant."

"This is so embarrassing," Hannah mumbles.

"Anyway, the next thing we knew, droves of people were showing up, most of them asking if you all were here yet."

Hannah and I look at each other and Stacia covers her mouth.

"Oh no! Was this supposed to be a surprise? I would feel terrible if I ruined an engagement surprise."

I stumble. "I'm out of here if I see a ring."

"I don't think that's the case," Hannah assures us.

"That's a relief." She claps a hand over her mouth. "Oh, I didn't mean it that way, I'm sure there will be a ring in your futures. I just didn't want to be the one who asked you. That didn't come out right either, what I meant was—"

"The hole is already deep, Stacia. Stop digging it," I say.

Hannah elbows me.

"Ouch," I mutter, and rub my side. "What was that for? I was helping her."

"Be nice," Hannah chides.

Stacia's face goes beet red. Hannah can elbow me all she wants, but Stacia was going to keep talking herself in circles until she passed out.

"Right. Sorry. Follow me." Stacia escorts us into the room, and Wyatt wasn't kidding about being dead center. I've only been to this restaurant a couple times, but if memory serves, the tables have even been rearranged for optimal viewing of ours.

Wyatt fidgets with his hair. He seems uncharacteristically nervous.

"You said the other day you would drop a hint that we'd be here tonight. You wouldn't know anything about the mosh pit close to forming out front, would you?" I ask.

"About that. Turns out, subtlety isn't my strong suit. I mentioned something to one of my mom's friends, and I think she made up flyers and activated the emergency phone trees," Wyatt says.

"All this time I thought it was just your parents and my parents that were bonkers, but now I think there's something in the water in Eagle's Landing," Hannah says to Wyatt.

"Sorry about all this," he says to me.

"You know, I think I'm starting to embrace the unexpected." I attempt more nonchalance than I feel as I wave at several tables peeking at us over their menus.

Stacia escorts a confused Quincy to our center-stage table. Quincy was a one-night stand who removed all his clothing and folded it into neat piles before approaching the bed, then proceeded to dive in with zero foreplay and lasted about thirty seconds before carefully putting his clothes back on, saying goodnight, and heading out the door. He was friendly and we hit it off at the bar, but his bedroom performance was anticlimactic. Hannah has no intention of going further than a good night kiss so I wasn't worried about her being disappointed. For one dinner and no long-term commitment, Quincy seemed like a good choice.

"Sorry I'm late. I couldn't find anywhere to park."

"No worries. It's packed. This is Hannah, and my boyfriend Wyatt. Wyatt, Hannah, this is Quincy." The word boyfriend bounces around like Pop Rocks in my mouth.

They all exchange greetings, and our server comes to take our drink order. Hannah, Wyatt, and I get our order placed quickly while Quincy plays a game of twenty questions about the wine list while our server keeps anxiously glancing at his other tables. They have a full house, apparently thanks to us, and he doesn't have this kind of time to spend with one guy's drink order. I can only imagine how long he'll take with the food menu. This identity crisis of a restaurant's menu is seventeen pages long, featuring an alarming amount of different cuisines. The kitchen setup must be absolute chaos. I'm about to take pity on the server and suggest he give us a minute when Quincy decides.

Hannah and Quincy are just starting to look comfortable talking to each other when a teenager wearing a manager's nametag taps on a microphone.

"I want to thank everyone for joining us here at the Fork and Spoon. We are honored that you have chosen to spend your special evening with us."

The restaurant is officially packed to the gills and it erupts in applause. The four of us awkwardly join in as a woman named Myra, whom Hannah explains in hurried whispers is the self-appointed reporter for the neighborhood, comes up to our table with her phone held out in front of her.

She speaks into her phone as if we're exhibits in the museum. "First there were the Hatfields and the McCoys, and now there's the MacGregors and the Nelsons. For years, the battles have waged on, from harmonicas tied to mufflers to shoveling snow onto porches. It all comes down to tonight, when the offspring come face-to-face. Can these two sweet kids bring harmony to Eagle's Landing? Only time will tell. Sit back and enjoy the show." Myra fiddles with her phone and turns her attention to us. "Hi kids! So nice to see you here." She shakes hands with Quincy and Moxie.

"What's going on?" Wyatt asks.

"You and Hannah are the talk of the neighborhood, so of course I need to report on it. Since it's so popular, I thought I'd do a podcast. Won't that be a hoot?" Myra says.

The giggle starts out slow. I try to stop it, but it quickly erupts into a fit of laughter. This is too much. My gut reaction was to run, but now I think I might need to join her podcast to document this absurd neighborhood's antics.

Hannah eyes me with concern. In fact, they all do.

"Thanks Ms. Leibowitz. We're going to get back to our dinner now," Hannah says.

"Of course." But instead of going back to her table, she slides over to Quincy. "I couldn't help but notice you spent some time with the wine list. Are you a connoisseur?"

Quincy looks at Hannah as if for approval before he answers. "I enjoy a good wine, and it doesn't hurt to show your interests on a first date."

"Oh, right you are. Well, good luck, honey. I'll leave you to it." She backs away giving thumbs up to several other tables.

"This is a nightmare." Wyatt holds his head in his hands.

Hannah sighs heavily. "Quincy, I apologize. This was

supposed to be an average, everyday date, but it has turned into mating season at the zoo. If you want to reschedule this, I totally understand."

"No!" I shout, surprising myself with my own vehemence. The absurdity of this evening has me cracking. We've come this far; it needs to work. "We can't walk away now. It will go through the neighborhood like wildfire. Quincy, your dinner is on us. We're going to do our best to ignore all these people. We can block this out."

"Can we, though?" Hannah asks skeptically with a wince. It's like we've swapped roles.

"I didn't say it would be easy. We just need to act like we're movie stars," I say, grasping at straws.

"You've got a point. Celebrities go through this all the time." Wyatt jumps to support me. Bless him. That earned him some brownie points I'm very much looking forward to granting later. I try to communicate this plan to him nonverbally with a covert, intense look and lick of my lips. His eyes widen, and while Quincy and Hannah debate the merits of various celebrities, he mouths, "Yeah?" I mouth back, "Later."

Quincy pulls out his phone and taps away at it. Hannah meets my eyes, and I shrug. He passes the phone around. "I searched for fun ways celebrities have dealt with paparazzi." When Hannah takes it, he grabs his napkin off the table, pokes eye holes into it, and throws it over his face like a mask. I have to give the guy credit for going with the flow and making the most out of a weird situation, even if he now looks like a bargain basement ghost.

"You might have to bail on that one when the food comes," I say.

"Yeah, but I'm going to enjoy the weird looks I get until then," he says.

"Dibs on hiding behind things that are obviously too small to hide behind," Wyatt says.

"Oh! That lady looks like she's taking a picture of us." I nod across the room, pull my phone out, and aim it at her for strategy number three: the "camera duels" tactic. Wyatt holds up a salt-shaker and very seriously hides behind it.

Hannah giggles. "I like the Emma Stone and Andrew Garfield method." She pulls out her ugly notebook and tears out a piece of paper. She writes down instructions to give attention to something more deserving and lists the local food bank and animal shelter.

It turns out Quincy's wine choice is pretty good and we all share a second bottle. Wyatt gradually scoots closer to me, and my heart thumps away in my chest when he holds my hand under the table and runs a thumb over the palm.

By the time we get to dessert, half the restaurant has come up to say goodbye. I don't know that Quincy will be looking for a second date with Hannah, but he certainly didn't act like he was being held hostage.

"Quincy, I hope this evening wasn't too much of a train wreck for you." Hannah, bless her heart, is genuinely concerned about her date.

"It was unusual. Do these people follow you around every-where you go?"

"Not usually, but I can't say it's out of the realm of possibili-ties." Poor Hannah looks a little sad.

Quincy gives her a chaste hug and heads out. Hannah looks relieved.

"See, that wasn't too bad for a first date," I say.

"It was a disaster, but being famous was kind of fun." Hannah giggles.

A woman grabs my arm as we make our way to the exit. "You and young Wyatt here make such a lovely couple."

"Thanks?" I answer and continue pushing my way forward.

Another woman comes up to Hannah. "I know I took Ms. MacGregor's side in this mess, but it's nice to see you two getting along. I'm hosting the chili cook-off this year. I hope to see you and your family there."

"Thank you, Ms. Sweeney," Hannah says.

The three of us break free into the parking lot. It's pouring rain, and our clothes are instantly drenched and plastered to our bodies.

"Holy shit, it worked," Wyatt says.

"It actually worked!" Hannah squeals, and the three of us dance in the rain until I slow to a stop.

If it worked, my time is running out. My heart drops. If the feud is over, will he still spend time with me? Wyatt is my best shot at pulling myself out of my boring life and experiencing more, but I also don't want to lose him. I put on a fake smile to dance with Wyatt and Hannah in the rain. These questions haunt me as I say goodnight to Wyatt, who has to work early in the morning, and while I towel off in my car. They haunt me all night while I stare at the ceiling above my bed in a fitful failure to sleep.

Chapter 21
Wyatt

"Look everyone, Wyatt finally decided to show up. I thought you might be avoiding the hard work," Dad says. A cheer goes up in the backyard where he and three of his friends have spray-painted part of the yard and look like they're drawing straws for who's going to start digging.

"I told you I had a hike this morning. You're going to wish you'd been nice to me when Mom and I are enjoying that giant sub I brought."

"You got here just in time, kid." Mr. Franklin cheerfully slaps me on the back and hands me a shovel.

Dad's friends drop their tools and head for the kitchen without another word. I chuckle and follow them.

"Can you believe we'll have a hot tub back here next week? It's a dream come true." Dad rubs his hands together. He's like a little kid.

"I can't wait for the daily calls from Mom complaining about you guys."

Dad rolls his eyes. "She gripes about it, but she's already talking to her book club about making their next book a 'beach read' and having their meeting out here. She's been out buying beach towels and those little umbrellas for drinks, so don't feel too sorry for her."

"You two better get in here before this sub is gone," Mom shouts out the back door.

Their house has changed very little since I grew up here. The small kitchen is overwhelmed by all the guys wolfing down cold cuts.

"Wyatt, I heard something about you and your girlfriend going on a double date with Hannah," Mom says.

"It's all over the neighborhood," Mr. Wong teases around a mouthful of food. "I saw them with my own eyes."

Mom drops her sandwich. "It's so funny that everyone is so interested. Here, let me show you the pictures. Ava got a good one of you and Moxie holding hands, and I thought this one was cute of the four of you. That Quincy was harder to get in a smiling picture. Why on Earth did he have a napkin on his face?" Mom scrolls through what looks like a full photo album of pictures from our date night, including an under-the-table hand holding shot. Geez, did these people bring professional telescopic lenses to spy on their neighbors' date?

"You all know being this involved in your kid's life is not normal, right?" I ask.

"Sure, but you aren't my kid." Mr. Franklin high fives Mr. Harris and they laugh.

"I'm going to talk to Hannah. I think we need to put on a little Ted Talk about boundaries for all of you."

"What do you expect from parents that have had a partially-built fence for twelve years?" Everyone looks at Mr. Wong as if he might have gone too far with his joke, but Dad waves it off.

"The fence does look messy out there. Do you think we should consider taking it down?" he asks.

A hush falls over the group and everyone looks down while Mom and Dad exchange a look that holds an entire conversation.

"That's a nice idea," Mom says.

Dad's friends throw their hands up in celebration behind his back. I want to scream from the rooftops, throw a parade, blow on a dozen of those New Year's Eve party horns all at once, but this is a delicate step toward a truce, so I settle for sending them all mental high fives instead.

We spend the next two hours digging up the grass so the hot tub oasis will have an even surface to sit on. More accurately, I dig for two hours while Dad's friends discuss their golf game.

I notice Mr. Nelson hanging around in his backyard like a kid on the playground hoping to be asked to join the game. I'm starting to think this whole scheme of Hannah's might work.

"Wyatt, you've been working pretty hard. Do you want some lemonade?" Mom calls from inside the house.

"Don't *we* get some lemonade?" Dad asks.

"I haven't seen any of you guys shoveling or picking up rocks. Get to work and maybe I'll bring you some."

I jauntily march inside for my refreshment. "Thanks."

Mom sits down at the table with me. "It's my pleasure. Thanks for helping us do this."

"You know I'll be stopping by, so I should help put it in."

"How are things going with you and Moxie? Did you have a good time at Fork and Spoon?" Mom sends out her fishing line. A picture may be worth a thousand words, but Mom's looking for the novel.

"It was amazing. The evening was a mess initially. Half of Eagle's Landing was there watching us, and I thought she was going to be upset and walk out. Instead, she made a game of the whole situation, and it saved the night."

Mom returns my smile.

"I've never been with a woman who's able to pivot so easily. There have been some unusual circumstances that have come up, and every time I think she's going to run, she gives me another chance."

"It sounds like she's pretty special."

"I think she is." I'm embarrassed to be sharing all this with her, but my heart is swelling for Moxie, and it's getting harder each day to contain the emotion.

"When do we get to meet her?"

"You have met her, remember? You came by the office when she was there, and then again at yoga."

Mom wails, "I'm hoping she's forgotten those meetings. Talk about a bad first impression. Does she hate me? She's going to think of me as one of those horrible mothers-in-law where you have to make up elaborate excuses to avoid spending time with them."

I can't help it. I laugh because there's no doubt that Moxie has a terrible impression of my mom, and if she knew that Mom was already considering herself Moxie's mother-in-law, she'd freak out. But my parents are both good people at heart, and I'm sure in time she'd win her over.

"Wyatt, this is serious. What if you get married and she doesn't want to spend any time with us?"

I've always held big dreams for my relationships and have had no problem imagining futures. However, I'm very aware that's not Moxie's style, so there's no doubt I need to nip this marriage talk right now. She must see it in my face because she jumps up from her chair and squeezes me in a tight embrace.

"She's incredible, but you seriously need to relax about this. She is a free spirit so she gets a little spooked by the idea of commitment. I'm doing my best to be Mr. Chill because I'm trying to respect her wishes. Can you do that?"

"Absolutely. It won't be easy, but I can see it's important to you, so I'll wait patiently for a chance to redeem myself. Please reassure her that I don't normally lose my cool like I did at your office."

Shouting erupts out back. We head out the door to see my dad dancing around like he just hit a walk-off home run. My mom rolls her eyes.

"Wyatt, you missed it!" Mr. Wong exclaims. "Your dad just

landed the frisbee in the recycling bin after throwing from the center of the future hot tub, across the yard, and off the garage"

"He's still got it." I start cleaning up the backyard mess while the guys take turns trying to outdo each other with trick frisbee shots until I notice Mr. Nelson standing on his side of the completed fence section. He has his arms draped over the fence, a beer in his hand, and a scowl on his face.

One by one the guys notice him and slowly quiet down.

"Hello, Arthur," mumbles Mr. Wong.

"I take it this is the kind of thing I have to look forward to with your fancy new hot tub." He takes a swig of beer.

Dad quietly studies him. "Yep, I think that's safe to say." The joking tone is gone from his voice.

"Have you gone through the HOA for this thing?"

Hushed groans go through Dad's friends.

"I've jumped through all the hoops and checked all the boxes." Dad's mood gets darker as the conversation goes on, and sweat breaks out on my forehead. I don't know how to slide in here and prevent this from escalating. I was riding high after our double date because it seemed like the ruse had worked. I dared to hope there might be an end to the childish battle, but these guys look ready to brawl.

"You remember I'm an engineer, right?"

"Of course I do. What, do you think we missed something? Have you been talking to the HOA?" Dad's hackles go up. Nothing would piss him off more than being dragged in front of the homeowner's association again. In the beginning, by unwritten agreement, they both used other means of battling it out and avoided weaponizing their mutual enemy, the HOA. But as the feud escalated, it became too convenient a weapon, and both have used it against each other a few times over the years.

"No, but I'm just not sure how your hot tub is going to get in the back yard with this fence here. You might want to double check those dimensions."

Mr. Franklin drops the frisbee. "You mean we did all this, and you won't be able to get the dang thing in here?"

"You did all what? I think it was mainly Wyatt doing the work."

"You can't go on the other side since the evergreen is in the way," Mr. Franklin points out.

My dad and I move at the same time. I grab the tape measure and we converge on the side of the house.

"I'll get the spec sheet," Mom calls as she beelines into the house.

Sure enough, the path is two inches too small between our house and the fence. Mr. Nelson takes another swig of his beer.

"It's later than I thought, Tim. I better get heading home," Mr. Wong says.

All three of Dad's buddies hustle their butts out of there in record time, and Mr. Nelson calmly eyes Dad.

"I've been meaning to come over there to have a chat with you, but time seems to always drift away." Dad turns toward Mr. Nelson but keeps his distance.

"You don't say. How long have you been thinking about that?" Mr. Nelson asks, a hint of sarcasm and distrust in his voice.

"For a couple months actually," Dad says.

"Would that have been before you decided to turn your back-yard into party central or after?"

Dad scratches his beard and sighs in frustration. "See, I knew you'd think that. It's one of the reasons I put it off for so long."

Mr. Nelson finishes his beer and turns towards his house. "Well, that's a real shame. Good luck juggling that thing."

Damn, this stupid feud is going to cause chaos in this neigh-borhood. If my dad got this close to having a hot tub back here and he doesn't get it because of Mr. Nelson, my life will be a living hell.

"Can't you throw out a peace offering?" I quietly suggest.

Dad sighs then whispers, "It's not like he'll listen. That fence is made of more than wood, son."

I glare at my stubborn dad. "Mr. Nelson, why don't you come over and have a beer. It's been a long time."

"I don't know. Every time we get together it seems like things get worse." He takes a step toward his kitchen door.

"Are you saying it's my fault?" My dad's words act like kindling on the conversational fire.

A muffled voice comes from the Nelson's kitchen window. "Hannah says it takes a big person to take the first step. Wait, I don't think that's right. I think it goes, the most important thing is to let people know you are doing the right thing."

That sounds kind of like the opposite of an inspirational quote to me, but I jump on engaging her while I can. "Hi Ms. Nelson. Why don't you and Mr. Nelson come over for a drink or two?"

"Doctor," Mr. Nelson corrects.

I wince. He's got me there, and honestly, mad props to him for demanding the proper respect of his wife. "I'm sorry, I meant Dr. Nelson, but the invitation stands."

"No I don't think we should come over. In fact, Arthur, why don't you come inside," she says. Then, as if a light bulb went off above her head, she adds, "Wait, was the quote, *if you do the right thing, you shouldn't have to tell people?*"

Mr. Nelson chimes in. "No, that one is, *If you're good at something, you shouldn't have to tell people. They'll see it.*"

"Oh, yeah, you used to tell me that when I was in little league," I say. Maybe a change of topic will help.

"Everyone knew you were great at baseball the day you started pitching," Mr. Nelson says, and I want to high five him not only for rolling with my topic change, but for doing it with a compliment to me that will surely win him some points with my parents.

Dad laughs. "He went through the neighborhood trying to

get everyone to play with him nearly every day. He got a little cocky for a while there, didn't he."

"After he broke our window for the third time, I decided he needed a little humbling," Mr. Nelson says.

"Yeah, I forgot about that. He struggled with those wild pitches. Hank at the hardware store started stocking windows in your size so I could replace them quickly." Dad shakes his head, but he's smiling. I can practically feel the egg shells under our feet. We're at the precipice. A truce is so close I can taste it.

"You were fun to watch, Wyatt," Mr. Nelson says.

I shrug off the compliment. "Thanks. It was fun to play, but I do feel bad about the windows."

"Arthur, why don't you come over here and have a beer with me?" Dad asks.

Mr. Nelson nods his head and moseys over while a reluctant Dr. Nelson watches at the window. I focus on putting away tools and hovering near the garage, trying to look busy. There's no way I'm leaving these two alone, but optimistically, I want to give them enough space to work shit out.

Two hours later, after another round of beer and countless stories about stupid stunts they both did over the years, the three of us tear down the fence. Dr. Nelson comes over to join them, and the group is soon full of tentative smiles and cautious but amiable conversation. Mouth agape, I quietly leave them to make burgers and bury the hatchet.

Chapter 22
Moxie

"Hey there, gorgeous." Wyatt leans in for a quick hello kiss that feels as natural as breathing when I let him in the door. I don't know when I shifted to being so comfortable with him, but it's scary and spectacular all at once.

When I step aside, my eyes catch on the object in his arms, and it's going to take everything I have to be polite about it.

"Whatcha got there?" I ask, attempting casual curiosity.

He groans, and I relax since it isn't something he's overly attached to. "My mom's love language is gift giving, but she's not particularly good at it. She doesn't know you, but she was convinced this would be a perfect fit for your place."

I grimace. I can't imagine this thing being a perfect fit for anyone's home. The only house it belongs in is the haunted kind. It's a painted statue about three feet tall. It's humanoid but not quite right. It sends a shiver down my spine in the same uncanny way that the animation in *The Polar Express* does. The thing is creepy as hell, with major Chuckie vibes.

"Are we sure this isn't some kind of maternal hazing intended to scare me away?"

"Oh no, she's stoked about you. This is a genuine attempt at an olive branch. She's paranoid that you think she's awful after she made such a bad impression the first two times she met you."

"And this is supposed to give me a good one?" I ask.

"She thinks so. This is the kind of stuff you get to look forward to." He runs a hand through his hair and laughs nervously, but I'm stuck on the last thing he said: *The kind of stuff you get to look forward to.* Wyatt is thinking about our future, and rather than that terrifying me, I'm excited by it.

He's oblivious to the revelations happening in my brain and is looking at the statue like he'd feel much more comfortable pitching it into a fireplace. "I promised I'd give it to you, but you're under no obligation to keep it."

"Maybe I'll keep it in a closet and just bring it out if she ever comes over here," I say. Wyatt's face lights up. From what I've seen of his mom, I'm certain she's coming over at some point. I'd better keep my apartment clean.

"You don't have to do that. She'll probably move onto other gifts and forget she even gave it to you."

"Here, you can set it in the corner for now."

He sets it down to face the corner in a ghoulish time out. I wince, and mutter "sorry" as I drape a jacket over it.

"Did you just apologize to it?" he asks.

"Yes, and now I'm paranoid it's going to be mad I covered it up and will seek revenge," I say.

"Calling it, 'it' probably isn't helping," he says.

"Sorry about the jacket, Chuckenstein. Just a little blanket for you." A shiver runs down my spine despite the room's warmth. Wyatt rubs my arms, the friction bringing heat to them. I lift onto my toes to give him a quick peck on the cheek.

"I don't know if I can sleep knowing that thing is in the other room," he says.

"Getting presumptuous about spending the night, are we?" I ask, but he can presume all he wants. I nearly said, "Good thing I've got plans that involve neither of us getting much sleep."

He blushes. He's usually so smooth and sexy, so when I

manage to put him just a little off-balance like this, it's a treat. "Maybe, but don't feel any pressure. We can hang for a bit and then I can head home for the night if you want me to. I just want to spend time with you."

And that's the crux of it. I want to spend time with him, too. No promised adventure as a trade-off, and no putting on a show for anyone, just him and me. I know I said I'd give us a real shot, but now I can't even pretend that any of this is fake. I don't even care if we get naked. I mean, I certainly would enjoy it if we do, and I'm hoping for that, but if we don't, that's okay too. I'm confident it would still be a good night. I clear my throat to rid myself of the emotional lump forming there.

"You don't have to go anywhere. Let's cross that bridge when we get there."

Wyatt smiles in return, and for a minute, things get a little awkward. Neither of us knows how to proceed until I find a way to break the ice. "Are you sure you're good with frozen pizzas?"

"You bet. Maybe in a little while, though, unless you're hungry now?"

"In a while is good. I'm not hungry yet." Hungry for Wyatt, yes. Food? Not so much. "Anything to drink?"

"Just a water for now, please," Wyatt says. Everything feels so stilted and formal, and it's making me worried that the casual ease with which we've interacted in the past is a trick of being in public, and now that we're alone, we won't mesh.

I lead the way to the couch, then watch his smooth movements as he takes a seat next to me. He sets his water down on the table, and my eyes are drawn to the way his muscles flex as he moves. I want to run my hand over his arm, but that'd probably be a weird thing to do out of the blue.

"See something you like?" he asks, the corner of his mouth lifting into a smirk. Not only did I get caught staring, my lower lip pops free of my teeth. I didn't even realize I was biting it. I'm far from embarrassed, though. My ogling finally broke the tension and brought out Wyatt's playful side. This is a game I'm familiar with, and I relax comfortably into our banter.

I give him a light shove, and he allows himself to fall back, his head landing on the arm of the couch. I crawl on top of him. "Always so cocky."

"You were the one staring at me. Was I wrong?" he asks without a trace of concern that he might have been.

"No, you were not." I kiss him, and we melt into each other. I'm not sure if five minutes or fifty pass while we make out on the couch like teenagers, all roving hands and rustling fabric. Eventually I rest my head on his chest, and he alternates between stroking my hair and rubbing my back while we tune into the movie for a while.

"Who's this guy supposed to be again?" I ask.

"I have no idea. Someone is distracting me," he says.

"Guilty." I kiss his chest and lay my head back down with a sated hum.

A few minutes pass, and while I try to focus on the movie, I'm beyond lost with the plot. Even if we hadn't missed half the movie thanks to our locked lips, the soothing sensation of his strong hands tracing my back has my full attention.

"Why are they fighting with those guys?" I ask.

"Not a clue," he says.

"And why can't that guy just use his powers against the bad guy? Seems like a plot hole to me."

He laughs, and his fingers gently scrape my scalp in just the right way. A moan slips out.

"Do you always talk this much during movies?" he asks, more curious and teasing than accusatory.

"No, but I'm usually pretty in the zone while watching them. You're making it a little hard to focus."

"Only a little? I'm going to have to up my game."

He doesn't need to do a damn thing to improve his game. His nearness is enough to heat my face and send a needy twitching between my thighs. His kisses have left me wet and anxious to move on to the next part of our evening. His hands' tentative roving has me eager to see all the ways he can be gentle and not so gentle with me. "Okay, a lot."

"I won't tell anyone if you ignore the movie," he whispers.

A wicked grin pulls at my cheeks. I swing my leg over his and pull his face to mine. He lifts his leg the slightest bit, pressing his thigh against me. I gasp at the contact and can't help but grind against him as his tongue teases mine.

My body burns hot with desire, but I'm wildly aware that it's Wyatt who's making me feel good. His name runs a loop in my head. I'm in the moment and also flashing back to flour rubbed off my cheek and dancing in fields. I marvel at how present I am in these kisses. In all my one-night stands, there were good nights and bad, but even during the good ones, my mind would go blank. I'd experience physical sensation and nothing more.

On our dates over the last few weeks, fake or not, I've fallen for Wyatt. My heart tugs in my chest as we lift off each other's shirts and our hands explore. My feelings for him drive my physical desire, making every throb of longing even more desperate than I thought possible.

"More," I gasp between breaths because kissing and touching is no longer enough. My need builds, and if I don't find release soon, I might combust.

We clumsily remove our pants and are just coming back together when he grimaces.

"What's wrong?" I ask.

"The Frankenchuckie Thing. I feel like it's watching me."

My laugh comes out as a completely unattractive snort, but apparently Wyatt doesn't think so because he laughs and kisses me like I've just done the sexiest of strip teases.

"Let's move to the bedroom," I say. We proceed with an awkward naked scamper because I need to be touching him sooner rather than later, but there is no non-awkward way to run when naked.

He follows behind me, and I pull the door shut behind him

and lock it for good measure. I turn to catch Wyatt smirking again, his eyes fixed on my dresser drawer. I climb on the bed to join him.

"I promised we'd explore the contents of that drawer next time. It's next time." As he says this, his warm chest presses into my back and his fingers blaze a slow trail down my arms. He kisses my neck.

I'm one of the lucky women who can get off with a man and without the assistance of a toy, but a toy sure makes it a heck of a lot easier and usually more enjoyable. If he's game to use one, I'm not about to turn him down.

"Did you have something specific in mind?" I ask, debating my options and pressing my ass against the evidence of his arousal.

One of his hands runs over the curve of my hips, up my side, and cups my breast. "Nope. Introduce me to my teammates. Which one is your favorite?" His voice is husky at my ear, and I tilt my head to give him better access to my neck.

"What a... healthy attitude..." I say between labored breaths, and I reach to grab my trusty vibe. It's basic but has the perfect speed settings to get the job done.

He gently nudges me to lay down. "Show me," he commands, and I obey, turning the vibrator on and bringing it to circle the area surrounding my clit. I gasp at the contact and moan as I roll it over my most sensitive spots, teasing myself in waves.

Out of habit, my eyes roll closed, but that doesn't stop my skin from prickling with the heat of his gaze. I open my eyes and meet his intoxicated stare drinking in my nudity. I spread my legs wider, and a husky groan resonates in his throat. I smirk, high on the power of putting on a little show for him.

"That's a good girl." Wyatt kneels next to me with a fist over his cock, slowly stroking himself. With his other hand, he teases my entrance, and the pressure mounts to unbearably blissful levels as I gasp.

"Please," I moan, and I tug the vibrator away, edging myself out of coming.

"Please, what?" he asks, pumping faster.

"I want you inside me, now."

In a blur, he has a condom on, and he's thrusting inside me. I increase the speed of the vibrator, and my mouth falls open in silent screams of pleasure as he pounds into me. The combined sensation of his thrusts and the vibration intensifies until I can't take it any longer. I crash over the edge as a powerful orgasm overtakes me.

I scream a blend of incoherent sounds and his name as he thrusts again, grunting his own release.

"You're incredible," he says, and kisses my forehead.

"You're not so bad yourself," I tease, thinking he's fucking amazing.

We clean up and return to bed. Cuddled together, I'm filled with a fizzy feeling, delirious off Wyatt. We pull the sheets over our heads and laugh together as we share secrets.

When we get hungry, I make the pizzas, and we pretend to understand what's going on in the movie that we've watched in snatches, while the food bakes.

We find our way back to bed for round two, and I don't even hesitate to whisper in the darkness, "Stay."

Chapter 23
Wyatt

In the back seat, a bottle of wine clinks against some of Noah's favorite "Old Ruffian" beer from a local brewery. I drum my fingers on the steering wheel as excitement and anxiety wrestle for dominance. Tonight is the big meet between my best friends and my fake-not-really-fake girlfriend. My worlds are colliding, and there's an anticipatory weight on my chest. It's vital that the most important people in my life hit it off.

I'd be less worried if I hadn't had such miserable luck with love in the past, and if Noah hadn't acted strange all week. He even forgot an appointment and had me covering the front desk while he bolted out the door.

Moxie buzzes me into her building, and I knock at her door. While I wait, I brush nonexistent dust off my shirt and flap my arms to air out where I'm already sweating through. Our relationship finally feels like it's taking flight. When we bumped into an acquaintance of hers at the store the other day, she even referred to me as her boyfriend, for real, with no one to put on a show for. A thrill ran through me.

I'm about to knock again when the door flies open. Moxie has on one shoe, an incorrectly-buttoned sparkly purple shirt, and the hottest leather pants I've ever seen. In one hand, she's clutching an assortment of clothing, and in the other is a cookie. Her face is ruby red, and she breathes like she just finished a hard-fought race.

"Are you okay?" I thought I was anxious, but I'm cool as a cucumber compared to her. She's like a guitar string pulled too tight.

"Me? Oh sure. I might be a tiny bit nervous. Come in, I'll be ready in a minute. This is fine, I always have–" she gestures wildly around without finishing her sentence. She walks back to her bedroom, running fingers through her hair. "This is no big deal, right? I mean it's just your friends, isn't it?"

I smile at how cute it is that she's concerned about making a good impression. "Oh yeah, you'll like them. You don't have to stress. Noah and Mindy are the best friends everyone wants to have. I'm sorry, I didn't know you were worried about this. Think of it as a backyard barbecue with another couple."

She waves me off. "Right. I mean it isn't like you're bringing me to some formal 'meet the family' grilling. Noah has already seen me! No big deal." She spins on her heel and disappears behind her door. Moments later, she reappears looking far more composed in a black skirt that falls at different lengths around her legs. It gives her a look like she's gliding on shadows, and her white shirt shows off a hint of cleavage.

"Oh, that looks like an even better idea," she says.

"What does?" I ask.

"The way you're looking at me now, maybe we should just stay here and entertain ourselves tonight." She suddenly sounds more confident, her voice tinged with the hope of an escape.

My brain freezes as my body seriously considers her proposition. I swallow hard, then nearly growl out my response. "You're a wicked temptress."

I glance at my watch. We've got a little room to spare.

I meet her eyes, and she grins wide.

"How do you feel about a quickie?" I ask.

"Hmmm... that sounds like it's in your favor."

I straighten. "Hey, not that quick. I can get the job done." I walk past her into the room and pull open the drawer of fun gadgets. "Especially with the help of one of these."

She pulls a vibrator from the drawer, clicks it to life, and I tackle her.

Moxie exits the bathroom, patting her hair back into place, her skin flushed.

"Do we have to go? Are you sure we can't keep doing that?" she asks.

"I don't want to stand them up. And unfortunately, we're running late." I walk over to her and rest my hands on her waist. "If you're uncomfortable there, I promise we can leave at any time, but you won't want to. Trust me, they'll love you. I'm sure you'll be best friends by the end of the night."

I give her neck a gentle kiss and wait until her eyes soften. Her breathing slows, and I take her hand and escort her to my car.

On the ride over, I turn the radio up, trying to keep to music choices of the "you can't help but sing along" variety. Moxie and I rock out to "Livin' on a Prayer" as we pull up to Noah and Mindy's small brick bungalow. Kids' voices cheer and shout at a park down the street, and a family waves to us as they walk by pushing a double stroller. The place is idyllic, and the family vibes are just right.

I hand Moxie the wine and grab the beer. Noah greets us with the warmest smile I've seen on him in a while.

"Noah, you remember Moxie." I dramatically wave my arm toward her, picking up her sweaty hand.

Her smile quavers, but Noah doesn't seem to notice.

"Moxie, it's nice to see you again. We'll try to keep you dry tonight. I think the first time I saw you, your hair was still dripping from the river," Noah jokes.

Moxie laughs. "Not my best look."

Mindy walks up, gently pushing Noah out of the way and waving us in. "What do you mean not your best look? You're gorgeous." She gives her husband a reproachful glare while accepting the wine from Moxie.

"Thanks. When I first met your husband, it was about an hour after Wyatt had to fish me out of the river on a rafting trip. I'm sure I looked like a drowned rat." Moxie rifles her fingers through her glossy hair as she talks, causing the light to shimmer across her locks.

"You looked fantastic." I freeze, realizing I said it aloud. Noah and Mindy turn to look at me and my face heats under their silent stares.

"Well, come on in. We're grilling black bean burgers out back. I hope that's okay for you, Moxie. I know Wyatt will eat just about anything." Noah directs us to the backyard.

"You make it sound like I'm a goat. I have a delicate palate." I put the beer in the cooler, then hand one to Moxie.

Her eyebrows go up. "That might be a stretch. From the fast-food wrappers I saw in your truck, I don't think discerning fits, either."

"It's not my fault that their offerings call to me as I drive by. You want a beer, Noah?"

He nods, and I toss him his usual.

"What about you Mindy? Do you want a beer, or I could open that bottle of wine?"

She shakes her head and holds up her water bottle. "No, I'm good, but tell me about this river trip. Is that how you two met?"

Moxie recounts the story animatedly, praising me along the way while Noah rolls his eyes good naturedly and Mindy laughs in all the right places. For someone who was so nervous to meet my friends, she has no trouble charming them. I catch an approving smile from Mindy, who drifts around Noah as they set up the grill. They move like they're so aware of each other, like they always know where the other is and what they're doing without a thought. Their casual touches are as natural as breathing.

The way they look at each other with such affection has always been a mixed bag for me. I'm over the moon that my best friend has his soulmate, and seeing them so happy together is incredible, but sometimes it's hard to play third wheel when I've always yearned for a companion of my own. Tonight, the ever-present twinge of pain I feel watching them together is absent as I admire the radiant glow surrounding Moxie. She catches me staring at her and winks. Warmth fills my chest, and I know in my soul I've found my person.

The conversation branches out, and soon Moxie and Mindy comfortably exchange book recommendations before heading inside for a tour of the house. While I can't hear what they're saying, Mindy tells a story that sends Moxie into giggles. I could see us getting together and doing game nights, backyard dinners, some bar hopping. The future is laid out before me, and it's beautiful.

When they disappear inside, I turn to Noah.

"So, what do you think? She's great, right?" I feel my face warm, embarrassed to be asking him like I'm seeking approval, but I can't help it. Things seem so perfect; I need someone else to verify that I'm not dreaming.

"Yeah, she seems nice." Noah takes a drink of his beer, and my stomach drops.

"But, what?" So many times, I've thought I had a good relationship with a girl only for her to dump me. Every step I take in life, the rug gets pulled out from under me, and I'm afraid to believe. Is this once again too good to be true? Baseball dreams race through my head. Does he see something I don't?

"But nothing, man." He chuckles. "Remember, slow and

steady. I'm trying to look out for you. That said, I do like her, and I think Mindy does too." Noah slaps me on the back.

My muscles relax away the tension I hadn't noticed I'd been carrying.

"I'm getting hungry. Are you ready to throw the food on?" Mindy calls out as she and Moxie return from their tour. The temperature gauge on the grill shows it's heated and ready, so onto the grill the food goes.

The conversation flows easily as our dinner sizzles. Mindy shares how they ended up finding their house and the endless list of improvements she's hoping to do.

Noah shakes his head. "One thing at a time or Wyatt's going to have to move in to help me get everything done on your schedule."

"Hey, as long as you feed me, I'm happy to help out." I hold Noah's gaze so he knows I mean it. He's my best friend. I'm glad to do whatever he needs.

Noah takes the plate from the table over to the grill. The savory scent fills the backyard as he opens the lid to flip the burgers and roll the corn.

"Moxie, if you ever need any heavy lifting at your place, all you have to do is wave a promise of food in front of him, and he'll follow you anywhere," Mindy jokes.

Noah gives me a subtle nod of appreciation and turns to Mindy. "Don't worry. We'll get it done, but there's a lot going on at work right now. Once we get that sorted out, we can get back to fixing up the house." Noah runs his hand through his hair, pursing his lips.

"I'm sure we will, but I feel like we have a little more of a deadline now," Mindy says.

I look from one to the other, clearly missing something.

Noah calls out, "Burgers are just about done."

"Okay, let me get the rest of the fixings out. Moxie, could you give me a hand?" Mindy asks.

I give Moxie's back a little rub as she gets up from the table.

She leans over to kiss my forehead. Her fingers drag down my biceps as she turns to go into the kitchen.

My eyes linger on her perfect ass as she struts to the house. Finally, I turn to Noah with a big smile on my face.

"Man, you are putty in her hands," he says.

"I know. It's probably embarrassing but I can't get myself to give a shit about it."

"Do you want another?" He nods toward my beer, already reaching into the cooler.

He pulls the burgers and ears of corn off the grill, and I clear the table. Mindy and Moxie bring a salad, seasoned crispy potatoes, and rolls to the table.

"Everything looks delicious." The melted butter hits my tongue with each crunch of the famous Olathe sweet corn, picked at peak ripeness. The burger is perfectly cooked and has the right amount of spice, and the potatoes balance it out perfectly.

We chat about everything from favorite bands to top TV series. Moxie must be damn good at her job considering how smoothly she fits into conversation with anyone.

"I was actually glad you set up this get-together, Wyatt." Noah reaches over and covers Mindy's hand.

"You don't see me enough at work?" I ask.

Noah turns toward his wife. He slides his arm around Mindy's shoulder, his face settling into an affectionate smile. "Don't interrupt me. I'm trying to do a thing here. We have an announcement."

There's an anticipatory silence as Mindy smiles at him and nods before he continues. "We're going to have a baby. We wanted you to be the first to know."

I swear the whole world shifts before my eyes. Suddenly the way he's been acting and stressing about the business makes sense. My best friend who would get wasted with me in college, the creator of more pranks than anyone I know, is going to be a father. He matures right in front of me.

An Ex-citing Proposition

He and Mindy gaze into each other's eyes as if in their own little world. I look from one to the other, then to Moxie. I jump out of my chair finally catching up with what he said and give my best friend and his wonderful wife huge hugs.

"That's fantastic! I'm so happy for you guys. Wow, you're going to be parents. Un-fucking-believable. Oh sorry, my language. I'll clean it up. Sorry, little one," I add in the direction of Mindy's belly. I stare in amazement and can't stop shaking Noah's hand. My favorite people will soon have a tiny life totally dependent on them. Wow.

Mindy laughs. "It's okay. I don't think you have to worry about your language just yet, but it's going to get weird if you keep staring at my belly for the next seven months."

We finish dinner, but everyone is a little distracted since the announcement. Mindy and Noah keep exchanging loving smiles. Moxie, who had seemed so comfortable before, now is more reserved.

"Mindy, do you think it's a good idea to trust this guy with your little one? I don't know," I say. I have to immediately bolt across the yard as Noah charges after me. Mindy and Moxie laugh as we revert back to kids.

Moxie congratulates Mindy and asks all the typical questions about how she's feeling, the due date, and more than I can fathom at this point. I'm still in shock, but the wave of responsibility crashes over me. This is why he's been stressed about the business. We can't fail.

Moxie gets up and gathers plates. "Mindy, you sit down and relax. I'll take care of the dishes."

"Oh, don't be silly. I'm fine other than some extra trips to the bathroom and some wicked morning sickness," Mindy admits. They gather up the plates and disappear into the kitchen.

"Wow, man, this is the best news. I'm so happy for you both. This is going to be one lucky little kid," I say.

"Thanks. I can't believe it myself. I wanted to tell you the other day, but we were going to the doctor to make sure everything was okay and Mindy didn't want to jinx anything. I couldn't even look at you because I thought you'd guess," he admits.

"It makes sense now why you've been so stressed about the business. I get it."

Suddenly Noah's jaw sets, and lines of tension appear on his forehead. "Do you get it, though? This isn't me being stressed because we have a change in our life. It's for real. This business is what my family depends on. We need to go over the details and come up with some ideas to get us back on track."

"I didn't move forward with that night hike like we talked about, and I've been trying to get more advertising going, but I guess I didn't appreciate the situation we're in." I probably should have pushed for him to explain his charts in more detail when they went over my head. I thought it had been more of the same, and my brain has been in a Moxie-tinted haze.

"That's why I've been on you about the partially-filled tours. Surely you've guessed that it can't be good to have so many empty seats on the rafts. This business is in trouble, and I'm starting a family."

"Shit, Noah ..."

"We're surviving, but we need to find a way to make it more profitable or I might have to consider other options."

My head spins, and I'm embarrassed because I didn't even worry about it. I totally trust Noah, so I have always kept my head down and done the tours while Noah has handled the money and the bills.

"I'm sorry, I didn't realize. It sounds like we have a lot to talk about, and you're right. I didn't understand. We should go over the numbers again. It's now at the top of my list."

I feel like I'm on a roller coaster that jumped the track. Everyone was so happy ten minutes ago.

"I shouldn't have brought it up now when we're celebrating, but you understand, right? What kind of a father will I be if I can't take care of my family?"

Chapter 24
Moxie

I step out to the soft glow of the fading sun and see Wyatt lay a hand on Noah's shoulder across the yard.

"What kind of a father will I be if I can't take care of my family?" Noah says.

I flashback to the night before my fourteenth birthday when I heard my dad ask Allison that very same question.

The patio bricks lurch underneath me, and I need off this emotional Tilt-a-Whirl. My parents threw everything into their business, and their shitty partner lost it all. We had to sell our house and move into a tiny apartment. Their dream was crushed and they lost all faith in other people. My life was never the same. My parents were shells of their former selves, and they approached everything with a large dose of skepticism. We learned the hard way that to survive, we had to take care of ourselves and never put our eggs in anyone else's basket. Distance is safe. In getting closer to Wyatt and Hannah, I'd forgotten that hard-learned lesson. I can't be the reason another family's dreams are crushed. I can't do this.

I look around the backyard at Noah and Mindy and fear they may have to endure the struggles that my family went through. The financial loss was bad, but the loneliness and distrust were much worse. It's been ten years and my parents have recovered financially, but we still haven't figured out how to get that trust back.

This might be different because I can't see Wyatt ever intentionally hurting his friends, but if he can't get his work done because of me, the result is the same. I can't separate the image of my lonely younger self from my fears for these people. I can't be with Wyatt if I'm distracting him from his business. Clearly, he needs to focus all his energy on work right now.

A breath of air escapes as I double over like I've been punched in the gut.

Wyatt and Noah turn toward the sound.

Wyatt's expression lifts into a smile when he sees me, but it quickly morphs into a concerned frown. Whatever it is that I'm feeling must be clear on my face. He steps forward, an arm lifted as though to steady me.

"Moxie—"

I shake my head rapidly. I try to speak, but the words don't come out. It's like the worst kind of déjà vu. I thought by being with Wyatt, I wouldn't have to be afraid of placing my trust in another person. He seemed safe because Hannah trusted him, and I trusted Hannah. What a fool I've been, believing in him, believing in her. I know better.

"I can't do this," I say.

His eyes search mine and his brows furrow. "What do you mean?"

"Your business. I'm getting in the way."

"What? You're not," he says.

"You said it yourself; you've been distracted by other things. Me. I'm the other thing." I'm suddenly cold, arms wrapped around myself.

"That's not what I meant," he protests.

"I should go." I spin on my heels, finally convincing my feet to move and digging my nails into my palms to keep back tears.

"I drove." Wyatt's voice is soft and dripping with concern.

I freeze, then pull out my phone. "I'll get a rideshare."

My eyes start to water, and I bite hard on my lip to force the tears back. I focus on my screen. A ten-minute wait.

"Come on, I'll take you home."

Waiting here in front of Mindy and Noah's for ten minutes would probably be worse than a ride from Wyatt. My shoulders sag.

"Fine," I whisper through gritted teeth.

"Let me say goodbye."

I nod and trail after him to thank our hosts.

He hugs Mindy then talks quietly but with intensity to Noah, probably about me. The floodgates are about to break. I take a bracing breath to fight back the tears.

"Congratulations again," I say to Wyatt's treasured friends. "It was so nice to meet you."

"It was great to meet you too, I hope we can—" her eyes dart between Wyatt and me, sensing the tension. "I hope we can do this again sometime," she finishes awkwardly. The words don't even try to take up their space in the air. They dissipate as they leave her mouth like they know it's never going to happen.

We walk out to the car. Wyatt lengthens his stride and opens my door for me. In the car, we sit in silence and stare at the road ahead of us.

Wyatt runs a hand through his hair and sighs. "I feel like I just walked into the movie theater halfway through the film. Catch me up."

"Your business is failing," I say.

"It's struggling, not failing. I'm sorry you heard any of that. I'll discuss it with him more tomorrow, and we'll come up with a game plan."

"You haven't been able to talk to him because you've been busy with me. I can't be responsible for both of you losing your dreams." Tears stream down my face but I'm too upset to stop them. I want to get home.

Wyatt goes pale as if sick, and there's no sparkle in his eyes as he puts the car in drive.

The ride home is quiet, the drone of the tires rolling over pavement echoing in the empty space that has opened between us. Wyatt keeps muttering that he doesn't understand. My heart aches as I feel the best relationship I've ever had crumble into dust.

I break the silence with a honking nose blow.

"Moxie, honestly, I know your parents had a bad experience with their business partner, but this isn't like that at all. We're still good friends; we just haven't had time to sort out some details. None of that has anything to do with you. Please don't be upset."

I'd been so stressed out to go there, and his friends were so nice. Even when they had a disagreement, it was calm. Without a doubt, I was the most upset in the group. They didn't seem especially mad at each other but rather upset with the situation and anxious to solve it.

After all these years of being on my own, I let Hannah and Wyatt past my walls. Or maybe, like determined insects, they found their way in through the cracks I didn't even know were there. Damn it, it felt good.

I've never had a friend like Hannah, and I don't think I can bear to lose her. Our friendship has opened my outlook to a lifestyle like flower petals in the spring. She truly seems to care about what's happening with me and wants to do what she can to help because she's a nice person who only wants friendship in return.

And Wyatt—my handsome, funny, kind, adventurous Wyatt—has been the boyfriend I never wanted but maybe needed. I don't think I can stop seeing him. My life has been more exhilarating and happier since I've known him. My old ways won't be enough. I'm sitting right next to him in this car, and I already miss him.

"Please talk to me. If there's a problem, we can solve it

together. I know we can. Trust me." Wyatt looks so earnest as he stares out the windshield.

"This is too much for me. This is not what I do. I don't do relationships, and it was wrong of me not to be upfront about that from the beginning. I never expected it to go this far."

"What do you mean?"

"I went out on a limb for you because Hannah talked me into it. I let it happen even though she said you were a relationship guy, and I don't do relationships. Then with your parents, we said it'd be a fake relationship, and every day it became harder and harder to pretend it was fake." I gasp as I realize the feelings I've laid bare. "Then you got me thinking that you were worth breaking my rules for. I started calling you my boyfriend and fuck if it didn't feel right." I shake my head. I shouldn't be telling him all this.

I try to catch my breath as I dry my eyes. "It all got complicated, but it doesn't matter now because it sounds to me like you have major business issues and your friends are counting on you to help them fix it. You can't do a relationship now, either."

"Moxie, I feel like we both have something to work out, but if you're thinking we can't date because of Shred and Tread or my friends, I promise you that isn't an issue." Wyatt pulls over to the side of the road. "I'm trying to be cool about us and not rush anything, but I can't. I'm falling for you, and I think you have feelings for me. I care about you and I want you to be my girlfriend."

His eyes are deep pools that I can't look at or I will fall into them. My head won't stop shaking from side to side because I'm sure that my parents' partner gave them every assurance that things were fine, too. My heart thunders in my chest. Every wall I've built to protect my feelings has been bulldozed. I need to run away.

In the driver's seat, Wyatt flounders. His mouth fish-flaps as he tries to work out the words to explain. "Moxie, please talk to me."

We're incompatible. I tried and look what happened. His business is on the brink of collapse. I bark a harsh laugh and shake my head disbelievingly.

"Every minute I'm with you, I fall further for you. From the beginning, I was fine with the fake-dating deal as long as I could spend time with you. My world is a better place when you're in it," he says.

He reaches over for my hand. "I've seen the hunger in your eyes and I think you want this too. I think we're both happier when we're together."

Tears roll down my face, and my chest hurts with the pain of holding back the violent sob that's desperate to escape. "It's not just about what you want. What we're doing is impacting Noah, Mindy, and my god, their baby."

"Noah knows about us. In fact, he'd probably say he knows too much about us, but I swear we are okay. I'm sorry you had to see us argue but I've got this."

"You don't understand. I told you what my life was like growing up. All of that happened because my parents trusted someone with their livelihood, and she screwed them over. I can't be the one causing that to happen to Shred and Tread. I can't do that to you or Noah and Mindy. They're having a kid! I don't want them dealing with the same things I did." My voice shakes. I can't bear to look at him.

"Can you please drive?" I wipe my face with the back of my hand and dry it on my tear-soaked top.

He frowns and watches me for another minute before shaking his head.

Wyatt and I have never had a shortage of things to talk about. Silence between us has been rare, and even then, it has always felt charged with this happy energy, like the conversation kept going even when we weren't speaking. It was bright and lively, like Wyatt's personality. That isn't the case now.

I try to keep my eyes off Wyatt and trained out the window, but they keep shifting back to him. His Adam's apple bobs as he clears his throat to speak, but then he changes his mind, over and over again. He must not be able to stand it any longer because as we near my apartment he cuts through the thick silence.

"Look. I can feel you pulling away. Please don't."

"I don't think I can do this. Maybe you should focus on the business for a while," I say.

"For how long? I can be with you and take care of Shred and Tread. Both are possible. It's not like business owners never have relationships. Am I expected to stay single forever if I'm going to own a business?"

"No, of course not. I don't know. Until the business gets back on its feet."

"It is on its feet. What's the benchmark? We're always going to be trying to increase business. While we're doing that, there's no reason we can't spend time together." Wyatt's voice is laced with emotion, and his eyes shimmer with tears threatening to fall.

I want to believe him. It scares me how badly I do. I didn't think I'd ever find myself wanting to commit to another person the way I want to with him. Faith is not a part of my vocabulary. Wyatt is an optimist. He sees the best in the world and in people. I'm a realist. I know the truth about people, or I thought I did.

It's hard to imagine that Wyatt would deliberately hurt anyone. If Noah's been trying to talk to him, that means Wyatt has been too distracted. I have pages of texts and our time spent together as evidence that I'm the one to blame.

"Maybe. I need time to process, and you need to help Noah. Let's cool things down for a few days. Take some time to evaluate. You said you wanted to take things slow, so let's take a break."

"I don't need time to evaluate what I already know. I want to be with you." Wyatt's voice is hoarse.

The words knife right through me and twist because they're what I want to hear yet exactly what I can't have. The decision falls over me like an eclipse shrouding me in darkness. I know what I must do, but I'm going to gut myself in the process.

We pull up to my building's entrance. He exhales slowly, his head tipping forward to rest on top of the steering wheel.

"I changed my mind. I don't want to go on a break," I say.

He meets my eyes, and the flash of hope shatters my heart into a million pieces. I swallow the bile rising in my throat to choke out the words I wish I didn't have to say.

"This isn't going to work. I'm sorry, Wyatt. This is over."

I yank open the car door and run for my building before he has time to protest. In my apartment, I toss my keys on the counter and collapse onto the floor where I finally give up and let the sobs overtake me. I cry until my throat is raw. I cry until the heaving of my misery leaves me sore from head to toe. I cry until my tears have drained me completely, and on the cold tile of my kitchen floor, I fall asleep.

Chapter 25
Wyatt

I'm late. On the day I need to be as trustworthy and responsible as a brain surgeon in the operating room, I didn't set an alarm. Noah laid all his concerns on me last night and I promised him we would sit down to go over every single digit in his ledger. He looked so relieved as I swore I'd be there early so we could spend a couple hours going over our current situation, but I was so upset about Moxie that I couldn't drag my ass out of bed. I'm an Asshole with a capital A.

My cell's ringtone bounces around my room as I frantically throw on clothes. It must be an angry Noah wondering where the hell I am. I lunge across the room to grab it off my nightstand. It's my mom, and I don't have time for this. I let it go to voicemail and grab my socks.

Last night was like a dream. Everything was flowing along beautifully like the current of the river, but then it was as if our boat came around a bend to a gushing waterfall and I got stuck underwater.

All night I imagined what I could have done differently, and it boiled down to doing my damn job. Moxie and Noah would both be happy with me if I just worked like I said I would. So what do I do? How do I show the people I care about most that I'm not a fuckup? I don't set my fucking alarm.

My phone rings again as I race across town. My frustration hits mountain peak levels as I see Mom's name across my phone's display yet again. She's not going to stop, so I punch the answer button on my steering wheel.

"Hey, I'm sorry but I can't talk right now."

"I'm having a hard time with this new buddy-buddy attitude your dad has toward the Nelsons. Marge acts like she *wants* to be friends, but I think she's still mad that Hannah's not in love with anyone. She says she would know if this Quincy guy from the restaurant was the real deal because Hannah tends to go on about stuff and she's not calling to talk about Quincy at all. What can you tell me about the two of them?"

Exasperation leaks out of my pores. I've never clenched a steering wheel this hard in my life.

"Mom, please trust me. Hannah's happy. I've got a few issues this morning and I'm late, but I promise I'll give you the full scoop after work today."

"Sure, it's just that last night at book club I got into it with Marge because she thinks you and Moxie forced Hannah into pretending that you had that double date."

Hearing Moxie's name twists the knife in the gaping hole that our breakup has left in my chest. Spots cloud my eyes, and I force myself to take deep slow breaths to bring the road back into focus. Oblivious to my turmoil, Mom carries on with her rant.

"She had Myra's pictures from the restaurant blown up to eight-by-ten inches, and she studied the video footage. Myra and Marge now are working together to 'uncover' the lie as some new mystery-solving spin on Myra's podcast. They say there was no chemistry between Hannah and Quincy. I need to know the truth. Is Hannah dating this Quincy fellow or did you set all this up for some reason? I hope you didn't because if you did, I'll never live this down."

I'm going to lose it. Our brilliant plan had worked perfectly. My dad and Hannah's dad were reunited. I thought this whole damn thing was resolved, so of course when I'm already having the worst twenty-four hours ever, it rears its ugly head.

Calling upon every drop of patience I possess, I stretch the truth. "In my opinion, Hannah had a good time on our date. I don't think Quincy is her person but I did not create an elaborate lie to trick you and the Nelsons."

"You swear you're being honest?"

I replay my wording in my head. I believe I've carefully avoided an outright lie. I know I'm guilty, but every aspect of my life is underwater right now and this is the best I can do.

"Yes, I told you the truth. But Mom, I can't tell you how crucial it is that I get off this phone right now, so please forgive me but I'm hanging up."

My tires screech as I pull into the parking lot. There's a line of people waiting to get their donuts from Penny's bakery. Taking a deep breath, I get out of my car and try to seem like a calm, professional tour guide and not a guy whose whole life is falling apart, again.

I burst through the doors but don't see Noah. "Hey Noah, sorry I'm late."

After clearing the store front, I call out to him again as I enter the storage area.

"Noah, where are you?" The room is silent. I look around and finally see him sitting in a kayak at the back of the big room. He doesn't look up or answer.

"Are you okay? You don't look so good."

Noah slowly looks up at me and takes a deep breath. "To be honest, I don't know if I'm okay."

I've never seen him like this, and I don't want to see him like this now. He has dark circles under his eyes and a scowl on his face. His shoulders sag and he looks like he wants to sail away to anywhere but here.

I creep over like I'm approaching a wild animal. "I'm sorry

I'm late, but I'm here now and I'm ready to go over those numbers. I know you're worried and I'm totally committed to doing whatever is needed to get things back on track. Come on, let's go to your desk and crunch those digits." I attempt a smile as I break out in a sweat.

"I made a mistake last night. I didn't want to bring all that up when we were celebrating and meeting Moxie, but it just came out."

"The night kind of got away from us, but we can get back on track starting today." I move a chair over by him since he doesn't seem able to move from his kayak.

He lets out a dark laugh. "Yeah, that's what I was thinking. It shouldn't have come out then, but I figured we would work it out today. You were surprised last night, but you acted like you really cared and that you wanted to do everything you could to fix Shred and Tread."

"Yes, I did. I still do. That wasn't acting. I'm determined to right this ship. We're a team. I was caught off guard last night, but—"

Noah throws his hands against his raft. "What do you mean you were caught off guard? For the past three weeks I've been showing you. Do you listen to anything I say?"

As a person who used to get in trouble a lot, I've had my ass handed to me in many different situations, but never have I felt as distraught as I do now. He's right. He's been expressing concerns over and over again, and I've assumed he was blowing things out of proportion, that it was nothing beyond any business's usual desire to grow. I try to speak but there's nothing I can say that he'll believe.

"I trusted you every time you said 'Don't worry, we've got this. We're a team, this is our dream, blah, blah, blah.' I wanted to believe it so bad. This is a great business. How many people get to spend their days making other people happy and do it with their best friend? I believed all your hype. It was working for a while, but the pressure is really on now with a baby coming and I don't feel like I can trust you anymore."

"You can trust me. I'm here. I know I was late and I totally get that it looks bad. There's no excuse for it, but I'm here now and I will never let you down again."

"You can't expect me to believe that. It was just last night that you said how important this all was to you and that you understood with the baby you needed to buckle down and help me get this place back on track."

"Yes, I meant every word of it."

"Bullshit. You are forty-five minutes late and didn't even bother to call and say so. We were supposed to spend two hours going over the books. You finally roll in and you think we can come up with a genius plan and get everything ready for the rafting trip in the hour before you have to head out."

"Yes. I mean, no. I didn't plan it this way, but I was freaked out and couldn't sleep last night. When I finally did fall asleep, I must have forgotten to set my alarm. You don't know what happened after we left. Moxie broke up with me. She was alarmed about the business issues, and I was—"

"Man, don't you think it' a problem that she cares more about our business than you do?"

"I care. I swear Shred and Tread means everything to me. You're important to me and so is Mindy and that nugget that will be the best baby ever. You're my family. I love you guys."

"I know you think so, but it isn't coming through in your actions. I love you and we'll always be there for you but I'm not sure we should continue with Shred and Tread." He sadly looks around at the equipment spread out in our storage room that has become my second home.

"Noah, we can do this. I fucked up this morning. Shit, I guess I've been fucking up for a while here, but please don't give up."

This is basically the same empty promises I was making to Moxie last night. I follow his gaze around the spacious storage room that I had imagined filling with more equipment as our business grew.

Noah gets up and heads into the front office. "I used my unexpected free time this morning to job search. You should think about doing the same. We'll keep the business going for a while so we have money coming in until we can both find something, but I need a steady income that I can depend on. It breaks my heart because we poured everything into this, but it's clear this isn't going to work. I have to put my family first. I'm sorry, but soon, we're going to have to close."

Noah shuts the door between the office and the storage area, leaving me alone in the room to process what he's said.

I look around at our dream business. I was so proud when we first opened our doors. When I lost my chance at playing professional ball, I thought I'd never be that happy again. Opening Shred and Tread was an even better dream. I took for granted how lucky I was. It only took me a few weeks to throw it all away.

But that probably isn't true. I wasn't paying attention, so who knows how long Noah has been worried. I thought he was over-reacting.

I can't run it without him, and even if I could, I can't afford to buy him out. Half of the appeal was running things with my best friend. I don't know if I'd even want to do it without him. I've lost Moxie, and I've lost my dream job. Hell, have I lost Noah too?

I stumble back, clutching at my chest as my vision spots once again. I gasp for air and put my head in my hands.

What have I done?

Chapter 26
Moxie

"You don't look so good," Simon says, taking his usual seat across from me at the blackjack table.

"And you've reached a new low on pickup lines. That's the worst one you've used on me yet." The corner of his mouth quirks up the slightest bit, but it looks forced.

"I have a few others I've been wanting to try out, but you didn't look like you were in the mood for it today. If it'd cheer you up though—"

"Why does everyone think I need cheering up?" I hiss, resisting the urge to turn around and make sure my boss isn't witnessing me chewing out a player. I'm not sure what I'd get in more trouble for: taking my eyes off the table and the chips or snapping at Simon. I take a deep breath. "Sorry. Long day."

The longest. The casino is dead today. My table has been empty for most of the first half of my shift. It'd been empty for the last ten minutes before Simon sat down. No players means no distractions, so I've had to spend this very long shift sitting with my thoughts and reliving the breakup with Wyatt.

I deal out a few hands and try to keep the conversation focused on Simon, but it isn't working.

"Quit looking at me like that," I snap, handing out his cards.

"Like what?" He taps the table for another card.

"I don't know, like I'm Josie Geller in *Never Been Kissed* after the popular kids egged her."

"Oh man, you do seem like that!" Genuine concern mars his features. He's clearly familiar with the movie. I hadn't even seen it until Hannah insisted on a slumber party, complete with the screening of multiple romcoms. "Is that what happened? You got stood up and egged?" I raise an eyebrow to remind him he needs to indicate whether he wants a card or not, and he unsurprisingly waves a hand to stay on nineteen.

"What? No. And I do not look like that," I protest. I flip my other card, pull another and, "Dealer has twenty-one." I swipe up his chips.

"Hey, don't take it out on me. You don't have to be so enthusiastic about taking my money."

He's right. I'm dragging Simon under my dark cloud, along with every one of the very few players who have sat at my table so far today. I'm a wreck. I hate that I let myself become so attached to Wyatt that I dared to imagine what might have been.

I quietly deal another hand, which he wins. "Yay," I say quietly but genuinely.

"Are you really okay?" he asks.

My lower lip threatens a wobble, and I nod. He's being kind, and I'm being a jerk. I still think he'd be a good option for Hannah if I can survive my own personal train wreck of a love life long enough to set them up. I'm spared from having to put on a happy face any longer by a tap on my shoulder.

"Break time. Boss wants to see you in her office," says Blake, today's break dealer.

In all my years working here, I can't remember ever being called back to the office for a talking-to. Maybe they picked up on my attitude with the players today after all. I probably should be freaking out, but I'm already too down to care. Let them write me up. I've never been in trouble before, and unless I'm pocketing chips, they aren't going to fire me over one bad day.

I walk past the rows of ringing and flashing slot machines to the back office. I ought to be filled with dread, but with everything else I'm feeling, I can't even bring myself to care. When I enter Sally's office, I expect to find a stern expression, but she greets me with a wide smile.

"There she is! Thanks for coming back. Take a seat." She gestures to the chair opposite her desk.

I force a smile and sit.

"How are you doing today?" she asks.

The question of the day. Sally's a good boss. I like her well enough, but we've never quite reached authentic friendliness. I'm not about to tell her I'm wrecked because I broke up with my boyfriend.

Boyfriend. I finally got close enough to someone to use that term only to discover that our relationship was dooming another family to go through what mine did. I'm so lost, it feels like my head is on crooked. I squeeze the arm of the chair for stability.

The worst part is, because I'm the one who ended things, it feels like I don't even have a right to be upset about it. I was getting in the way of his business. I did the right thing. At least I think it was the right thing.

"I'm doing okay," I finally tell Sally. Better if I could get this over with, get through my shift, and go figure out how to get Wyatt off my mind. Belatedly, I remember my manners. "How are you?"

She beams back at me. "I'm doing great, and we'll see if we can make your day even better."

I straighten in my chair. I'm not in trouble after all. "What do you mean?"

"How long have you been working here?" she asks.

"Almost seven years."

"I wanted to return to our discussion from family night. You've gotten a lot of experience under your belt. We've noticed what a great job you're doing. The players love you, you're quick with numbers, and you know all the games inside and out. I know you were considered for advancement a few years ago, but it says here in the file that you turned it down. I believe we asked you about it, but I don't recall what your reasons were." An unasked question hangs in the air.

I nod along, beginning to see where this is going. My heart beats faster as I swear the walls are moving towards me. Sally gives up on me explaining my past choices.

"Since Dylan left, we have a floor supervisor opening and we think you'd be perfect for the job. You'd still have some dealing shifts, but you'd have a raise for the shifts you supervise, and after some time training, you could supervise full time."

I can't move, like I'm frozen in carbonite. She folds her hands on the table in front of her and watches me expectantly. I know the appropriate response to this is to be squealing in delight. Okay, squealing isn't really my thing, but I should be high-fiving her or something. This is a good thing. I know this, or at least some part of my brain does, but my body is having the complete opposite reaction. My muscles tense, and my stomach lurches with a sense of dread and panic.

"Moxie?" she frowns, clearly puzzled by my lack of enthusiasm.

My chest squeezes. *Smile. Say thank you. Do something.*

"I—" I choke on the word. One letter is all I can manage. *Come on, pull yourself together.* "Thank you."

Sally's forehead smooths out and she gives a hesitant smile.

"It's well deserved, but I get the feeling I caught you off guard. We'd love to put some training shifts on your schedule in the coming weeks."

I nod mechanically, knowing I should be saying more or asking questions, but the lump in my throat threatening to make me vomit is back. I want to get out of this room so I can calm myself down and try to figure out why I'm freaking out.

"Are you alright? You don't look quite yourself."

I pull myself out of my stupor and force a smile. "Yes, sorry, just surprised. I came in today expecting a regular Tuesday."

Sally chuckles thinking I was making a joke. "I'm glad we were able to surprise you with good news. It's a change and I know that can take some adjusting, so feel free to take a few days to consider."

We talk for a few more minutes about scheduling and expectations. Rather, she mostly talks at me, and I nod and smile, trying to process what she's saying. Finally, someone knocks at the door, and she excuses me.

"Let's talk in two weeks and you can let me know what you've decided."

I run from the office and straight to the break room where I hide in the corner to have a meltdown.

This was never supposed to be a career. I was supposed to breeze around town, exploring new possibilities. I thought I'd made it clear a few years ago that I didn't want to move up. Advancement means being responsible for other people doing their job. Putting my trust in others is not what I signed up for. I ran from home to start a new life and avoid having everything and everyone I care about in one place. A promotion and more responsibilities will only entrench me further in this job that has already not been what I thought it would be. In fact, the only excitement I've had has been Wyatt.

"You all right over there?" asks a colleague whose name I can't remember. I hope she's new and not someone I didn't notice before. Hannah would know everyone's name.

"Fine," I snap, immediately annoyed with myself for my inability to be civil. The clock looms down at me. I have to get back out there.

I return to my table and go through the motions, robotically dealing out cards and tugging at my collar. It's all too fast. I can still back out of the job. If I take it, I might get stuck in a rut I'll never escape. I might wind up losing that job when I'm older with no skills to do anything else. Talk about locking myself in a box.

My chest constricts further. I can't breathe.

"Pit!" I shout to call the pit boss over. When there isn't someone at my shoulder immediately, I yell again.

"What is it?"

"I have to go," I say. "I need air. I have to—"

She must sense my panic because she steps in for me.

"Don't worry, your shift is almost over. I'll cover for you."

I check out, and when I make it out the door, I gasp in the fresh air as if I haven't had it in days. My breathing eases, but I'm staring down two huge decisions. Two pieces of my possible future weigh heavily on me. I collapse into sobs.

Chapter 27
Wyatt

I knock on the door while juggling a box of donuts and two cups of coffee, then step back to grin at the peephole.

Hannah pulls the door open and looks around me, clearly assuming I wouldn't visit alone. "Wyatt, what are you doing here?"

"What are *you* doing?" I ask in return because even though I'm the one who showed up unannounced, she's the one who looks out of character right now, acting all cagey and peeking around the door.

"I'm kind of in the middle of a project. Don't you know people don't do pop-ins anymore? You're supposed to text."

"How about you let me in? I brought high-quality bribes, and I need to talk to you."

"You do?" She slowly opens the door, still searching the front yard for reinforcements. "Wait here, I need to put a few things away. Give me a minute."

As instructed, I wait in the entryway while listening to the clanging sounds of frantic cleanup going on inside.

"Okay, you can come in now." Hannah sniffs the air. "Please tell me that coffee is for me."

There's a large red plastic bin in front of the TV that I assume holds all the items she was hiding away. Her jumbo white board and bookshelf crowd the small eating area and couch. Looking around, it's clear this woman's brain is a stack of graph paper. I can't help but smile at her piles of binders, notebooks, bins, and impressive rainbow of markers

Hannah grabs her coffee and embraces the cup. Her table is covered with Post-it notes with arrows connecting them together in an elaborate spider web of directions.

I pick up a red sticky note with the word "police" on it and look curiously at some tinsel hanging off her whiteboard.

"Are you planning to rob a bank?" I ask. She gives off a sweet vibe, but with her incredible research and organizational skills, she could be a criminal mastermind. No one would ever suspect her.

"Oh, please, do you really think I'd rob a bank? No, I'm planning a murder," she retorts, completely nonplussed.

I gape at her.

"Just kidding. Well, sort of. I'm planning a murder mystery party. Do you want to come? Because if you do, you can't look at any of this. What am I saying, of course you're going to come." She drags me approximately six feet into the living room and unceremoniously shoves me onto the couch with my back to the plotting.

Hannah is a huge planner, and she's very visual. You give her a problem and leave her in a room with a dry erase board and some crafting supplies, and she'll come up with a NASA-level solution.

I hand her the donuts. "You might need a bigger lair."

"Don't judge me." She gives me a sassy smirk and tests her coffee.

"No judgement. It's just a question. I take it things didn't work out with you and Quincy."

"No, but that's fine. I think he's convinced I'm some minor celebrity and left it open if I want to call him. But no sparks."

"Can't say I'm surprised. He didn't seem quite right for you, but don't give up. The right guy is out there, and Moxie seems like she wants to help you find him."

Hannah nods her head but without conviction.

I drop that subject because she's usually a chatterbox and her silence is giving clear "leave it be" vibes. She sets two plates on the coffee table and drops onto the couch, carefully opening the donut box. She falls silent as she deliberates. Time for what I came here for.

"I need your help, and the way I see it, you owe me." I smile and snag a donut for myself.

She studies me. "I'm happy to do you a favor, but why do I owe you?"

"You set me up." I let that hang there for a minute. "Don't even try to deny it. You plucked me out of your past and waved Moxie in front of me so you could solve the feud and work this pact with your new friend. I was an unwitting pawn in your elaborate game. The last couple months of my life have been a Hannah Nelson production." I wave my hand at her whiteboard.

Hannah sits back in her seat and wipes her face with her napkin, her head tilting as she looks off to the left. "But did I?" She smiles an evil little grin and leans forward. "If you really think about it, all I did was tell Moxie about you and then get her to the Expo so she could sign up with Shred and Tread. The rest was nature taking its course. She asked you out and you said yes, my friend, so I think it's all on you." Hannah eyes the rest of the donuts, clearly proud of her explanation.

"Are you denying responsibility?"

"For you falling head over heels for her? Absolutely."

She's downplaying her role, but I let it slide because she's just sunk an arrow straight into my heart and doesn't even know it. It's true; I fell hard and fast, and then I blew it.

Hannah, distracted by her donut, doesn't notice the change in my mood. "I think this has worked out great for all of us. The feud is over, and you've got Moxie. If anything, you should be thanking me."

I thought Moxie might have told Hannah about the breakup, but clearly not. It worries me. She isn't close to her family, and I'm pretty sure Hannah's the closest friend she's got around here. If she hasn't talked to Hannah about us, that likely means one of two things: Either I never meant as much to her as I thought and I'm not worth mentioning to her friend, or she's hurting without a support system. Neither is great.

Hannah still hasn't looked my way and continues talking even with a mouth full of donut. "It's like if a friend says, 'I could go for some Mexican food,' and I know this little place on Hilltop Drive that has a great enchilada. Of course I'm going to tell them they should check it out. That's all I did."

My mouth drops open. "Hannah Nelson, were you telling Moxie about my enchilada?"

"What? No!" She whirls around, her face turning a tomato red.

She's so easy to rattle.

"Don't worry, I'm giving you a hard time. You were right to set us up. She's fantastic."

"I knew it!" Hannah drops the last of her donut and bounces up and down like she won the lottery.

I let her have her moment before I break the news to her and ask for help.

The smile dies on my face. "It *was* going great, but I take it you haven't talked to her or your mom today."

Hannah checks her phone with a groan. "I missed a call from my mom, but it's too early for me to face Stitch 'N Bitch drama. I haven't heard a peep from Moxie, but we worked different hours yesterday and she's not really a morning person. What happened? Did the dinner with Noah and Mindy not go well?"

My muscles tense as my fight-or-flight mode activates. No part of me wants to relive our argument. I've tortured myself with enough mental reliving already, but I have to bring her up to speed.

"It started off great. Everyone hit it off right away, and Noah and Mindy told us they're expecting. Can you believe that? They're having a baby."

"That's great for them." Hannah's smile for this news is genuine, but her eyes are still full of concern.

"Then the conversation took a turn." The whole story pours out of me. The argument with Noah that Moxie overheard, her dumping me because of it, and my failure to show up on time to work the next day. While I can barely bring myself to even think it, I even tell her about Noah's plan to close Shred and Tread.

"Oh, shit." Hannah drops down on the chair, her face turned down. "That's a lot. I'm so sorry. I know Shred and Tread was everything to you."

My eyes well up, and I try to discreetly wipe the moisture away. For the last twenty-four hours, I've felt myself falling into the same pit of despair I got lost in after my injury. That same drowning sensation has overtaken me. Pulling myself out of bed and coming here to Hannah's was more of a monumental effort than I can say, but it's my cry for help.

"He's been trying to tell me. He's been telling me constantly, and I still somehow missed it."

Hannah bites her lip and puts a gentle hand on my shoulder before tentatively saying, "Maybe you didn't want to see it."

I look up at her, waiting for her to continue.

"I've known you a long time. Besides Shred and Tread, I've only seen you so passionate about one thing before."

She waits for my reaction, and I grind my teeth, instantly feeling defensive. "I don't want to talk about baseball. I've got enough terrible shit going on right now. Don't make me relive my old nightmares, too."

She winces and says the rest like she has to power through it. "I'm not great at this, but I think this is a tough love moment. Maybe you *need* to talk about baseball. Maybe if you'd talked about baseball anytime in the last several years, you wouldn't be where you are right now with Shred and Tread."

"I fail to see the connection."

"It took a lot for you to get excited about the business after everything you lost with baseball, but when you did, you jumped in with both feet. I wonder if maybe, because of all that loss, you were so afraid of losing everything again that you couldn't admit to yourself what Noah was telling you."

Begrudgingly, I work my way past my raised hackles to consider this. It's one thing that's been plaguing me since my conversations with Noah. I may not be great with numbers, but how could I still not have heard what he'd been so plainly telling me? Shit, Hannah might be onto something.

"That... actually makes sense," I admit. My head sinks into my hands.

"I'm sorry. I know it's not what you want to hear."

"I can't go down this road again. You and Noah pulled me out of it, but it's my life. I can't give up on that yet. I'll figure something out; I just need more time to think."

She nods, her weak smile understanding. "Just to be clear, we were there for you, but you fought your way through the pain and disappointment. We just stood behind you so it was harder to slip back."

Hannah gives my hand a squeeze.

"And Moxie?"

"She hasn't called you?" I ask.

"No. You know how she is. She's a closed book. She's not going to rely on anyone unless they force her to."

"I don't want to lose her. I'm falling for her, and I swear she was happy with me. I'm sure of it." I get up and pace the living room. "I don't know what to do. I thought you might be able to help. I don't want to be the jerk that doesn't take no for an answer, but I'm worried. Can you check on her and make sure she's okay?"

"I'll call her."

"If she needs time, I can give her whatever she needs, but I don't want her to give up on us."

"I know. I'll see what I can do, but she's a private person. If she doesn't want to talk to me, I need to respect that." She looks across the room at me, her eyes full of concern.

I wipe my hand across my forehead. "I didn't want to do the fake dating thing, but that was all she was willing to do. From the beginning it's been real for me. Now I don't want to imagine my life without her. I'm sorry I'm dumping all this on you, but I don't know what to do." I get up and start pacing. "I was trying to go slow and not rush the relationship thing, you know? I thought I was hanging back, but then she flipped out."

Hannah's brow furrows in concern. "I'm so sorry. I'll let her know that you're worried about her."

"You agree I should give her time to sort out whatever is stressing her out? You don't think I should try to help her?"

"No, let me talk to her. Maybe she just needs time to process. Like you said, she had a hard time getting on board with a relationship to begin with. I know it's hard because you care about her, but try to put her to the back of your mind for right now. Give her space. You've got other fish to fry. It sounds like you need to focus on Shred and Tread. Is there any way I can help there?"

"Actually, yeah." I hold up a thumb drive. "I snagged some of the stuff from work that I failed to deal with before. Noah's given up. I don't blame him, but it means I can't talk to him about it. I want to salvage things, but I have to understand them first and I'm not good with numbers. These spreadsheets go over my head."

Her eyes light up at the word spreadsheets.

"Will you go over them with me?" I ask.

She extends a grabby hand out for the flash drive. "Of course. This is right up my alley."

We spend the next two hours reviewing Noah's budget documents, and finally I get it. I know what we need financially not only to get back on track, but to stay there. Now I just need to figure out how to make it happen.

"Do you want me to brainstorm with you?" she asks. "I love brainstorming."

"No, thanks. You've done more than enough. I think I need to do that on my own. Can you forget that I came here all pathetic and needy?" I ask.

"You aren't pathetic. Just don't tell anyone about the murder party yet," she says.

"Deal. I haven't even asked, how are things going with you?"

She shrugs. "Pretty good, I guess. Glad the parents are finally getting along."

I groan, and her mouth falls open.

"No, not them too! What happened?"

I tell her about my mom's suspicions. "It didn't sound promising."

Hannah sighs. "If I could find somebody for real, maybe they'd let this go."

I pat her shoulder. "If it makes you feel any better, once they find out about me and Moxie, it'll be both our faults. And really, their fight shouldn't be the reason you want to find a partner."

"I know, but I'd have been dating anyway. I'm just not any good at it. I have no luck."

"You're still doing the pact, right? Maybe you'll hit it off with one of Moxie's exes," I try to reassure her, even though I'm not confident that Moxie will want to continue setting her up after she and I broke up.

"We're kind of a mess, huh?" she says.

"Yup," I agree, staring into space and rubbing at my chest where my aching heart is pining for Moxie.

"Come here and let me give you a hug. Have faith. Things will work out."

"I hope so. I'm going to take off, but thanks for your help."

"I'll let you know what she says, and I'm putting you on the guest list for the party!" she calls out as I walk toward the door.

"I'll have to think about it. Last time you killed me with an icicle to the head."

"Oh, that's right. That was some of my best work!" She chuckles. "They can't find the murder weapon if its melted."

"Want me to drop that in the recycling?" I nod at the now-empty donut box on the table, but I don't even hear Hannah's response because the box has given me an idea.

Chapter 28
Moxie

Tears of frustration leak out as I peel away from the curb. If I wasn't upset enough, the fact that I'm crying is maddening, which only makes me cry more, and *damn it*.

A few months ago, my biggest problem was being bored. If I'm honest, I was a little lonely, but I wouldn't have even considered a relationship. Today, I'm barely holding myself together and am completely heartbroken.

My eyes go blurry, so I pull over before I get into an accident. I throw the car into park and look down at my phone and think about calling Hannah. That's another problem—I used to be completely independent, but now when a problem comes up, I want to hash it out with her.

A thick teardrop falls from my eyes, landing with an earth-shattering thud on the steering wheel. I stare at the tiny puddle for a moment as frustration boils within me until that energy needs a release.

"Ahhhhh!" I yell, banging my palms against the sides of the steering wheel. I'm going full Tarzan, and I don't even care. My hands ball into fists and I beat against the dashboard until my knuckles ache and the pent-up energy fizzles. "What the hell am

I doing?" I whimper. This time when the tears fall, I know there's no holding them back.

So much has changed, and I have so many emotions that I don't know how to deal with. I don't want to get hurt any more than I already am.

I need the Moxie coping method, and I need to stop trying to face this alone.

I breathe in the piney scent of the surrounding trees and allow the dizzy sensation from looking down at the forest floor to rush over my brain and drown out my thoughts.

"Aren't I supposed to bring you soup, force you to bathe, and clean up the mountains of tissues and ice cream containers littering your place from your three-day wallow or something?" Hannah asks, a tinge of hysteria to her voice.

She's been surviving the high ropes course, clinging to me most of the way, but just barely. We've made it to the final obstacle: jumping off a platform and being lowered to the ground.

"You've watched too many sappy movies," I say.

"No." The word is drawn out and shaky. "I don't think so. I think you have unusual coping methods, and as your support person, I have to say I'd prefer if you reverted to the stereotypical ones. I'd be more than happy to bring you an assortment of Ben & Jerry's finest."

"Quit your whining and jump," I snap. My emotions have had the night to bubble back up while I tossed and turned in bed. First thing this morning, I rounded up Hannah for an early-bird high ropes course. All that emotion needs somewhere to go. I don't *want* this adrenaline rush; I *need* it. If I don't get her to jump off the damn ledge before me, she's never going to.

"Okay." She nods to the guide, closes her eyes, and heaves a few deep breaths. She holds one foot over the edge. "But this is unhealthy—" the "Y" turns into a scream as she steps off and rings the bell on the final challenge of the course. The operator on the ground unhooks her, and it's hard to say from way up here, but I'm pretty sure Hannah's glowering at me. Let her. My broken, disappointed heart is going to burst out of my chest if I don't do something.

I fidget impatiently as our guide hooks me up and asks, "Ready?"

I don't bother with a response. I run the two steps to the edge and leap. Wind pushes at my face as I ring the bell and fall, whisking away my worries. All the anxiety in my heart feels momentarily free as my pulse quickens with the adrenaline coursing through my veins.

Then, the rope catches me.

In the blink of an eye, I'm helped out of my harness, and it's over. No sooner have I walked over to Hannah than my misery rises back up to choke me. Although her face is still ashen from her own jump, Hannah's eyes crinkle in concern. "Do you feel better?"

I shake my head. "I did. For about five seconds."

Five freeing seconds, and then it's straight back to Wyatt. His infectious laugh and cocky, playful attitude. He likes me for who I am. He's like pure adrenaline, and while I can't get enough of him, I'm still convinced that being with him would destroy us. It would be the downfall of his career and his passion. It would take all the light out of him, and watching what that does to him and to Noah would kill me.

Hannah links her arm with mine. "I'm sorry. I can still get that Ben & Jerry's."

I feel like I'm about to explode. "I need a bigger cliff."

What little color was left drains from Hannah's face. "No. We need to find you a less terrifying coping mechanism. I'm sorry, but I draw the line at cliff jumping. A high ropes course was more than I was comfortable with, if we're being honest. Besides, I hate to say it, but we need to get ready for work."

"No," I whine. I'm crawling out of my skin here. I can't stand still at a blackjack table for eight hours. I will explode. Spontaneous combustion. Human bonfire, right there in the casino. I haven't made a decision about the promotion. I'm just avoiding everything. "I shouldn't have to work when I'm in crisis."

"I couldn't agree more. You could take another sick day, but I'm a little worried what you'd get into without supervision. Do you need me to take the day off?"

I mentally count my days off in my head and decide that this is not the way I want to spend another one of them. "No, I can't afford to use another personal day for this, and I'm definitely not making you use one of yours," I say, even if I feel like my heart has been torn right out and stomped on.

Hannah sighs. "Welcome to America."

We walk toward my car among the shadows of the tall trees. We're mostly quiet except for the snapping of twigs and crinkling of dry leaves beneath our feet. I try to keep my eyes focused on the path, but in my periphery, she's watching me as if trying to determine if I'm going to ditch work and attempt to go hang gliding as soon as I'm out of her sight. Every time I catch her, she quickly looks away as though she's been looking at the brilliant blue sky the whole time. After three occurrences of this, I snap.

"Quit studying me. I'll be fine."

"Mmhmm. This is what fine looks like? Showing up at your friend's doorstep at seven a.m. with an Egg McMuffin and dragging them to a high ropes course that's somehow supposed to be therapeutic."

"Stop judging my coping mechanisms."

"If you need mechanisms, you're coping with something, which means you're not fine."

"You're a real pain in the ass sometimes," I grumble.

"A pain in the ass who's trying to help you." Hannah swears

on occasion, but it's rare enough that it sounds unnatural. It's usually accompanied by hesitation, as if the words are stuck to the roof of her mouth like peanut butter.

She's right. I know I'm being shitty, but if I'm not angry, then I'll be sad. I'd rather be mad than devastated, so that's where we are. When the path spills out of the forest into the parking lot, she drags me to a nearby picnic table.

"Are you ready to tell me what happened with Wyatt, and why you ran out of work yesterday?"

Over the course of a few short months, Hannah has gone from someone I barely knew to someone whose presence can calm me from an absolute panic. She was the right person to call today. I don't want to have this conversation, but maybe it's necessary.

"I'm so ridiculous." I squeeze the life out of the steering wheel in frustration with myself and my circumstances.

"Why do you think that?" she asks gently.

"I was offered a promotion."

"I'm guessing from our current situation here that we're not happy about that, but I'm not sure I understand why."

"That makes two of us." My voice comes out weak and cracks.

She frowns in confusion. "Let's try to piece it together. How are you feeling right now?"

"Like crap." Thank you, Captain Obvious. She doesn't even roll her eyes, just patiently waits. "Okay, I feel like… have you seen *Star Wars*?"

"Of course."

"I feel like I'm in that trash compactor scene. Like my life is mostly a steaming pile of garbage that I'm swimming through and the walls are closing in on me."

She considers this. "The job offer could have a major impact on the trajectory of your life. I can see how that would feel like the compactor walls, but why is the rest of your life garbage?"

"Maybe that was an unfairly strong metaphor." I laugh,

swiping at a rogue tear. All the cells in my body are rebelling against leaning on Hannah, but if I'm going to let her help me, I've got to talk to her. "When I was a kid, I spent a lot of time at my parents' wedding barn. I have so many vivid memories of watching the brides and thinking they were all beautiful princesses. I loved it there, and so did my parents. My mom... you should have seen the way she would light up, getting to be a part of someone's big day. She would always remind the staff at the beginning of every event that for them it was just a day at work, but for the couple, it was the biggest day of their lives."

"It sounds like she loved what she did," Hannah says.

"After the business shut down, it was like a light went out of her. I remember one Saturday, standing in her room and watching her pull her hair back in her mirror before work. I thought that I would normally be watching a bride do this. Instead of seeing one of those princesses tearing up seeing themselves in their wedding gown, I was seeing my mom with bags under her eyes about to head out to a job she hated."

The haunted look on her face etched itself into my brain. My parents tried not to let me see how hard things had gotten for them after Allison's betrayal, but it was impossible to miss.

Hannah shakes her head sadly. "That's terrible."

"Putting all their trust in that one person and in that one business destroyed them. I swore I wouldn't let something pin me down like that, yet somehow, without realizing it, I've gotten myself involved with a man who's struggling through financial issues in business with his best friend. I've settled into working the same job for years. I stand behind a table and flip cards all day, every day."

Hannah opens her mouth like she's ready to defend our coworkers who have been doing this for even longer than me and happen to love it. I wave her off.

"There's nothing wrong with that, but it's so far from where I imagined myself. A promotion means committing more to this job that I don't love. It means turning it into a career."

"I thought you liked being a dealer."

I shrug letting out a long sigh. "I do. As a job it is fine. I just thought it would be more exciting."

Hannah makes herself comfortable, laying down on the picnic table and letting the sun warm her face. "No job is without some level of redundancy. I doubt there's anyone out there who couldn't name something they don't like about their job. You're good at what you do, and the players always seem like they're having fun at your tables."

She sits up. "Imagine for a moment that you take the promotion. You learn some new things and take on a leadership position, so that even if you decide it's not for you down the line, you have that experience. In a year you could say, *I'm sorry this didn't work out.* Would that be so bad?"

I ruffle my own hair and breathe out another sigh of frustration with myself.

"You're not your parents, you know," she says gently.

"I know."

"Do you?" she asks.

"I'm working on it," I admit. "Do you think I was too hard on Wyatt?"

Her head tilts to the side with a tight-lipped *What do you think?* smile.

"It's scary, trusting someone with your heart," I say.

"It is."

"I can't believe I threw away my chance with him." I drop my head in my hands

"Are you sure you did? When I saw him looking at you, he had that dreamy look in his eyes. I could practically see the cartoon hearts circling his head."

"I think you're exaggerating, but even if he was, I lost it at the barbecue."

"It's kind of funny how these double dates have been complete nightmares for us."

I laugh as my mood lightens a little, but I think Hannah is

wrong. When he dropped me off that night, he was angry and disappointed. He's not forgetting what I did to him anytime soon.

"How's he doing?" I finally ask.

Hannah bites her lip and darts her eyes all over the place. "I don't know. You're going to have to talk to him about that."

Bullshit. She knows, but she isn't going to tell me, which means he's either doing great without me or is a total wreck, too. She wouldn't be afraid to tell me if he was just going along. But it's not fair to put her in the middle. I need to put my big girl pants on and deal with it, but it's also not right if I get his hopes up just to walk away. When I try to imagine my life moving forward, I see him there, but he feels far away while I keep grasping at straws.

"Maybe, but I think I need to sort myself out first. I need to figure out how I feel about work and what I want to do with my life before I bring someone else into it."

"That's fair. I'll let him tell his own story, but I think he's got some figuring out to do as well."

I look at my friend, this sweet girl who came into my life and who I don't deserve. "Thank you. Really."

"I'm here for you. Always. But maybe next time, let's keep our feet on the ground."

Chapter 29
Wyatt

If things hadn't recently imploded with Noah, I would have begged him to take today's tour. He's still set on closing the business. I think I have an idea to significantly cut down our costs, and I've been taking steps to make that happen, even enlisting Hannah's help in putting together a presentation for Noah. I just haven't shared it with him yet.

It isn't enough. It might have been if I'd come up with it weeks ago, before I screwed everything up so badly, but now I need more. I've been racking my brain for another opportunity to bring in extra revenue without drastically increasing our costs, but so far, I've got nothing. I will. I have to.

Still, despite usually loving leading tours, I don't want to do this one. I booked a trip for a guy named Marcus and his about-to-be fiancé to Alberta Falls. That spot is probably responsible for more engagements than there are rocks up there. It's a spot that I had hopes to show Moxie someday.

I've tried to bury my head in the business and put her out of my mind. To some extent, it's worked, but as soon as whatever was pulling my focus is gone, the pain flares up as fresh as ever. This guy is going to propose, and I'm going to have to "share in their bliss" when I'm fucking miserable. I can't take it.

An Ex-citing Proposition

I plaster a smile on my face as Marcus and Adelyn walk up. I do my best to maintain the facade as I go through the first leg of their tour. Sweet mountain air seeps into my lungs, and even with my determined misery, I can feel it trying to lift my spirits. It might be good that I'm out here. This is a spectacular hike if you ignore the aura of bliss surrounding Adelyn and Marcus.

Trying to dazzle the lovers with the beauty of nature on the walk up, I point out animal tracks and birds along the way, my mood only souring a little as thoughts of how Moxie would react to each tidbit creep in.

As we crest a ridge, a field of lupines peeks through the pines. Adelyn and Marcus hardly notice because they're so focused on each other, and all I want to do is tuck one of those flowers into Moxie's hair. I wipe my face as if I can scrape off the envy as I watch the tourists hold hands.

Two-thirds of the way to the waterfall, we come across an older couple guzzling water and struggling to catch their breath. I point out the picturesque mountain ridges in the distance to distract them while I make sure these two are okay. I don't want to leave them in this shaky state.

"George insisted that we see the waterfall in person. He proposed to me up here forty years ago." The older woman rubs her husband's back as he wipes his brow.

"That's so romantic." Adelyn unconsciously strokes her boyfriend's arm. The fifth wheel on a brand-new car would be more relevant than I feel right now.

"I thought it would be something special for our anniversary, but now I think it will be a way for her to remember my heart attack." The older man attempts to laugh, but I'm a little too concerned the joke will come true to find it funny. As someone whose recent romantic attempts failed, I feel like I should help this poor guy out.

"I have an idea; what if we set you two up on a log over here, and we can do a video chat. I'll take you up the rest of the way on my phone and we'll share the view from the top," I suggest.

The two of them exchange looks and reach out for each other's hand. "That would be so kind."

We spend a few minutes connecting the call, and then my young lovebirds and my older video sweethearts join me as I continue the tour to the falls. I resume pointing out all the gems our mountain has to offer, and Adelyn takes my phone and points it at me so that our new video friends have a good view. George keeps asking about different wildlife as we climb higher, and I continue to answer all his questions as if he were hiking with us. Fortunately, my young couple doesn't seem to mind the extra company. At the top, I retrieve my phone and do a slow circle to show George and his wife Grace the breathtaking view.

"Oh George, it's just like I remember. What a wonderful treat this is. Wyatt, put the phone down and take a picture of Adelyn and Marcus. It's so pretty, they need to capture this."

"Don't worry. I'll get some good pictures for them." I find a nice spot to prop my phone so they can still enjoy the waterfall.

"Do you two want me to take some pictures of you?" I ask.

Marcus rushes over and hands me his phone. He discreetly reaches into his pocket and pulls out a jewelry box. I take his phone, winking to assure him I'll get the big moment.

They pose in front of the waterfall, and I snap pictures of them. Adelyn is giggling at something he shouts over the roaring of the falls. It's so easy to see myself exploring the falls with Moxie and making her laugh like that.

Then he visibly summons his courage, and I switch to video to record as he sinks to one knee. My heart wrenches with joy for them, and I'm touched by George and Grace, who are cheering from their log a half mile down the mountain.

I'm overflowing with happiness, but I also feel a pang of jealousy and a deep longing to have a happily ever after of my own. So often in the past, I've wanted that, and if I'm honest with myself, the image of the woman by my side has been interchangeable. Now, I can't imagine it being anyone other than Moxie.

An Ex-citing Proposition

I walk away from Adelyn and Marcus so they can have some privacy to revel in their joy. They seem to be floating on air.

"Grace, do you remember where you were standing when George proposed?"

Grace laughs. "Actually, I was leaning over to look at the waterfall, and as I started to lose my balance, my Prince Charming swooped me in his arms and asked me to be his." She hugs a blushing George.

With the camera in my hand, I walk toward the edge and pan the view of the waterfall for them. I snap a few pictures to share with them later.

"George, it sounds like you were quite the Casanova in your day," I tease him.

"I was trying to get a kiss but got a little carried away."

"Oh, you rascal," she says.

"I was all caught up in the moment and wanted to spend the rest of my life with you."

I look at the breathtaking view that has inspired such devotion and feel like my fucking heart is going to burst.

I'm grateful to our chatty new friends for the distraction from the bliss that rolls off the newly-engaged couple. We pick up George and Grace on our way down.

"Before we get back, can we get a picture of all of us? We really appreciate you sharing this with us. I can't tell you how much it means. I know we weren't with you, but it felt like we went up there together." Grace looks like she's about to attack me with a hug.

"What a great idea! This has been such a romantic day. I'll never forget it." Adelyn plants a kiss on Marcus. As I take a selfie dripping with other people's love, the tiny seed of an idea begins to form.

Chapter 30
Wyatt

I came down from Alberta Falls two weeks ago feeling like I might have a break in the clouds over my head. George and Grace enjoyed their video hike up the mountain so much that I thought there must be other people who want to experience all Mother Nature has to offer but can't due to physical limitations or lack of time. This isn't the first time I've had an idea that I've presented to Noah. In fact, I've had lots of ideas. Most of them he's thankfully talked me out of, but there was that one idea after college that he thought was good. Now, I've just got to see if he can give one more of my brainstorms a chance.

I fiddle with my tie for the hundredth time and rearrange papers on my desk. My feet tap anxiously under the desk while I wait for Noah. I've made a point to be not only on time but early and as professional as possible.

He's still determined to close the business. I want to make sure there aren't garage sale stickers on the equipment, but nothing's been sold yet because he hasn't found another job. I think there's a part of him that hasn't given it his all because deep down he doesn't want to let this dream go any more than I do. At least, I hope that's true.

I've spent weeks putting together numbers and—with

Hannah's help—making a kickass presentation. It all comes down to today, which explains the suit and tie. This is my last-ditch effort, my last chance to salvage what we've built together.

The door swings open and Noah walks in, his steps heavy and his shoulders slumped. I feel you, buddy. It's not easy coming to work at a place you love when you know you're about to lose it.

I clear my throat. "Good morning."

"Morning," Noah says without looking up.

"How you doing?" I ask.

"Alright, I guess. You?" Our conversation is stilted and formal. If we have to close, it'll be tragic, but losing Noah as a friend would crush me. We've been trying hard to maintain civility and keep things normal, but they aren't. How could they be? There's a discomfort that will take time to mend, but I have to believe we'll get there.

"I'm good."

He finally glances at me and his eyebrows furrow. "What's with the suit? Do you have an interview?"

Admittedly, the suit may have been overkill, but if I want him to take me seriously, it felt right to dress seriously, too.

"No, no interview, but I've been working on something that I want to show you. Do you have a few minutes?" I ask tentatively. We used to be the perfect team, but I know I dropped the ball, and it's shifted the balance of power. I'm at Noah's mercy.

He gives me a pitying look and shakes his head. "You know we've got to close, man. I didn't make that decision lightly."

I take a deep breath and try to steady my shaking hand as I fumble to bring my laptop over to him. "I know. But I've worked really hard on this, and all I'm asking is for you to take a look with an open mind. If after this you still think that's the right decision, I won't fight it anymore. I'll start filling out applications today. But I'm asking, as your friend, for you to let me get this out. Please."

He holds my gaze for a long, tense beat. "Alright, but don't get your hopes up."

I nod, because this whole month has been like trying to keep a flame lit in the pouring rain. There's been so little hope, but I refuse to give in until I know I've done everything possible to make it work.

I start by expressing what we need. I cover our current financials and where we need them to be. This isn't news to Noah. He knows it far better than me. I was worried he might cut me off, but I decided to lead with it anyway because I need him to know that *I* understand it now.

He rubs at his neck impatiently, but my friend can see I'm trying so he quietly waits me out.

"The first thing I wanted to do was find a way to cut our expenses significantly. This will bring us more stability so that even if we have another rough patch, we have the cash to comfortably get through it. That's where Penny comes in."

"Penny? As in our neighbor, the baker Penny?" he asks.

"I haven't pitched this to her. I didn't want to make a move until I'd run it by you. She's outgrown her current spot and is considering relocating, but she doesn't want to lose the foot traffic she currently gets. Our warehouse is larger than we've ever needed. We can condense things, and I have more than enough space to store some things in my garage at home to free up enough space to sublet the back half to her."

The tolerant, even expression he had been wearing shifts to something more thoughtful. "That's... not a bad idea," he admits.

"Thanks," I say, "but there's more."

He raises his eyebrows. "Carry on."

I tell him all about the hike and my encounter with the elderly couple that still enjoyed their virtual trip to the summit. I share how they were able to talk to me as we explored and how I could move the camera to show them exactly what they wanted to see. It was something they couldn't get from seeing the spaces in a documentary or photos.

"It got me thinking, since we sometimes have a hard time filling open spaces, maybe we could be creative. What if we could tap into another market and fill those spaces virtually? I did a few proof-of-concept tours with my parents and some of their friends already. Take a look."

I press play on the laptop to start a video with excerpts from another hike, a climb, and a whitewater rafting tour. My parents and their friends were laughing and sipping margaritas as I paddled over the rapids while my buddy Mike filmed. Not one of my dad's friends' backs would have been able to handle those rapids, but they got the live feel of tipping on ledges, bouncing off rocks, and splashing each other for dramatic effect—all from the comfort of their new jacuzzi.

I included a video testimonial from Hannah's mom about how she wanted to plan a trip with a friend of hers from Connecticut. Things are still a little shaky between the parents, but her willingness to help me went a long way with my parents. Hannah and I have kept at it, and they're beginning to come around.

"It allows an opportunity for people whose mobility concerns might otherwise prohibit them from experiencing these types of things. We can be accessible, and that would open us up to a new customer base. Not only that, but people can join us from anywhere in the world. I think we'd still want to limit the number of people we have join so they can ask questions and create an enjoyable a live experience, but our total addressable market is practically limitless."

Noah's eyes widen. "Look at you, throwing out TAM."

I'm scared to hope, scared to fan that little flame I've been desperately nurturing for the past month. But Noah hasn't shot me down yet. He's leaning forward, his body language telling me he's at least interested in what I'm saying.

"And it's scalable. I didn't want to introduce too many costs at first, but if it proves to be successful, down the line we could look at virtual reality options, though I see that being more distant future possibility."

"The ideas sound great, but I'd need to look at the numbers," he says.

"I've got that!" I spring out of my chair and hand him a binder. Hannah was so excited about this project she gave me one of her favorites, a royal blue cover with green folder tabs.

He flips through, and I sit on top of my desk drumming my fingers on my leg. Please let this work. *Please.* The binder has a detailed budget, including potential rental money from Penny. There's a bit of a startup cost for my digital tours idea. It requires equipment, but I've allocated for that in estimates for selling some of our other equipment from some of our less popular tours. This has the bonus of ensuring we're no longer operating those unpopular tours at a loss. I did my due diligence. I crossed every "t" and dotted every "I". I'm all in. He has to see that.

"I don't know what to say," he says, and my heart sinks. After all the research and organizing I've done over the last month, it still wasn't enough.

"I'm really impressed."

My head shoots up. "You are?"

He laughs. "I am. This is great work. I don't want to close, but I couldn't keep doing this with a partner who wasn't invested. This? This is you all-in."

My eyes start to water, and I breathe in deep to hold the tears from falling. I actually did it.

"I want to run it by Mindy, and we have to get Penny on board to rent the space, but if you can do that, I'm in."

The flood of immense relief that washes over me at those words does me in, and I let the tears fall.

"Aw, buddy, come here." Noah pulls me into a hug, and I know we're going to be okay. We've got a long road with a lot of hard work ahead of us, but I've got my best friend by my side again.

"About Penny," I say, once I've regained my composure.

"Yeah?"

"I was really hoping this would work, and I invited her over this afternoon. Is that alright?"

"Well, shit. No time like the present, I guess. And Mindy will probably feel better if I can tell her we've got this in place. Let's get ready."

Penny, Noah, and I sit at Noah's desk, the sweet smell of cinnamon filling the air as she sets out a tray with three mouth-watering rolls on it.

"I'm not sure if I should be nervous. I don't know if I've ever seen Wyatt look this professional and serious," Penny says.

"Oh man, these rolls are so damn good," Noah says around his gooey mouthful.

"They're my top seller." She grins proudly and takes a bite of one.

"I think you rigged the ventilation system to pump cinna-mon-scented air into the street," Noah says.

"What did you guys want to meet about?" Penny asks.

Noah sits up at his desk and switches over to professional businessman. While we were prepping earlier, Noah encouraged me to lead the pitch, but this is still his wheelhouse. There's too much riding on this for me to prove a point by running the pitch.

"We were talking about our needs here at the office and your needs for your bakery. Wyatt says you're having difficulty with your space?"

"I need to expand to meet demand. There's only so much room in the current kitchen, and our storage area is already over-flowing. I'm worried that we might have to move to a bigger store. I love this location, but I'm not sure what to do about it."

"We don't want you to go either. Let's be honest, Wyatt is

hooked on your treats, and I can't lose him to a muffin detox program."

I nod in agreement. It's more than that. Her foot traffic is good for us, and we value her friendship, too.

"We can't have that, can we?" Penny grins.

"Wyatt has been inventorying our equipment, and we have more space than we need. We thought we could rent out part of our storage area to you. What do you think?"

"Are you serious? You guys could do that?" Penny sets down her fork and sits up in her chair.

"We were thinking it's a good solution for all of us. Come on, let's take a look back there and see about how much space you think you need," he suggests.

Penny's eyes light up as she surveys the area. She wanders around mumbling about shelving and boxes and finally proposes how much she thinks she could use.

We review the numbers that I put together. The math will never come easily to me, but thanks to some help from Hannah, I've gotten to a place where I'm comfortable enough to get by.

"Let me think about it while you finalize the numbers, but this is brilliant. You don't know what a relief this would be. I don't want to move." We formally shake hands and return to the front office to see her out.

"That reminds me." Penny drapes her arm around our mannequin Zelda's shoulders. "I want to be clear that there will be no pranks with your sawdust-filled assistant here. I start work early in the morning and if I get the snot scared out of me, you'll both be banned from brownies for the foreseeable future."

We've still got old footage from the security camera from the time we left Zelda by the baker's back door. Penny screamed, punched the mannequin, and sprinted across the lot.

Noah holds up his hands. "No problem. I promise we'll cut the pranks and Zelda will be limited to strictly promotional activities at Shred and Tread." He turns to me, his face stern. "Right, *Wyatt*?"

I raise my right hand. "I promise that I'll announce my arrival in the back of the store and that I'll keep all Zelda pranks directed at Noah."

"How about we stop the pranks?" Noah suggests.

I look from Penny to Noah. "Do you think we need to go that far?"

"Yes," they say in unison.

I shrug. "Fine. I need brownies in my life." Shred and Tread, too.

Penny retreats to her bakery. When the door shuts behind her and she's no longer in ear shot, Noah and I throw our hands up for a high five.

Chapter 31
Moxie

I'm hit with the old familiar smell of beer, sweat, and the stale remnants of cigarettes—aromas that haven't been allowed indoors in years but the scent of which never quite faded. My entrance goes unnoticed, even though it feels like the music should have screeched to a halt with strange looks from the customers. I haven't been here for months.

"Where the hell have you been?" Murray scolds as if I'm a delinquent employee.

"It's good to see you too." I sit at the barstool that used to be my favorite spot every week.

"Usual?" he asks, already pouring a beer for me.

I nod as I look around the room and note a couple of guys whose attention I caught. I briefly consider prowling for a rebound hookup, but the thought makes me sick. It feels like cheating on Wyatt. I'm not over him and maybe never will be. Maybe I don't want to be.

"I have to cash those guys out, but don't go anywhere. I want to hear what's been going on with you."

I came here tonight out of habit and because I have to decide about the promotion. Sally gave me the better part of the month to consider. I promised her an answer tonight, and I don't feel prepared to give one. I'm hoping a drink will help me stop over-thinking it, and my feet lead me back to Murray's.

He dries his hands on a bar towel, tosses it aside, and leans on the counter. "Spill."

"Nothing to tell." I shrug.

"Bullshit," he says. "Where were you?"

"I met someone." I guess technically two someones.

He snorts. "Yeah, I know. You meet someone every night."

I roll my eyes. Okay, I deserved that one, although I have no shame in my hookup past. I'm allowed to like sex whether I'm in a relationship or not.

"No, I mean I dated someone. And made a friend? I don't know. Shit's been weird." The last couple of months started off feeling strange because I was out of my element, but every time Hannah imposed her friendship on me or I'd find myself spilling my life story to Wyatt, that wrongness felt a little righter.

Murray's eyebrows shoot up. "No kidding?"

"Would I lie?" I ask.

"Definitely," he says.

I flip him off and he chuckles, then sobers and shakes his head. "Alright, I believe you. You went and got yourself a life."

His words strike me. Before I can figure out how to respond, a man further down the bar flags down Murray.

"One sec," he says and goes to take the order.

Was I not living before?

Murray makes his way toward me but doesn't quite get there, muttering, "Oh no, not again" and backpedaling. I turn around and see Hannah tentatively poking her head into the bar, her eyes searching. Her face lights up with recognition when she finds me.

"It's okay, Murray. She doesn't bite," I say.

He reluctantly takes her order, a more confident request for wine than her once absurd ask for "some alcohol."

"I'm not even crying this time." She winks at him, and it looks like she's trying to flush a bug out of her eye.

Murray's face morphs into a grimace, and he ducks into the back room to pretend he's busy.

"So, these dates you've been going on that haven't gone well... how many of them have you winked at?" I ask, as casually as I can muster.

"A few. I was trying to be flirty. Why?"

Yikes. "No reason." We're definitely going to have to work on that, but I'm not going to get her spiraling in Murray's again. He might kill me. "I'm guessing from his reaction you haven't become a frequent patron. What are you doing here?"

"Don't be mad, but you looked stressed when you left work, so I kind of... followed you."

I laugh. I probably should be concerned, but it's so Hannah. I know she's only looking out for me.

"You're good. Don't worry."

Her shoulders relax and she takes a sip of her wine. "Are you, though?"

Today was fine. F.I.N.E. fine. Entirely stress-free and very much like it has been for the last several years. And *that's* what's stressing me out. I was bored before, sure, but how has it suddenly become unbearable and so lacking in hope? I can't keep doing what I'm doing.

I look at Hannah watching me with earnest patience and count myself lucky to have a friend who cares enough to stalk me. The me of two months ago might have tolerated work, but she wouldn't have let Hannah get so close to me. Wyatt either. And with what I thought were good reasons. Given the way I've been hurting the last few days, I should feel reassured in those reasons, but while I had to give up Wyatt, Hannah's been there to pick me up. It's been nice to have someone to lean on.

The breakup was painful, but for the first time in a long time I felt something. Maybe Murray was right—I went and got myself a life. I let people in. I let myself feel, and having been through that, I wouldn't trade it for the numb way I was walking through the world before.

"It looks like there's a whole lot going on in that noggin of yours," Hannah says, absently spinning on her stool while I perform mental gymnastics. From the outside it probably looks more like I'm holding a pose while someone paints a contemplative portrait.

"I need to text Sally. I'm going to take the job."

Hannah fist pumps. "Yes! I would have supported you no matter what you decided, but you'll do great."

My thoughts race, and my mouth runs to catch up. "But I still need more variety. I don't know why I waited so long to get out and do things. I'm going to sign up for more activities. Or join a club. Or do some volunteering."

"I like where this is going," she says. "I would totally ask Murray to get us some celebratory champagne, but the bubbles give me burps and I have a sneaking suspicion it's not really your drink."

I shake my head, barely processing what she's saying because my heart is thrumming in my chest. Adrenaline is flooding my veins, and I suddenly feel like I need to get up and go. Do all the things. "I'll take a pass on the champagne."

I feel good. Great. The room feels brighter, sharper, and suddenly everything is crystal clear. If I was so wrong about keeping people out before, how much else was I wrong about?

My stomach lurches. What have I done? I look up at Hannah, and sensing my shift, she snaps to attention.

"I think I've made a big mistake."

"With Wyatt?" Her voice is tentative, like she's terrified I'll say no. She has nothing to be afraid of.

"Yes."

She practically collapses onto the bar in relief. "Oh, thank god. I knew you'd come around eventually."

"I didn't."

"But you did," she sing-songs.

"Let's not get obnoxious about it," I warn.

She's giddy, bouncing in her seat. "Remember how I said I

didn't want to tell you how he was doing because it was his story to tell?"

"Yes."

"Well, I'm a lying liar who lies because I'm going to tell you."

The words pour out of her. My high is crushed as she tells me that Noah wanted to close the business, but then it's pieced back together as she tells me about Wyatt's business plan and Noah's agreement to give it another shot. If I was at all unsure about wanting to go back to Wyatt, she's erased any lingering doubts. He's nothing like Allison. He never was.

"My mom heard that Shred and Tread had so much immediate interest with their new digital offering, Wyatt thinks they are going to have to hire someone to work a few hours here and there. It might be perfect for someone who's looking for something adventurous to do on the side of her new job."

"Really?" My old wounds will never disappear, but being able to spend time with Wyatt at work would go a long way toward easing my nerves. I look at Hannah and shake my head. I don't know how I got along without her. "You're a genius."

She clinks my glass. "I know."

Chapter 32
Wyatt

The next few weeks are a whirlwind. We formalize our process with a few more practice runs on Dad and his breakfast buddies, and I sell some of our old equipment so we can upgrade to a better camera. Noah launches a marketing campaign, and Mom lights up her gossip lines and tells everyone over sixty that she's ever met. There is such a large immediate response that I'm exhausted from so many runs a day. We can barely keep up.

You'd think that with all this going on I wouldn't have time to think about Moxie, but she's like "Baby Shark" on my brain. I'm itching to tap out a text to check in, when like a magician's parlor trick, my phone chirps with an alert. My heart jumps as I yank my phone out of my pocket, but it's Noah.

"I don't know what you're doing, but you've got to get in here. *The Denver Gazette* called. They want to do a story on our cozy couch hikes."

"That's great! Are we calling them cozy couch hikes?" I ask.

"I'm trying to come up with a creative name. Take your La-Z-Boy down the river or get your Rocky Mountain high while in your boxers. I know, it's not my thing. Just get in here. We need to figure out what to say."

"The extra publicity is great, but we can't keep up with what we've got. And it's kind of tricky to film myself. We might need to bring on some help."

"A month ago, I thought we'd be shutting our doors, but you're right. Even just a few hours a week would help. I'll make a job posting for it, but in the meantime, get your butt over here to charm these reporters."

A few weeks later, I catch Noah smiling at the ultrasound he has clipped to the side of his monitor as we wait for the previous candidate to clear out. He's looking a lot less stressed these days. Business is booming and Mindy, well into her second trimester, is feeling much better.

I've stopped by their house a few times to help him paint the nursery and put together a crib. The two of them together is a thing of beauty, and the guilt gnaws at me with every pang of jealousy. I haven't been on a single date since breaking up with Moxie. Work has kept me so busy there's been little time. Even if time allowed, all I want is her. I keep biding my time, hoping she'll come back to me.

I look over the applications for the people we've interviewed so far. Noah, who usually runs the show with things like this, has been looking at his watch.

"I guess that last guy sounded like he might be okay. He seemed stiff, but it could work out. You said we have one more applicant today? I don't have their paperwork." We've been interviewing for two days, and Noah usually hands me everyone's information at once.

"I didn't print it out for this one. She applied yesterday," he says. It's an uncharacteristic lack of organization. He hasn't been himself all day, but I don't know why.

An Ex-citing Proposition

We're hiring a much-needed cameraperson who will also be able to answer questions as needed, do all the activities, and fill in at the office or on trips when needed.

So far, no one has clicked. Noah and I get along so well, we want someone who'll be able to jump in, work hard, and have fun.

"Can you print it now? I don't know what to ask without seeing her job history."

"One sec." Noah fumbles around with the computer while I fidget in my seat.

The bell on the front door chimes as my mouth drops. Moxie freezes in the doorway. In the month-and-a-half we've been apart, I've had to rely on my memories of her, the selfies from our cooking class, and a five-by-seven photograph from our date with Hannah and Quincy. She's as beautiful as ever, and my body aches to hold her. I've been waiting and hoping for this moment, and now that it's here, it doesn't feel real.

She lets out a breath, then seems to garner her courage and walks slowly to our table. Her hands are clenched. In fact, her whole body looks coiled to spring.

"Hey." Her beautiful brown eyes dart between me and the floor. "This isn't a proposal," she blurts, then frowns, then curses. Smooth and romantic as ever. I curl my lips to bite back a laugh.

"I didn't mean… that wasn't… this isn't going well," she says.

I fold my arms. "Really? Seems like it's going great to me."

She sticks her tongue out at me. I'll take that over seeing her walk away any day. Giving me a hard time is Moxie's love language, and we've fallen back into it as if she never left.

"Don't tell Hannah because I'll never hear the end of it, but in the parking lot I pulled out her dating binder and read the section on communication. One of the most important parts of good communication is setting realistic expectations or something, so I—" she runs out of air and takes a deep breath.

"Got it. No impending proposal, but we're coming back to that dating binder."

"Right." She smiles at me, and her hands stop shaking. "Can I try that again?"

"Please," Noah teases and I step on his toe under the table.

"I've missed you. A lot. And I've been thinking about my life. I haven't made the best decisions, and I think I'm ready to start making changes." Her voice shakes. I wish I could steady her, but I have a feeling she needs to get this out.

"I'm not ready for this to be more than dating yet. Anything beyond that feels too big for me to fit into my emotional stability shape sorter right now. Being with you scares the shit out of me."

I grimace because I understand that, but it's hard to hear that she's afraid to see this through. She must clock my reaction because she waves a hand and hurries on.

"Lots of things have been scaring me lately, but I think I might have really fucked up when I walked away from you. I think you're worth being brave for. I want to keep chasing new adventures with you. I want to show you that I'm serious about us even if I haven't caught up to you yet. Even if it might take me a while."

My chest swells with hope. I nod my head to make sure she knows I'm good with everything she's saying. If she's willing to give it a shot for real, I can be patient.

"I got a promotion at work. I'm going to try to let myself enjoy that, but when Hannah mentioned that you had this job posted, it seemed kind of... perfect? It would provide a few hours a week for adventure so I don't feel too stagnant at the casino, and I'd get to spend that time with you without taking away from your focus on the business. What I'm trying to say is that I care about you. I'm sorry I was too scared to trust you. Can we try this again?" Moxie's hands nervously move around as if she's shuffling invisible cards.

I'm frozen in place while my brain tries to catch up. My eyes flick to Noah. The corners of his pursed lips twitch while he tries to keep his head down to his pile of papers. She's the final applicant. Noah's behavior today, combined with the lack of application, finally makes sense. I look back at this beautiful woman who has managed to take me completely by surprise, again. I'm torn between asking her for references and swooping her up in a kiss.

Moxie shifts her weight to her other foot and bites her lip. "Okay," she says, her voice still a little wobbly. "I know that was an abnormal interview, but if you could say something, that'd be great because you're freaking me out."

"I'm not sure if I can take you back during a job interview. Surely that crosses some line in our code of conduct." I smile as I stand up from the table. My eyes hold her smoldering ones. "What do you think, Noah?"

Noah clears his throat, scraping his chair across the floor as he rushes to the back of the store. "I don't know, I will… go look for that. It might take me an hour or so to write the policy, so I'll see you around."

Moxie stands up, her lips parting as I close the distance between us. My hand caresses the side of her flushed face as I slowly move in for a kiss. "I've missed you so much. I wanted to give you space, but it's been terrible without you."

"I needed some time to sort things out. You have been such a delicious surprise. When Hannah came up with this drunken idea, I thought I would do it just to get her to stop crying, but then she introduced me to you. From the time you yanked me out of the river, I've wanted to be with you."

"I'm so happy—"

"Wait, let me finish or I might never get this out. Fuck it, I've got to kiss you." She wraps her arms around me, and finally I get the kiss I've been craving for weeks.

"Shit, I'm messing this all up." She pulls back and straightens her shirt as her eyes soften. "I want to be with you. I want to go on dates, explore the mountains, and rip off your clothes. Hell,

I'll even do game nights with you. I don't care what we're doing as long as I can spend time with you. I've never wanted a relationship before, and I can't promise that I can jump to the L word. But Wyatt, I need you back in my life."

A wave of affection rolls over me, followed by the sheer disbelief that she's here in front of me, wanting me back. It's a dream come true. I'm at a loss for words as I trace the edges of her face with my thumb, reassuring myself I haven't imagined this.

"What do you say, cowboy? Will you take me on an adventure?"

I hoist her up, and she wraps her legs around my waist. "Buckle up."

The End

Epilogue

My water shoes squelch on the pavement as my boyfriend —my fun-loving, super-hot boyfriend—leads the way across the street and into the small and overflowing club house. The supervisor position has been going well, and on my days off from there, I've gotten to spend every waking moment (and most of the sleeping ones) with Wyatt, whether it's guiding a tour together or snuggling up on the couch.

We wrap up a rafting tour where I successfully manage to stay in the boat when Wyatt's Mom calls and insists there is some kind of emergency and that we are needed to come right away.

"Do you think they're okay?" I ask.

"I'm sure they're fine. You know how they are. Their emergency could be anything from a loose tube on the hot tub to the grocery store no longer stocking Mom's favorite candies." He's casual about this, but lots of time in his company has taught me that Wyatt cares deeply for people. I know he'll feel anxious until he's laid eyes on both of his parents.

Many of the faces in the crowd are familiar to me now. After creating such a buzz about Hannah and Wyatt at the restaurant, Myra has created a monthly podcast where I've been a guest twice. It has no discernible theme, and our discussions have ranged from whether ghosts are real to how to count cards at blackjack. She sprung that one on me without warning and was annoyed when I didn't want to lay it all out for her. I don't want to lose my job, which I've actually come to like.

I destroyed several of these people at poker at Hannah's parents' house just last week. I wasn't about to go easy on them just because my job gives me an abundance of experience. When my pile of chips at the clubhouse grew, Hannah nudged me to be kind to my elders, and Wyatt said, "Forget that. Mr. Shellecky has a mean streak in him. Take no prisoners. Get 'em baby."

That night, the clubhouse had been lively, but nothing like today. The room overflows with hard chairs that have been set up to accommodate the masses. Hand in hand, we weave through the crowd until Wyatt spots his mom and drags us over.

"What's going on?" he asks.

"It's your dad and Arthur"

Wyatt catches my eyes, and I know we're both thinking, *Oh no, not again.* Not when they've gotten along for so long.

I scan the crowd looking for the dads and try to make out the issue from the conversation around us. There are so many people talking at once, though, and I can't make sense of any of it. Hannah pushes her way in from the opposite entrance. She and Dr. Nelson gradually make their way over.

"Did you two also get summoned?" she asks.

"Yeah, we haven't figured out what's going on yet."

"The board placed a one-birdfeeder-per-household limit," Dr. Nelson says.

This strikes me as an absurd rule to enforce, but I can't remember seeing any birdfeeder at the MacGregors' house.

"So? Do either of you even have birdfeeders?" Wyatt asks.

Ms. MacGregor and Dr. Nelson exchange looks. "We didn't use to. I take it you haven't driven past this week."

Hannah bites her lip, and when she speaks, her voice is full of dread. "How many?"

"Seventeen," Wyatt's mom admits.

"Each," Dr. Nelson adds.

My eyes bug out. Thirty-four bird feeders between two houses?

"It's irresponsible is what it is!" A woman shouts.

"Mind your own beeswax, Elaine!" Mr. Nelson shouts.

"I know you said I need to stop qualifying everything as an emergency, but they're about to riot."

"All the spilled birdseed attracts other animals. My garden is a wreck!" someone shouts.

"There's squirrel poop all over my lawn," another person proclaims.

"You don't even know what squirrel poop looks like," Wyatt's dad says. Come to think of it, I've always lived in neighborhoods full of squirrels, and I don't remember ever coming across squirrel poop. What *does* it look like?

"I can talk to Dad about the birdfeeders, but he won't back down in this setting. I'll have to confront him later," Wyatt says.

"We just need to get them to move onto the next agenda item," Hannah says.

I've got this. I don't know how I ended up coming to so many homeowners association meetings for a place where I don't even own a home, but I know the ins and outs. I also know that the president, Janet, runs a ludicrous ship but is anal about keeping things on time. I turn to Wyatt's mom.

"Do you have the email with the agenda?"

"They send an email with the agenda?" she asks bewilderedly. How do I know this but she doesn't?

"Yes. Can I see your phone?"

"Of course, sweet girl," she says, laying it on extra thick. All this time and she's still paranoid about what I think of her.

"Four hundred and ninety-six unread emails. Geez, Julie. How do you sleep at night?"

"In the old guest room, you know that. I know it's controversial to sleep in my own room, and you know I love my husband, but that man sure can snore," she says, entirely missing my point.

I quickly search for the email and see that the birdfeeder agenda item's allotted discussion time ended fifteen minutes ago.

"The neighborhood vigilantes for decorative freedom stand in the corner, their oversized t-shirts flapping in the breeze like capes for the superheroes that they are," Myra says enthusiastically into a miniature microphone.

I push my way through the crowd and over to Janet.

"Hi," I say, bursting out of the mass of bodies and rubbing at my shin where Mildred whacked me with her cane for accidentally bumping her shoulder.

"Hello, dear," Janet says. "I'm afraid our agenda is closed today. I can't put you on the list for any additional topics, especially since you aren't technically a resident."

"I wouldn't dream of it. I merely wanted to check the schedule with you. It looks like we're running fifteen minutes behind."

Her jaw drops, and she checks her watch. From the absolute horror that paints her face when she realizes this is true, you'd think I'd just told her wolves have trampled her daffodils.

She bangs her gavel on the folding table, but nobody seems to hear it over the arguing. "Desperate times..." she mutters and pulls an air horn from her pocket.

She blasts the horn. Hands fly to cover ears, and people scream left and right.

"We're tabling this topic. We need to move onto the next agenda item. Mildred, the floor is yours." Her tone leaves zero room for discussion, and with only a few quiet grumbles, people who had wandered around make it back to their seats. I take the opening to move back over to Wyatt and take his hand. He gives it a squeeze.

"Aren't you the little senior citizen whisperer," he says and kisses my cheek.

"It's a talent." I shrug, and Hannah smiles at us in a half-formed way that's a little wistful. Her dating life is still a work in progress, and none of my exes have panned out yet. But I've got plans, and she's got herself a dating coach. I'm optimistic.

"I would like to propose we invest some of the HOA funds in a spiritual cleanser," Mildred declares without an ounce of irony, and arguments flare up from all around the room.

"Oh, come on."

"My hard-earned money is not being wasted on your superstitions!"

"What hard-earned money? You inherited all your money. You haven't worked a day in your life!"

"It's still my money!"

"Easy, people. Let's hear her out," Janet says.

"It's time we all acknowledge there's an evil spirit in our midst. I think you all know what I'm referring to."

A series of hushed whispers goes up around the room, and I pick out the words, "The statue." *Oh no.*

"Maybe we should get out of here," Wyatt whispers.

"Good idea," I say.

"I've been tracing the paranormal occurrences for my podcast.; The curious happenstances of Eagle's Landing/knitting with Myra, new episode every Tuesday and Thursday. I believe that haunting Victims Zero are the Nelsons.

"Wait a minute, was that you two?" Hannah hisses.

I stored the creepy statue that Wyatt's mom gifted me for a while, but after she stopped in a couple times and didn't seem to notice it, it had to go. I was all for setting it on fire, but in a not-so-sober decision, we decided to play a harmless little prank and leave it at the Nelsons. We wanted to see how long it took for word to make it to Hannah, but then I kind of forgot about it.

"For anyone unaware, the statue has been placed in the trash a minimum of fifteen times, once even being driven all the way to the landfill. It somehow keeps appearing in different people's homes," Myra says.

"Clearly there's an evil spirit at work that needs to be dealt with," Mildred adds, bringing us back around to the spiritual cleanser proposal, which launches the whole room into a spiraling argument once again.

"You're *haunting* the neighborhood?" Hannah whispers. She's quiet enough to barely be audible, but her pitch is reaching hysterical levels.

"Noah and Penny banned me from pranks at the office, so I needed an outlet." Wyatt shrugs.

"We only did it to your parents," I say. "Maybe the thing really is haunted."

Hannah's face goes red, and my jaw drops. "Hannah Nelson, did you move the statue?"

"Maybe? Just twice! My mom tried to get rid of it twice and I brought it back because she was kind of getting on my nerves. I was feeling a little petty, but then she started really freaking out and I didn't know what to do. Trevor saw me toting it around and said, 'Woah, that thing's creepy as hell. Can I borrow that?' I said, 'Take it.' I didn't know he was moving it around, too."

"Alright," A man in the corner shouts. "I admit it. I moved the statue."

"Quit taking credit for my jokes. You were never the funny one. *I* moved the statue."

How many people have moved this damn thing? "I think that's our cue," I say, and the three of us duck out the door.

"Well, that was eventful," I say.

"Yes, and as much as I'd love to stay and watch it devolve, I've got to get going," Hannah says.

"Are you working tonight?" I ask.

"Nope, I've got a lesson." Her cheeks go pink again. Wyatt's hand squeezes mine in that silent way we've managed to develop. "You?"

"Not today. I've got a supervisor shift tomorrow," I say. That sentence doesn't come with the same sense of dread that it used to carry. Now that I'm making better use of my time outside of work, I'm starting to look forward to working at the casino. I've learned a lot in my new supervisor role and am even thinking about enrolling in a program they have for senior leadership. That's way down the line since I haven't been a supervisor for long, but for once, staying in one place isn't so scary.

"Yeah you do, boss lady," Wyatt says, his voice husky and seductive. Working with him at Shred and Treat has been incredible, and we've made a date-night pact to take classes in things we've never tried to always keep us on our toes. I lean in to kiss him and throw in plenty of tongue. Wyatt's hand runs down my back, and he pinches my ass.

"On that note, I'm out," Hannah says and hurries away.

"Woops. Forgot we had an audience," I say against his lips.

"I don't mind an audience." He tilts my head and pulls me in closer with one hand, deepening our kiss while his other hand slides under the edge of my shirt.

I slap his hand and pull back. "Naughty."

"Guilty as charged. Come back to my place?" he asks.

"About that."

He raises an eyebrow, and I brace myself to say the thing that's been on my mind for the last couple weeks.

"You know how I keep a toothbrush there?" I ask.

"Yep."

"I was thinking... maybe you could set a drawer aside for me, too?" My chest constricts as that old claustrophobic feeling tries to take the wheel. But I force myself to breathe, and as I do anytime this happens, I remember all the amazing things that have ocurred in the last few months when I finally took some chances and got myself a life.

I study a crack in the sidewalk, a leaf on a nearby bush, a cloud that looks remarkably phallic—anything to avoid looking at Wyatt's face. Never one to let me get away with my shit, he raises a finger to my chin and gently nudges me to look at him. He's got the goofiest grin.

"That…" He dips his face and plants a peck on my lips. My heart flutters. "Sounds like a wonderful idea."

I didn't actually think he'd say no. If I expressed a hint of readiness, he'd probably drop down on one knee tomorrow. He's known from the start that I need to take things slow, and he's been incredibly kind and patient.

I just might love that man. Maybe soon I'll even work up to saying it.

The pact continues with Hannah's story in:
An Uncharted Ex-perience

Acknowledgments

From Linda:

I've dreamed of being a writer since I was a kid reading, Nancy Drew when I was supposed to be sleeping. There were attempts over the years, but nothing that I'd be proud to publish until I got to write with my daughter.

Kelly, I'm so proud of you as an author, mother, and as a person. I have loved writing with you and am so excited about our book. And we managed to do it and still like each other!

Thank you to my family for always being there and supporting our efforts through the long writing and editing process. Even when I had my doubts about whether I could do this, none of you ever questioned it. I love that we live the GalaxyQuest mantra, never give up, never surrender.

We had help along the way and let me just say, man, do I love writers. Creating stories can be such a solitary activity, but writers stick together like frosting on cake.

Specifically, Meika and Lyssa who are very busy writing their own incredible books. Your kindness, editing help, late night suggestions and emotional support were key to making this book a reality. We can't thank you enough, but if we could, I'm sure dessert and drinks would be involved.

I want to mention someone who took time out of their busy schedule to offer publishing advice and story suggestions. Tara, you are a true gem. Your insight and perspective helped provide the roadmap to get us through the publishing process.

Jen, thank you for doing an incredibly thorough read-through and offering detailed suggestions without crushing my spirit as a new author.

Joel, you are an exceptional editor who did a fantastic job on our copy edits. This poor guy has corrected so many grammar mistakes and incorrectly placed commas by me, I'm sure I've given him nightmares.

From Kelly:

Thank you to my reader group for being so supportive and helping spread the word about my books. Naming things is so hard, and I get paralyzing indecision over these things, so I love playing the naming things game with you all! Big shout out to Claire for her great suggestion of Fork and Spoon for our restaurant name. Thank you to Jessie Heins for naming Simon. We can't wait for everyone to get to see more of him in the next book! Thanks to Angela Coan for naming a character in another project that isn't quite ready to make its way into the world yet. It will get its time eventually!

Side note: if you haven't joined the reader group, please check the link in any of my social media bios and join us, so you can play the naming things game with us, and get insights into the writing of the books, and other fun bookish conversation.

I know Lyssa and Meika were already mentioned, but it bears repeating, thank you to you two for all the writing dates and encouragement. To you two, as well as Erin King, Annie Isaacs, and Victoria Solomon, I was deeply discouraged and that weekend up north saved me in ways I can't possibly put to words. Thank you for dragging me out of my despair, inspiring me, convincing me not to give up, and helping me brainstorm.

To the Forge and the Write Squad, thank you as always for your unending support. I couldn't do this without you. Thank you Rachael for sharing so much of your self-publishing wisdom with me.

Thank you to Ali Shearer, our incredible cover artist. The cover is beautiful and you were a dream to work with. We are so fortunate to have had your help bringing Moxie, Wyatt, and Hannah to life.

As always, thank you to my family and friends for all of your support, and to the readers, booksellers, creators, and librarians who do so much for this industry.

Inevitably I'll have missed someone, so to anyone who picks this book up to give it a read, who helped bring it to life in the first place, supported us on this journey, or supports this book at any point moving forward, thank you. From the bottom of our hearts, thank you.